"Please don't go," Nadine pleaded.

"Stay with me through the night. Never have I needed you as badly as I do now."

"Are you sure, darling?" Lloyd whispered, his mouth sweet and gentle as he kissed her, slowly easing the robe from her shoulders.

Nadine moaned as her robe fell away from her and lay at her feet. Lloyd's hands filled her with such wondrous desire she could not help but give in to the rapture. It was a raging hunger that must be fed. All sadness, all that was ugly in the world, was being swept away from her as though on a high, rising tide.

Twining her arms around Lloyd's neck, Nadine clung to him. A strange, sweet pain pulsed through her body . . . and this man whose blue eyes had stolen her heart was the cause.

Passion in the Wind

Cassie Edwards

Harlequin Books

TORONTO • NEW YORK • LONDON
AMSTERDAM • PARIS • SYDNEY • HAMBURG
STOCKHOLM • ATHENS • TOKYO • MILAN

For my friends, Bill and Lee Bell,
producers of "*The Young and the Restless*",
the staff and cast,
with appreciation for all that you mean to so many

Harlequin Historical first edition September 1988
Second printing May 1989

ISBN 0-373-28605-8

CASSIE EDWARDS

is the author of over twenty romances and has traveled the U.S. doing research for her books. When she's not on the road, Cassie spends seven days a week writing in her office in the Illinois home she shares with her husband, Charlie.

Chapter One

SAN FRANCISCO 1852

A brisk, damp breeze blew in from the bay, and slanting beams of sunlight broke through the threatening clouds and fell on the crowded waterfront. Montgomery Street, plagued by mud from an earlier rain, was full of horse-drawn buggies and men on horseback slowly making their way through the mire. Beneath the square false fronts that lined both sides of the street lay a motley collection of gambling halls, general stores and saloons. Men loitered in groups up and down the sidewalks.

Her arms laden with heavy packages, Nadine Quinn hurried along the wooden sidewalks, dodging the mud that oozed from the wide cracks between the boards. Her long auburn hair shimmered like spun silk in the wind, and the skirt of her cotton dress whipped around her legs. She was finding that she had not only the encumbrance of her dress to wrestle with, but also the threat of unruly men. The men who had come to California to quench their thirst for gold were always seeking the pleasure of women.

Nadine had learned to avoid them at all cost. None were like the gentlemen she had known in Boston and New York. "Gentle" was a word that seemed to be missing from their vocabulary. She would never understand why her father had dragged his family to this wild city by the sea.

Her father's restless and ambitious nature made him do many things, but it had also made him a rich man. With his partner, Sam Parsons, he could boast of owning a vast fleet of ships and an impressive stagecoach line. He had become even wealthier since the move to San Francisco.

Before San Francisco, there had been New York. And before New York, Boston. And before that, other cities too numerous to mention.

Nadine shifted the packages in her arms, grimacing at the thought of her father's most recent decision, to travel to Australia. The godforsaken country was half a world away!

In her frustrated state Nadine had gone shopping, knowing that there would surely be no opportunity to shop in the wilds of Australia! She would be separated by a vast body of water from life as she had always known it. At eighteen she was an adventurous sort, but she did not welcome what Australia offered her.

Complete isolation!

The sound of angry words and breaking glass from a nearby saloon drew Nadine's attention away from her self-pity. She pulled back in alarm as the swinging doors in front of her burst open and a man sailed from the saloon, closely followed by his hat, and landed clumsily at her feet.

Nadine groaned at the sight of her packages, dropped in her surprise, now scattered on the muddy sidewalk. Mud ran down the skirt of her dress in brown streaks.

She glared down at the man responsible for her mud-soaked packages and her ruined dress, ready to berate him with harsh words.

But when he looked up at her from where he lay, sprawled clumsily at her feet, she could not speak. Never had she seen such compelling eyes, such handsomely sculpted features. His face was marred only by the slight slant of a scar high across the right cheekbone. His golden hair was flecked with red, as though it had been burned by the sun. His face was tanned bronze, and his eyes were the deep blue color of the sea.

As the stranger rose to his feet, Nadine saw that he was tall and lean. His blue cotton shirt and tight breeches did little to hide the muscles of his broad shoulders and long legs, and he towered over her own diminutive five-foot height. She caught herself wondering if he saw her flaws. Did he notice her eyes were too widely set? Was he looking at her tiny, upturned nose? Her father called her his petite vision of loveliness, but she had always thought him too kind.

Feeling foolish for wondering what this stranger might be thinking about her, she dropped her gaze lower, to the frighteningly large ivory-handled pis-

tols holstered at his hips. She paled, thinking that he
might even be an outlaw!

"How's it going, ma'am?" Lloyd Harpster said in
a slow drawl that was thick with an accent Nadine was
not familiar with. He leaned over and grabbed his hat
from the sidewalk. It was a strange wide-brimmed felt
hat with a wide band of pale brown hide.

Seemingly unaware that mud stained the hat, Lloyd
swept his gaze over Nadine. He had been in San
Francisco for only a short time, but he had seen
enough American women to know that this one was
special. This was a lady.

It was the best of combinations for a lady—breed-
ing and looks. Lloyd would have liked to know more
about her, but this was a very odd way to begin an
acquaintance!

Shaking herself from her reverie, Nadine glanced
at her soiled dress and her muddy packages, and her
anger rose. Placing both hands on her hips, she
straightened to her full height, forcing herself to forget his strange way of speaking and his handsome-
ness. Though he made her heart almost stop beating
with his attractiveness, it was obvious that he was of
no account. Why else would he have exited the saloon in such an unconventional way?

"I demand an apology!" she stormed, and continued on without giving him a chance to reply.
"Waterfront riffraff like you don't know the meaning of the word apology, do you?"

She glanced up at the sign hanging just above her
head and read the inscription aloud. "Al's Saloon!"
she said, again glaring at the stranger. "You're too

much riffraff for even the likes of a place like this, or why else would you have been thrown from it?''

Lloyd raised his eyebrows, surprised to discover that he was enjoying the scolding from the lovely, high-spirited lady. Her wide-set green eyes were filled with fire, and her smart cotton dress revealed a slim, lithe body.

Yes, she was a woman he should get to know. And, somehow, he would!

"Sorry about the mishap, ma'am," he said with a slight bow.

Nadine stiffened, disturbed by his lazy sureness and his slow, magnetic smile. He did not appear to be riffraff, and he did smell fresh and clean, as though he had just bathed and shaved.

Yet she had caught what was surely mockery in his half bow, and she did not appreciate it. She chose to ignore his apology.

As she bent to pick up her packages, her gaze was drawn to his boots. They were made of the same sort of hide as the band on his hat.

The man was most peculiar.

A loud, familiar voice drew Nadine's gaze quickly upward, and she slowly straightened to a standing position, momentarily forgetting her packages. She watched in disbelief as her father stepped from the saloon, rubbing a fist that was raw and scraped from having just hit someone. Not just any someone but quite obviously the stranger, for his eyes were alight with fire as he glared at the two of them.

There was a moment of strained silence as Nadine waited for her father to lash out at her for being on

Montgomery Street. How often had he forbidden it, warning her of the men who loitered there? She had chosen not to listen. If he could change her life so severely by forcing her to travel to Australia, she had the right to some sort of excitement before leaving!

But she had never thought to find this sort of excitement, had never thought to meet anyone like this man who moved her so, with what was surely passion.

Harry Quinn was tall and hefty, with graying black hair and eyes as dark as midnight. He was in a black suit with a white ruffled shirt. A diamond stickpin glittered in the folds of his maroon silk cravat, and a gold watch chain looped from one pocket of his waistcoat to the other.

His face was wrinkled and ruddy, giving him a hard, pinched look, yet deep within him lay a heart of gold where his daughter was concerned. She was his only child, and he adored her. Nadine returned his feelings. She idolized her father, though not always his disturbing habits or decisions.

"What in the hell are you doing here, Daughter?" Harry stormed, taking a step closer to Nadine. He glared down at her from his towering height. "I've warned you and warned you against coming to Montgomery Street." He gestured with a hand toward Lloyd. "Do you now see why?"

Harry turned on his heel and faced Lloyd. He resumed rubbing his sore knuckles, his mind on the poker game that had just ended. Damned if he hadn't proven again that he was a poor loser. The cockiness of the Australian had gotten to him. He had not been able to control his temper, or his fists, and the thought of coming face-to-face with the bastard over and over again for the next several months only made him madder.

But there was no getting around it. The Australian had won, and Harry had lost.

Lloyd's eyes twinkled as he realized what fate had just handed him. He looked from Harry Quinn to Nadine. Not only had he beaten Quinn at several hands of poker, he had been given the chance to pursue his lovely daughter because of it. The voyage to Australia would take several months!

Rubbing his jaw, he was reminded of just why it hurt. His gaze swept over Quinn, stopping at the graying hair and the pinched expression on his wrinkled face. He had been right in deciding not to come up swinging. The man had to be in his early sixties.

"Quinn, if I hadn't been taught by my parents at an early age to have respect for my elders you'd find out that poker is not the only thing I'm good at," he said in his slow drawl. "You would be lying flat on your back, wondering what hit you."

Lloyd plopped his hat on his head and cast Nadine a lazy smile, his eyes saying to her more than he dared say aloud. "But my sore jaw is well worth everything I won in that game of poker," he said, tipping his hat before he turned and slowly walked away.

Nadine watched the slow confidence in his walk. She could not help herself. She had never met a man of such mystery.

Her pulse raced as she wondered at the meaning behind his last statement. What had he won from her father, and what had he done to outrage her father so much that he had had the need to hit him? The stranger had proven that he was a gentleman. If not, he would surely have hit her father.

In a state of wonder, Nadine watched the stranger mount a beautiful strawberry roan. Even the way he sat in the saddle was different. His back was so straight, his shoulders so square. He was so tall in the saddle.

He swung the horse around and began riding away. Nadine's heart lurched when he turned and gave her a soft smile and a wink.

"That blasted foreigner," Harry Quinn said, stepping in the line of Nadine's vision. "Don't you get to thinking crazy things about that man. I'll not have the likes of him for any daughter of mine."

Nadine's face grew hot with a blush. She swept the windblown strands of her hair back from her eyes and stooped to rescue her packages from the muddy sidewalk. Her father bent to assist her.

"Father, who was that man?" she dared to ask, giving her father a sideways glance as he picked up the last package from the sidewalk. She straightened her back, hugging two of her packages to her chest as her father grabbed her by the elbow and guided her quickly to her waiting horse and buggy.

"Father, who is he?" she persisted when she realized that her father was ignoring her. His eyes were dancing with anger, and a nervous twitch jerked at his left cheek.

"Never you mind who that man was," Harry said with a stern look. Taking her packages as they reached her buggy, he placed them at the back and helped her up onto the seat. "You just hurry home. I think you've had enough of Montgomery Street for one day, don't you?"

Seeing her father's cream-colored horse tied to a hitching rail close by, Nadine reached for her own reins and coiled them around the fingers of her gloved right hand. More than likely her father would return to the saloon and play another game of poker, for he was known not only for his acquired riches but also for being a notorious gambler. He had a lot of money to lose—and he had lost plenty!

"Perhaps I *was* wrong to come to Montgomery Street unescorted," Nadine said, her hair blowing in coppery wisps about her oval face. "But, Father, soon I won't have the opportunity to go anywhere. We'll be in Australia. I wish you would reconsider."

"The plans are made," Harry said, patting her hand. "Sam Parsons and I have sold all of our ships except for the *Lady Fortune*, and we have a buyer for our stagecoach line. We'll be leaving for Australia quite soon. There'll be no turning back."

Nadine sighed, for she hated even the mention of her father's partner. Sam had become a leech, living with the family as though he were one of them. Of late he had begun to try to expand his claim by pursuing her affections. Thus far she had managed to elude him.

It wasn't all that simple, though, for her father and mother both favored him as her intended. They were blind, it seemed, for only she saw that Sam's only true goal was to have sole possession of the business.

Nadine had seen his schemes for what they were. Why couldn't her father? Why did he trust so easily where Sam was concerned?

It was as though Sam held her family hostage, but she had never been able to put her finger on just why.

Nadine shook her troubled thoughts of Sam from her mind as she got another glimpse of the blue-eyed stranger as he turned down another street and was lost behind the buildings.

"Why don't you want to tell me who that stranger was?" she persisted, giving her father her most winsome smile. "What did he win from you, Father?"

"I guess you'll know soon enough what his name is," Harry said in a low growl, staring down at the toe of his boot as he angrily ground it into the mud. "His name is Harpster. Lloyd Harpster."

"Where is he from?" Nadine asked, recalling his odd hat and boots. "Some of his attire is most peculiar."

"No more peculiar than the man," Harry said, growling over his shoulder at the renewed thought of being forced to travel with the low-down gambler.

"You didn't say what he won from you at poker," Nadine prodded. "Nor did you say where he is from."

"You'll find out soon enough where he's from and what he won from me on my unlucky draw of the cards," Harry said, frowning at her. With a harried look, he nervously raked his fingers through his thick hair, pulling it back from his eyes. "He's from Australia!"

Shock registered on Nadine's face. She opened her mouth to question her father further, but he was already headed for his horse. The stranger was from Australia and was now in California, while she was leaving California to go there.

"Come along, Nadine," Harry shouted, reining in beside her. "I'm going to see to it that you get home safe and sound. There's something I want to give to you."

Nadine's eyebrow lifted with curiosity. What more could he possibly give her than she already had? She had never wanted for anything, except for the chance to live in one city and one house long enough to grow roots. She had come to the conclusion that she would never have such a life unless she married a man who was not as restless as her father. A man who could give her what she had never had. A house that could be called a home.

Smiling resignedly at her father, Nadine flicked her reins and drove stiffly behind him through the crowded streets. She guided her horse carefully up the street, afraid to turn and look over her shoulder at the waters of the bay that threatened those who lost control on the steep hills.

She was glad to follow her father's lead into a driveway that led to a grand three-story house. The mansion was built of stone and stood on a bluff two hundred fifty feet above the bay, offering a splendid view of the ocean as far as the eye could see.

Her father stopped to tie up his horse at the hitching post while Nadine drove along the circular driveway to the massive porch. Gazing up at the large columned portico that gave the mansion its distinctive appearance, she wondered what to expect of houses in Australia. Perhaps they would even live in a grass hut.

Sighing, she grasped the hand her father offered and let him help her down from the buggy. Now she had another reason for not wanting to travel to Australia: the stranger who would be left behind in California. His startling blue eyes would haunt her dreams the entire voyage.

But she was foolish for even thinking of him. Today's meeting was only by chance. Fate would never bring them together again. And it was best that it didn't. He most surely was not the sort to fantasize over. It was obvious that he was a gambler, and what else might he be involved with, she wondered, recalling the large pistols holstered at his hips and the scar on his right cheekbone.

"Nadine, let's go straight to my study," Harry said, interrupting her train of thought. "What I have to give you is in my wall safe. I should've given it to you long ago. There's no telling when you'll get a wild idea and go prancing about on your own," he muttered, filling his arms with her packages. "Was the shopping worth the danger you put yourself in?"

Nadine reached toward her father to help with the burden, but he jerked away from her and climbed the stairs to the porch. Drawing the hem of her skirt up into her arms, she followed along behind him into the house. They entered a foyer paneled in Norwegian pine from floor to ceiling. A graceful stairway with bronze rails and delicately turned balustrades led to the second and third floors.

Off to the right was the parlor, a large, airy room illuminated by a crystal chandelier.

Harry placed Nadine's packages on a side table, motioning to her with his hand. "Come along with me," he muttered.

Nadine nodded, smiling at her mother as she appeared at the parlor door. She began to say hello, but her father broke in abruptly.

"Make sure there's another plate on the dining table this evening," he ordered. "We're having a guest."

"Darling, who?" Mariel Quinn asked eagerly. Mariel's eyes were a vivacious green, almost a reflection of her clinging satin dress. Her auburn hair was swirled into a tight bun atop her head, and diamonds sparkled at her throat and earlobes.

Tiny and frail, she made scarcely a sound as she followed along beside Nadine, placing an arm around her daughter's waist. "Harry, who is coming to call this evening? Is it a business acquaintance?"

Harry lumbered on into his study, ignoring his wife's questions. With steady fingers he dialed the combination to his safe and swung the door open wide. Determinedly he reached in and grabbed a tiny pearl-handled pistol. Holding it in the palm of his hand, he turned and faced Nadine and his wife as they stared openly at him.

"Nadine, you take this pistol and use it for protection whenever you feel threatened," Harry said, knitting his dark eyebrows together into a frown. He held the pistol out to Nadine. "You never know when some low-down varmint is going to try and take advantage of you."

"Good Lord, Harry," Mariel gasped, taking a surprised, unsteady step backward. "You surely don't feel that anything warrants Nadine carrying a pistol?"

"No," Harry muttered, fitting the gun squarely in Nadine's hand. "She doesn't need to carry it with her. Just keep it handy." He cleared his throat nervously. "Especially while traveling on the ship to Australia. It's a damn long voyage, you know."

As she took the pistol from him, Nadine's hand felt threateningly heavy, even *hot*.

But of course it was neither. It was just that the gun made her feel vulnerable, frightened somehow!

"Now let's not talk any more about it," Harry said, drawing his wife next to his side and giving her a comforting hug. "Nadine needs a pistol. She has one. That's that. Now what did you say we were having for dinner, Mariel?"

Mariel laughed softly, accepting her husband's comforting arm. She looked up into his dark eyes with affection. "I didn't say. But if you want to know, it's your favorite, a roast," she said softly. "Darling, you didn't say who was coming to dinner. Surely you aren't going to make me wait and see. That's not fair, you know."

Harry sighed heavily, giving Nadine a troubled glance. He knew that he could not keep his transaction with Lloyd Harpster a secret forever. He might as well break the news now, or at least some of it.

"It's a man I met while gambling," he said hoarsely. "Seems he's won his way to our dinner table."

Nadine's eyes brightened and her heart began to race. She curled her fingers around the forgotten pistol, anxious to hear who her father was talking about.

Mariel stepped away from her husband, her eyes wide. "Why on earth would anyone play for such stakes?" she asked softly, resigned to her husband's bad habit of gambling. His good habits outweighed his bad, twofold! "Who is this man, Harry?"

"His name is Harpster," Harry continued icily. "Lloyd Harpster. He plays a mean game of poker, that one does. Why did he do it? I'm afraid you're going to find out the answer to that question soon enough. For now, though, let's speak of more pleasant things, shall we?"

Hearing the name Lloyd Harpster spoken aloud made Nadine's insides quiver anxiously. She had thought never to see Lloyd Harpster again, and here he was going to eat at the same dinner table with her tonight.

She cradled this knowledge close to her heart, ashamed of wanting these added moments with him.

When her father studied her expression, Nadine lowered her eyes, for what he might see frightened even her.

Chapter Two

A crystal chandelier hung low over the dining room table, its dripping pendants sparkling with candlelight. The room was sumptuously paneled from floor to ceiling and set off by a granite fireplace and red draperies. It was a room of elegance, with the furnishings of a family that knew the meaning of wealth.

Never had there been such an awkward, strained silence at the long oak table as now. When a fork accidentally clanked against a plate, everyone jumped as though shot. Everyone but the stranger.

Lloyd Harpster sat squarely at the table, confidently, eagerly eating the roast beef, carrots and potatoes, his blue eyes never leaving Nadine, who sat opposite him. Each time she glanced his way he gave her his slow, lazy smile. He could not remember when he had last had a genuine homecooked meal. Surely not since he had been shipped from England to Australia on the prison ship.

Nadine sat stiff backed on her plush red velveteen chair at the table, seeming to blend into the setting in her red silk dress, with its little puffed sleeves trimmed with lace ruffles. The bodice was cut very low, displaying the splendid whiteness of her bust. The dress was tight at the waist, the skirt long and very full.

Her mother had scolded her for choosing such a daring dress when a stranger was coming to dinner. But Nadine had ignored the scolding, knowing that once Australia was reached no occasion would ever warrant such a dress. She would probably never have an opportunity to join in any social function, *ever*!

Her hair tumbling across her bare shoulders in a satiny auburn cascade, Nadine toyed with the food on her plate. Lloyd Harpster's constant attention made her much too nervous to eat.

Even now she could feel the heat of his gaze from where he sat opposite her at the table. She had only dared to return his set stare a few times, but that had been enough to make her wonder about him anew. He still wore the same clothes he had worn earlier in the day. Was he so poor that he had no change of clothes? If so, why hadn't he gambled for money instead of the chance to come to dinner?

It made no sense at all.

His plate emptied twice of food and his stomach comfortably full, Lloyd dabbed his lips with a lace-trimmed linen napkin, placed the napkin on the table and stretched his muscular arms above his head.

"It's been a long spell since I've had such a meal, ma'am," he said, addressing Nadine's mother, who seemed in a state of shock over the visitor. Her eyes shone a vivid green in her pale face, and her low-cut satin dress revealed the nervous heaving of her bosom.

"I want to thank you for your kindness in having me at your dinner table," Lloyd continued, slowly lowering his arms and resting his elbows on the table. "It's been a privilege to be in your company."

His gaze warmed as he looked over at Nadine. Never in his life had he seen such a vibrant and glowing young lady, nor such enchanting curves. In red she was breathtaking! He could smell her perfume. The sweet aroma made his senses reel as it wafted across the table, teasing him. The long voyage to Australia would not be long enough to suit him, and once there, it would not be easy to say goodbye.

"It's been a double pleasure meeting your lovely daughter—"

He was interrupted by a voice at his side.

"Let's get this mockery of a meal over with," Sam Parsons demanded, doubling a fist in his lap. He had seen the stranger eyeing Nadine throughout the meal. Though Nadine had yet to be convinced that she would one day be his wife, Harry Quinn and his wife both approved of his intentions, and Sam didn't want a handsome drifter spoiling his plans. The long voyage to Australia would give him the opportunity he had been waiting for. It would become boring for Nadine. She would seek out the comfort of someone's company. He was going to make sure it was his.

"You won this evening's meal because of Harry's unlucky turn of the cards," Sam said, glowering at Lloyd. "I'm sure you'll have the grace to leave now that it's over."

Nadine's hands went to her throat. "Sam!" she gasped. "Though Mr. Harpster is here by unconventional means, you have no right to treat him so. You are my father's partner, but that gives you no right to interfere in anything but his business affairs!''

Sam returned her glare across the table. Though he was thirty, his face bore no signs of hard living. He was educated and wise beyond his years. His coal-black hair framed a square-jawed, handsome face, and his thin black mustache gave him the look of a gentleman.

His suit of brown velvet, his white satin waistcoat and the diamond stickpin in his cravat spoke of riches, yet there was something in his dark eyes that detracted from his near-perfect looks.

Riches seemed wasted on him.

Harry Quinn leaped to his feet. He angrily slammed a fist down onto the table, causing dishes and silverware to bounce. "That's enough from all of you," he said, his voice strained. "You all know that there's more to this evening than the meal, and it's best that you all hear what it is."

He glanced over at Lloyd, who was twirling a long-stemmed wineglass between his fingers as though he belonged there. The next several months would most surely be a test of Harry's nerves and willpower.

Nadine scarcely breathed, her insides trembling from the added tension in the room. Her gaze moved from Lloyd Harpster's pistols, which were draped over the back of an empty chair at his side, to the scar high on his cheek.

Outside, a sudden clap of thunder warned of an approaching storm. A slow mist was already covering the window glass, and the sound of the waves slapping against the cliff was ominous.

Nadine wondered if Lloyd Harpster might be the devil in the guise of a handsome man, his face dark and finely chiseled, his eyes as blue as the heavens as he again smiled at her across the table. As he stirred she caught the movement of his muscles down the length of his lean, tanned body, and her insides sparked with an excitement she had never felt before.

If he was the devil, she had most surely already lost her soul and heart to him, and he had yet to even touch her.

"So tell us what you know about Australia," Harry said, leaning his full weight on his hands and staring intently at Lloyd. "If you must travel on the *Lady Fortune* with us to Australia, you will have to contribute something. Your knowledge of the country will be all that I ask for. When Harry Quinn loses at poker, Harry Quinn pays his debts. You won a meal ticket here tonight, *and* free passage to Australia, but never ask for more than that, Lloyd Harpster. Never ask for more than that!"

Gasps rippled around the table. The faces of Sam and Mariel registered deep shock.

Nadine grew radiant with the news. Her blood quickened at the thought of Lloyd Harpster traveling with them on the *Lady Fortune*. The realization might be dangerous, but it was also unquestionably exciting. She could not help it. If she were ever to be with him alone, wouldn't it be almost too much for her heart to bear? Might not its wild beatings swallow her whole?

She leaned closer to the table, her pulse racing, her face hot with an anxious blush. The voyage to Australia, and the idea of being stranded there, no longer troubled her. She now had a reason to look forward to both. Hopefully, while on the ship, she would find out how and when Lloyd Harpster had received the scar on his face. She would find out everything about him!

But what if she found out that Lloyd was an outlaw, a man of no morals? He most surely represented everything she *wasn't* looking for in a husband. She wanted someone who could give her a home and a family.

Surely this man could never give anyone either.

But it was Nadine's fascination with him that made her grow even more anxious to hear him respond to her father's questions.

Lloyd continued spinning the glass between his fingers, silently staring down at it. Though he was willing to give Harry Quinn answers, his mind was drifting back to another time, another place.

He could still feel the whip cutting into the flesh of his back, the blood hot as it ran in tiny streamers across his bared buttocks. He could feel his lungs straining as he forced himself not to scream out as the flogging continued, lash after lash.

One day he would make Captain Grover Grenville pay for the beatings. One day he would prove that he had been wrongly imprisoned. Australia lured him back to its shores for only that reason. He could not

continue to be a wanted man. Nights were too restless that way. . . .

"As you already know, there is much adventure
and the promise of wealth to be made in Australia,"
Lloyd said, looking up at Harry, casting him his lazy
smile. "You're wise to plan to have a stagecoach line
in Australia. There's been a rush of people arriving
since the cry of gold. In fact, I might even try my own
luck at it one day."

He paused, as though weighing his next words.
"Anyhow, as I was saying," he then said, "the rush
of people to Australia has made the demand much
greater for all sorts of transportation."

He looked over his shoulder out the window. "As
you found in this country as the rush for gold became so maddening," he said, slowly returning his
gaze to those who watched him silently. "I would ad-
vise you to make your residence in Melbourne."

He looked down at his hand as he resumed twirling the glass between his fingers. "Most of Australia
is hard, dry and stubborn. It misses the softening,
life-giving quality of rain. Rivers and streams are
few," he said in a monotone, "but you will find that
it is heavily forested around Melbourne, with alpine
flowers and rushing streams."

His gaze moved to Nadine, and his eyes locked with
hers. "But in Melbourne you will find something else
not all that attractive to the ladies of your house-
hold," he said thickly.

"And what is that?" Harry asked smoothly.

"There are prison hulks moored in the bay," Lloyd
said, watching closely for Nadine's expression to

change to one of horror. The knowledge of the existence of the floating rat holes sent most ladies into a state of shock. Most didn't even want to know that such things existed.

Lloyd was glad of the compassion he saw registered in Nadine's eyes. He had been right about her from the start. Perhaps she might even understand when he explained his own personal history.

"My God," Sam said, his words sounding strangled. "Think of the danger to the citizens of Melbourne."

Harry's thick brows knit together in a frown. "What are the dangers?" he asked dryly. "Seems we missed being informed of the prison hulks being there. We're going to take up residence on the outskirts of Melbourne. I've been told there are some nice ranches there, vacated by officers of the British militia. Sam and I've already made arrangements to purchase one of the finest spreads," he said with a strange sort of hiss, startling Nadine.

That was not all that startled her. So did what her father had said. He had said that he *and* Sam had made arrangements to purchase a ranch. Were they going into partnership in the buying of a house?

Nadine glared at Sam before looking at her father wonderingly. She was becoming more and more confused about the arrangement between her father and his partner....

"There are few dangers to the local citizenry," Lloyd said, his lips pursed in anger as he thought of what had happened to him in Australia. "The dangers are for those unfortunates who have been 'transported' to Australia as punishment. The prisons are a place of organized terror, where brutal, unjust guards punish men in every cruel way known. Where pity is unknown and the voice of mercy never heard. In the hulks, even to smile when spoken to is punished by the lash.''

Nadine's insides grew cold at the thought of what Lloyd was describing. She had a feeling that there was more behind his description of the prison hulks than what he was actually saying aloud.

Something made her look at the scar on his right cheekbone. Could it be that he was speaking from experience?

"Do men ever escape?" Mariel asked in a weak voice, her face pale.

"Very rarely," Lloyd said, shaking his head. "But when there *is* an escape, convicts have usually been *allowed* to, so those in charge can play a cruel game of hide-and-seek."

"Good Lord," Mariel said, scooting her chair backward and easing from it, trembling. She held a limp hand to her brow. "Please excuse me. I feel so faint."

Nadine rushed from her chair and went to her mother. "Mother, you look so pale," she gasped. Placing an arm around her mother's tiny waist, she began to lead her from the room, giving Lloyd a nervous glance over her shoulder. He boldly returned her gaze, unnerving her.

Her pulse racing, Nadine escorted her mother from the room.

* * *

After helping her mother to her room and into bed, Nadine felt the need of a breath of fresh air to help clear her thoughts. Rain was falling in torrents, yet she stood on the porch looking out to sea, oblivious to the lurid flashes of lightning that danced along the horizon, turning nighttime into day.

A fierce clap of thunder caused the boards beneath her feet to tremble, and she drew her fringed shawl more snugly around her shoulders and hugged herself against the wall of the porch. Her mind was a jumble of thoughts, thoughts of the long sea voyage that lay ahead of her, thoughts of the handsome stranger.

The door beside her suddenly swung open. She nestled closer to the wall, hidden in the darkness, listening to her father telling Lloyd Harpster just when and where to board the *Lady Fortune*.

Then the door closed behind him and Lloyd was there, alone, fastening his gun belt around his narrow waist, unaware that Nadine was watching. He positioned his hat on his head as he peered out into the thundering rain. He began to walk toward his horse but stopped, startled, when out of the corner of his eye another flash of lightning revealed Nadine.

"Ma'am?" he gasped, turning on his heel to face her. "What are you doing out here? The weather is fierce."

His gaze swept over her as he wondered if she was waiting for him. Was she going to tell him how much she disapproved of having to be on the long voyage with him after meeting him in such a crude, uncivil manner earlier in the day?

Or would her eyes reveal that she was no longer angry with him, that she was sympathetic? She had defended him in front of her family. Why was that, if not that she was just as attracted to him as he was to her?

Nadine's insides quivered at his probing stare. At this moment, Lloyd Harpster was making her feel the same way he had when they had first met and his eyes had held her captive. Though she was chilled by the rain and wind, her insides were melting with a strange sort of heat.

Lloyd scratched his brow idly. "Don't you have anything to say?" he asked, laughing awkwardly. "Or are you expecting another apology like the one you did not accept outside the saloon this afternoon?"

Gallantly he swept his hat from his head and bowed. "Sorry, ma'am," he said in a slow drawl. "It won't happen again."

Nadine inched close to him and spoke up into his face as he straightened to a standing position. "Who *are* you, truly?" she asked in a harsh whisper. "Why have you chosen the *Lady Fortune* for your return voyage to Australia? Why did you even come to America in the first place? What draws you *back* to Australia?"

Lloyd placed his hat back on his head. "First you have nothing to say and then you can't stop talking," he said, his eyes twinkling. "Such a little lady for such big questions. Do you drill every man who comes to dinner in such a manner?"

Nadine gasped, and her eyes widened. "You are not just any man coming to dinner," she said dryly, pulling nervously on the shawl around her shoulders. "Do you forget so quickly just how you happened to be here? Perhaps I was wrong in defending you when Sam Parsons tried to put you in your place. Perhaps he spies a rogue much more quickly than I."

"A rogue?" Lloyd chuckled. "That's interesting. I haven't been called a rogue for a very long time."

Nadine's breath left her as he grabbed her and enfolded her in his steely arms. "If I'm accused of being a rogue, I guess I might as well live up to the reputation. Wouldn't you think so, ma'am?"

He drew her more roughly into his arms and, bending over her, sought her lips with his mouth, kissing her with an easy sureness. She wanted to fight back, yet the euphoria that filled her entire being was so sudden, so intense, it was almost more than she could bear. She could do nothing but respond in kind to his kiss.

Too soon, he released her, looking down at her with his haunting blue eyes. "Did anyone ever tell you how lovely you look in red?" he said thickly.

He spun on his heels and moved quickly from the porch, leaving Nadine alone and shaking with desire. She tried to bring her breathing under control as she watched him mount his strawberry roan and ride away in the rain. Lifting her fingers to her lips that still tasted of him, she held the wondrous feelings he had awakened inside her within the protective cocoon of her heart. She knew that no matter what his reasons for kissing her, she would always cherish this brief moment with him. She wanted him, yet she feared her own desire.

Nadine looked into the distance as Lloyd disappeared into the rainy night. A sweet current of warmth swept through her, for she knew that soon they would be together, bound by the vast stretches of ocean. With his kiss so fresh on her lips, she welcomed the time to come.

Chapter Three

ONE MONTH LATER...

The snowy sails of the *Lady Fortune* billowed before the favoring wind. In a high-necked cotton dress, Nadine stood alone on the top deck, watching the foam that silvered the sea at the ship's side. Overhead, stars sequined the dark heavens.

Clutching the fringed shawl around her shoulders, Nadine looked out across the dark stretch of water, seeing nothing. The sea breeze left a faint taste of salt on her lips, and there was no sound except the steady slapping of the waves against the sides of the powerful clipper. She was thankful that the two-masted *Lady Fortune* was faster and more comfortable than the average vessel. Most were built only for cargo, and passengers were crowded into makeshift bunks in the hold.

The *Lady Fortune* was a passenger ship, designed with cabins that gave passengers a great deal of comfort and privacy. It had windmill ventilators that kept

a constant current of fresh air running throughout,
and it was kept immaculately clean. Its hull was
painted scarlet, and her oiled mahogany decks
gleamed in the sunlight.

Yet, though the ship was a luxury vessel, Nadine
felt that nothing would be as good as having both her
feet on solid ground. Weeks—months—of sea travel
lay ahead of her.

Her thoughts drifted to Lloyd Harpster. She had
tried to avoid him, and she did not know any more
about him than she had before, but his friendly smiles
and easy nature had made it hard to resist him. He
was a most intriguing man. She didn't believe that she
would ever truly get to know the man behind the fa-
cade of gentle smiles.

"Lovely night, isn't it?"

The hair at the nape of Nadine's neck bristled at the
sound of Sam Parsons's voice as he stepped up beside her at the ship's rail. Since the night Lloyd
Harpster had made his appearance at the Quinns'
dinner table, Sam had not wasted any time pursuing
Nadine's affections. She had to wonder if Sam had
spied on them that night on the porch. Had he seen
Lloyd kiss her?

Refusing to give Sam the satisfaction of being able
to look her square in the eye when he talked to her,
Nadine stared out to sea with renewed dread of the
long voyage. When Sam Parsons decided he wanted
something, he usually pursued it until he got it. How
else had he cinched this partnership with her father?
He was the first man who had ever gotten this close
to Harry Quinn. He might have won her father's

confidence but Nadine would never let him sway her into liking, much less loving, him!

"The evening was lovely," Nadine said icily. "But now I find it quite dull."

She swung the skirt of her dress around and started to walk away but was stopped by Sam's firm grip on her wrist.

"Not so fast," he growled, his thin, sleek mustache and black suit making him appear even more sinister than usual in the gloomy darkness of the night.

Nadine's shawl fluttered to the floor as he pulled her toward him, and her green eyes filled with anger as she glared up at him.

"I don't see you running away from that Australian when he approaches you," Sam persisted stubbornly. "You look damn starry-eyed when he comes near you. Nadine, what is it with you? What have I done to deserve such treatment? You've known me much longer than that damn shifty gambler."

Nadine felt an instinct to defend Lloyd, as she had done at the dinner table that first night, but thought better of it. Sam already had enough jealousy to last him the entire trip to Australia.

"Sam, when you chose to behave as a suitor instead of just my father's partner, everything changed between us," she said, lifting her chin haughtily. "I care for only a casual acquaintance with you. Nothing more. Why can't you understand that?"

"You know that I won't give up all that easily," he said huskily. "I've waited patiently for you much longer than I've ever waited for anything that I decided to make mine."

"You're going to have to wait until hell freezes over before getting me," Nadine snapped.

She tried to jerk herself free from his grasp but winced with pain as his fingers tightened on her wrist. "Unhand me, Sam. If you don't, I'll scream. Father would not approve of your behavior tonight. He might even sever his partnership with you."

Sam let out a low chuckle, and his dark eyes glittered. "I doubt that."

"Without Father's wealth to back you up you'd be nothing, Sam. Nothing!" Nadine threatened.

"How naive you are," Sam said. "Perhaps it's time for you to learn the ways of the grown-up world."

He yanked Nadine so close that their bodies pressed together as though one. "I'll teach you the wonders of a kiss."

His lips brushed teasingly against hers. "Then, later, I'll teach you even more."

His mouth bore savagely down onto Nadine's lips. She pushed at his chest and tried to work her mouth free, but Sam was holding her immobile. One hand held her head, the fingers coiling tightly through her hair, while the other slipped around and pressed firmly against her buttocks, shoving her against the outline of his risen manhood.

The feel of Sam's hardness caused Nadine to panic. She tried to kick him, but her feet became tangled in the skirt of her dress. Her eyes were wild as she searched for someone to come and rescue her.

A quick movement through the darkness and a shuffling of approaching feet caught Nadine's attention just as Sam moved his hand to cup one of her breasts. Everything seemed to become a blur of motion. Suddenly Nadine was freed and Lloyd was there, hitting Sam with his doubled fists.

"You bastard!" Lloyd exclaimed, wrestling Sam to the deck and straddling him as he held his wrists to the sea-dampened flooring. "You obviously don't know how to treat a lady."

Nadine placed a hand to her mouth, stifling a sob as she stared down at Sam, whose eyes were wide with fright and whose lip and nose were bleeding. Her lips stung from his savage kiss, and her heart was thundering wildly.

She was grateful to Lloyd for having rescued her. She did not want to think about what Sam had been planning to "teach" her. Maybe now he would stay away from her.

"Let me up, damn you," Sam spit, his whole body aching from the beating. His eyes glinted as he looked up at Lloyd. "You'll be sorry, Harpster. Somehow, someday, I'll get you for this."

Lloyd laughed, his eyes twinkling. "A man like you making threats?" he said, laughing again. "I welcome the threat. It'll make life a wee bit more interesting, wouldn't you say?"

He released Sam's wrists and pulled away from him, moving to stand beside Nadine. He slipped an arm possessively around her waist and glowered down at Sam, who was slowly picking himself up from the deck. "Listen to my threat," he drawled. "Never lay a hand on this lady again, or I won't waste time playing with you."

Wiping a stream of blood from his chin, Sam hunched over and walked away backward. Glancing from Lloyd to Nadine, he turned and rushed away into the void of night.

Nadine wiped a stray tear from the corner of her eye. She felt a current of warmth spread through her as Lloyd placed a finger to her chin and lifted it so that their eyes could meet and hold.

"I don't know what to say, except thank you," she murmured.

"Are you all right?" he asked thickly.

Nadine's face warmed with a blush. "I'm fine," she said, smoothing the wrinkles from her dress. "I am now, that is."

"I think I put the fear of God into him," Lloyd said, raking his eyes over her, again taken by her vulnerable loveliness. Then he frowned down at her. "I'm surprised that someone so close to your family would try to take advantage of you."

"Perhaps he is close to my father, but not to me," Nadine murmured. She could still taste Sam on her mouth and feel the pinch of his hands on her buttocks. She welcomed the spray of the salty seawater as it settled on her lips, erasing any claim Sam had made on them. "He is a leech. He clings to my family as though he were kin, and he won't be happy until he is. He's determined to marry me."

Lloyd laughed. "I think he needs a few lessons in how to woo a lady," he said, his eyes twinkling. "Perhaps I could give him one or two."

"Please don't," Nadine gasped. She laughed absently when she realized what she had just said, then cleared her throat nervously, suddenly feeling awkward. The times she and Lloyd had chanced to meet on the voyage had been in broad daylight, in view of everyone. Somehow, being alone in the dark enhanced the sensual feelings she had for him. Should he try what Sam had just tried, she would welcome it. She could so easily fall hopelessly in love with him.

"Before I saw you struggling with Sam, I was on my way below deck to check on my horse," Lloyd said, nodding toward the companionway ladder. "Would you care to join me?"

Lloyd was feeling the dangers of staying in the darkness with Nadine for much longer. He could not help but feel the same sort of urges that had most surely driven Sam Parsons to kiss her. He hungered for more than a mere kiss. He ached to fully consume this lovely lady with the cute nose and the intriguing, wide-set green eyes. Though he had tasted the sweetness of her lips only once, that had been enough for him to be certain that he had most surely been destined to go to America. He had made good his escape from his tormentor, Captain Grenville, and he had met the lady who would have possession of his heart for eternity!

"I'd love to," Nadine said, hoping she didn't sound too eager, for she did not want him to be aware of her feelings for him. In truth, she was confused by them herself. "Your horse is one of the loveliest I have ever seen."

Lloyd bent and swept Nadine's shawl up from the deck, gently placing it around her shoulders. "He's a fine horse, but I've another that's teased my mind for some time now," he said, snaking an arm around Nadine's waist and leading her to the stairs. "It's the damnedest wild thing on four legs."

"Oh?" Nadine said, giving him a sideways glance as she followed him down the companionway ladder. "Where did you see it?"

"He haunts the hills and valleys around Melbourne," Lloyd said, envisioning the black stallion even now, with its long mane and sweeping tail and the white patch of hair on its chest in the shape of a star. He stood apart from all other horses Lloyd had ever seen. "He doesn't know it, but I have already laid claim on him. Mark my words, he will be mine."

"Do you truly believe you will see it again?" Nadine asked as they went down other steps that took them deeper into the bowels of the ship. "How long have you been gone from Australia? Why did you leave?"

She paused, weighing her next words.

Then she blurted, "Why are you returning?"

The ensuing silence made Nadine uncomfortable. She was about to repeat the question when they reached the hold and the sweet smell of hay wafted through the air. It was a welcome change from the smell of the sea.

Lloyd took her into an area sectioned off from the rest of the cargo, and she saw the cattle and horses stabled in separate areas. Her father had a reputation for being kind to all his passengers, even the animals who were forced to make the long voyage across the sea. All the animals were well kept. Most looked content.

"He is so beautiful!" Nadine sighed, stepping up to Lloyd's strawberry roan. She began stroking the horse's thick, flowing chestnut mane. "Surely no wild horse could compare. Perhaps it is because you cannot possess the wild horse all that easily that it is more alluring in your eyes."

Lloyd plucked a handful of hay from the floor and began feeding it to his horse. "He's no brumby, that's for sure." He laughed. "But he'll do in a pinch. If it's spirit and fire you want, it's the brumbies you go after."

"Brumbies?" Nadine asked, lifting an eyebrow questioningly. "What on earth are brumbies?"

"Wild horses," Lloyd said, almost dreamily. "A stallion is the wildest. They can tease worse than a woman!"

Nadine continued stroking the horse. "So you think women are teases?" she asked softly, not sure she should guide the conversation into such a delicate area.

A whale-oil lamp hung on the far wall. Nadine's hair spilled over her shoulders, taking on a brilliant red cast in the lamp's glow. "Do you?" she persisted, avoiding eye contact with Lloyd, afraid that he might think she was flirting with him, when in reality she was just trying to find a way to pull the truth from him.

"Would it matter if I did?" Lloyd asked, drawn to her as though she were a magnet. He twined his fingers eagerly through her hair, his free hand lifting her chin so that their eyes could meet.

"Would it?" he persisted huskily.

Nadine was taken aback by the suddenness of his movement. She looked up at him, keenly aware of the slope of his hard jaw, of the fire burning in his eyes and of the golden hair that framed his handsome face.

Suddenly she forgot what they had been discussing. Being so near to him, with his lips drawing closer, closer, she was robbed of all thought except that she wanted his kiss. She wanted to be held within his muscular arms. Nothing mattered but the hunger eating away at her insides, a hunger that was caused by him.

"Would it what?" she asked, her voice trembling, feeling foolish at her sudden show of absentmindedness.

"Would it be all right if I kissed you?" Lloyd asked, his lips brushing lightly against hers.

"I don't believe that was what we were discussing at all." Nadine sighed, delicious shivers of desire running through her.

"Does it truly matter?" Lloyd whispered, now kissing the hollow of her throat. "You are so damn beautiful."

His mouth finally found her lips. His kiss was hot and demanding, spinning a delicious web of passion around her pounding heart. Twining her arms about his neck, she clung to him, the wondrous feelings overwhelming her even more than the first time he had kissed her. A tingling sort of liquid heat was spreading deep inside her.

When his hand cupped her breast through her dress, everything that had ever been beautiful in her life before this moment dimmed, for the pleasure that his touch evoked outshone them all.

A great roar of a voice wrenched Nadine from Lloyd's arms. Trembling, her face colored with a deep blush, she turned and faced the threat of her father, who stood only a footstep away in the darkness of the corridor, his fists doubled at his sides.

"What the hell is going on here?" Harry demanded loudly, stepping into the light of the whale-oil lamp. His eyes were brimming with anger as he glanced from Lloyd to Nadine, seeing a deep guilt etched on his daughter's face. "It doesn't take much common sense to figure it out, does it?"

Not wanting to make another scene with this damn Australian in front of Nadine, Harry grabbed her by a wrist and jerked her to him, trying to keep his temper under control. "I've been looking all over for you," he said, his eyes dark with emotion. He was oblivious of Lloyd, who was standing silently, looking on. His hands clasped her shoulders, and he turned her to face him. "Your mother needs you, Nadine. She's not feeling well. She's burning up with some sort of fever."

"Mother, ill?" Nadine gasped, shaken by the news. Then her eyes grew wary. She wondered if her mother was truly that ill at all. Perhaps her father, having found her in a lover's embrace with a man he detested, was trying to alarm her unduly.

"A person can't pick and choose when a sick spell takes hold," Harry growled, giving Lloyd an angry sideways glance. "But one can pick and choose whom to associate with! And, Daughter, I've warned you about this scoundrel."

"Father, please..." Nadine said, casting her eyes downward. "This isn't the time...."

"Any time is the right time to warn you against a man who is wrong for you," Harry said, glaring at Lloyd. He took his hands away from Nadine and took a bold step closer to Lloyd. "Harpster, you stay away from my daughter, do you hear?"

"I believe she's old enough to make her own choices in life," Lloyd growled, challenging Harry with an angry, set stare.

Nadine looked from her father to Lloyd, infuriated by the way they talked about her as though she were not even present. Both of them seemed to have forgotten that she did have a mind of her own.

"Will you two just stop it?" she stormed, her voice so loud that the horses in the stalls whinnied nervously. "I am perfectly capable of taking care of myself! I am old enough to know what I want, and right now, at this moment, it's not to be near either of you!"

Holding the shawl securely around her shoulders, she began to run, her feet barely seeming to touch the steps as she climbed upward. Her mind was floating between the memory of Lloyd's kiss and the fire of his hand through the cotton of her dress, and her father's troubling words about her mother.

Never had she felt so torn as she did at this moment.

Chapter Four

The whale-oil lamp emitted only a faint glow of light upon the pale face of sickness. Nadine sat at her mother's bedside, smoothing a damp cloth across her mother's feverish brow, feeling a bit more confident at the moment that perhaps the strange fever that had gripped her mother these past several days was lessening in its intensity. Mariel lay on the bed with her auburn hair spread out across the pillow like a delicate halo. Her cheeks were no longer flaming with color, and her eyes were peacefully closed in what appeared to be a restful sleep.

Harry Quinn's tall shadow fell across Nadine as he moved quietly into the dusky cabin. He placed a comforting hand on her shoulder. "Daughter, why don't you go to your cabin and rest a bit?" he said hoarsely. "I've already ordered a tub of hot water readied for you. Go soak the smell of sickness off your flesh. I'll see to your mother. It's my duty to do so, you know."

Nadine turned her eyes to her father. She covered the hand that rested on her shoulder with one of her own, smiling warmly up at him. "I've not minded at all sitting vigil at her bedside," she said in a whisper, not wanting to disturb her mother. "I've understood why you found it hard to. It must hurt terribly to see your wife so full of life one minute, so ill the next. I feel totally helpless. It must be worse for a husband."

"It seems you're stronger than me under these circumstances," Harry choked out, tears brimming in his dark eyes. He drew Nadine up from the chair and into his arms. "Honey, how come I was so lucky as to have two such special women in my life?"

Nadine returned his affectionate hug, then eased from his arms with a heavy sigh. Kneading her brow, she rolled down the sleeves of her cotton dress. "A bath sounds grand," she said, her voice weak with emotion. "You always seem to know what I need."

Her words faded as she recalled just how little her father understood her need to feel free to make her own choice of men. If it were up to him, she would eventually marry Sam. But she wondered how he would feel if he knew that Sam had forced himself upon her.

Thus far, Nadine had chosen not to tell her father about what Sam had done. She didn't believe it was necessary. Lloyd Harpster had warned Sam against trying anything again, and it seemed Sam had taken the threat seriously.

"But you don't always listen to my advice, do you?" Harry said, haunted again by the vision of Nadine in the arms of Lloyd Harpster.

Damn the turn of the cards that had made it possible for the Australian to be on this long voyage. Before her mother's illness, Nadine had been too spirited not to seek some sort of excitement to pass the time of day. And damn the Australian for recognizing this restless trait in her and taking advantage of it.

"I'll be going on to my cabin now," Nadine said softly, ignoring her father's last question. It was a question that he already knew the answer to. She did not wish to get into a discussion of Lloyd or her feelings toward him. It truly did seem that sometimes love had no choice at all. It was the heart that made the final decision.

"You need this time alone with Mother," she added. "Though she's fast asleep, perhaps she can somehow sense your presence. I am sure it will give her some comfort."

Nodding, Harry slipped into the chair beside his wife's bed. He took one of her limp hands from beneath the quilt, lifted it to his lips and softly kissed it before replacing it beneath the warmth of the covers. Then he held his head in his hands and began a quiet prayer.

Touched deeply, Nadine stifled a sob. Turning away from him, she moved out into the sunshine, inhaling the sweet, fresh fragrance of the sea. Somehow, out there, drenched by the sun, splashed by the seawater as the perfumed breezes filled the *Lady Fortune*'s sails, death seemed very far away!

Walking along the deck, the weight of worry now less burdensome on her heart, Nadine hurried to her own cabin, anxious to bathe and slip into a crisp, clean dress. She had no plans to take a nap. Her mind was recalling the lovely strawberry roan down in the hold of the ship, surely lonesome for company.

Glad to be in the private confines of her own cabin, Nadine closed the door behind her and latched it. She spied the copper tub in the middle of the room, steam hanging like fog over it. The aroma of perfumed soap wafted through the air, and a luxurious towel lay on the bed.

Nadine could not get undressed quickly enough. She stepped gingerly into the steamy water and relaxed, enjoying the warmth of the water soaking slowly into her weary muscles.

After soaping herself, she scooted farther down into the water. Relaxing at last, she let her eyes wander, admiring the cabin her father had assigned her.

It was large and furnished with a red plush settee and an overstuffed leather chair. The doors were framed in mahogany, and the built-in bureau had a metal rail around its top to hold objects when the ship pitched. Upon the bureau sat an enameled basin and ewer, and on the floor was a tin chamber pot. A small bed, spread with a white eyelet covering, sat at the far side of the room.

A massive trunk sat at the foot of the bed, filled with Nadine's beautiful silk and satin dresses. Nadine eyed the trunk for a moment, her mind drifting to the red dress that lay snugly between the others. It was the one she had worn the night Lloyd had come to dinner. It made a strange sort of warmth surge through her to recall how he had commented on how lovely she looked in red.

"One day, perhaps, I shall wear the same dress for him again," she whispered as she rose from the tub.

She dried herself and drew on a fresh, clean cotton dress with delicate lace bordering the low bodice. She brushed her hair until its copper strands shone and then left the cabin.

Momentarily pausing outside her mother's closed door, she felt saddened, but reassured herself that her mother was finally on the road to recovery. Moving on, she headed down the steps that took her deep into the bowels of the ship.

When she picked up the scent of hay, she knew she was drawing closer to where the horses were stabled. Her heart began to race as she recalled the first time she had been there, and with whom. She suddenly realized that it was not the horse drawing her back there, but the horse's owner. Perhaps he would come, just as she had, drawn by the memory of their previous meeting.

Her long hair hung like fine spun silk down her back and her ripe body trembled beneath her cotton dress as she hurried from one dark passageway to another. She dared not look over her shoulder for fear that someone might be following her. She wished now that she had remembered to carry her pistol. This was the reason her father had given it to her, for her daring moments of wandering on the ship alone.

Now beyond reach of all human sounds, Nadine heard only the timbers of the ship creaking and the steady slapping of the waves against the ship's hull.

The neighing of a horse came from somewhere close by. She felt her way along the dark wall, heading toward a dim light just ahead. She sighed with relief when she finally reached the section of the hull where the horses were stabled.

Glad that the whale-oil lamp anchored to the wall afforded her enough light, Nadine stepped across a cushion of spread straw and went to Lloyd's horse.

"Hello," she whispered, running her hand down his sleek neck. She warmed inside as she felt his soft, whiskered lips brush her hand, searching for something to eat.

"Yes, I should have brought you something," Nadine purred. "How thoughtless of me. But I will next time."

Nadine's hand wandered farther, smoothing down his flanks. The roan was a big, splendid animal, with solid legs. She could tell by the way his hair glistened that someone had spent much time grooming him lately. Had Lloyd walked him today, to give the horse the exercise he needed to stay healthy on the long sea voyage?

The horse whinnied softly as she moved on to stroke his broad shoulders.

"It's all right," Nadine reassured him. "I'm your friend. I'm your friend forever, if you will allow it."

"And also mine, I hope."

The familiar voice made Nadine draw a ragged breath, and her heart fluttered strangely. She was shocked by the intensity of the feelings his voice caused inside her.

She wheeled around to face him. "I didn't hear you come into the stall," she said in a rush, clasping her hands together behind her so that he would not see them trembling.

"That's not good," Lloyd said, taking a step closer, his boots making no sound on the straw beneath them.

"Oh?" Nadine said. "Why would you say that?"

Her gaze absorbed him. His blue shirt was half unbuttoned, revealing thick golden chest hair where it gaped open in front. His dark, snug breeches displayed his manliness to an extreme, almost shameful degree.

Feeling a rush of heat to her cheeks, Nadine forced her eyes quickly upward. His waist was void of his pistols, making him look somehow half-naked.

"Ma'am, anyone could have sneaked up on you," he said in a low growl. His gaze raking over her, he saw everything about her that pleased him, everything that could cause a man to lose control of his senses. "You shouldn't be here alone. Have you gone crazy?"

The fact that he still called her "Ma'am," and the fact that he was implying that she was foolish, sparked Nadine's anger. She placed her hands on her hips and glared up at him. How could she even think she could love a man who wouldn't even call her by her name? Did that mean that he did not separate her in his heart from all the others he had surely known before her?

"I'll have you know that I have a name and that I am perfectly capable of taking care of myself," she spit angrily.

But then he smiled at her—it was an amused smile, she thought—and she could not restrain an answering smile of her own.

Again she stroked the roan's neck. "Your horse. Have you exercised him today?" she said absently, aware that Lloyd was now standing close beside her. She could smell his clean, familiar scent. It was like the outdoors, fresh and new. He alone seemed to lay claim to that smell, a smell undisturbed by the expensive colognes worn by the rich.

She adored the difference. Oh, Lord, she could not deny that she adored him.

"Yes. He's been exercised."

"And fed?"

"And fed."

Nadine's pulse began to race as Lloyd bent his head to kiss her delicately tapering neck. "And watered?" she murmured, her breath catching as his hand cupped her breast through her dress, causing a strange, curling heat at the pit of her stomach.

"Yes, watered," he said huskily.

Nadine turned with a start to face him, her skin on fire where his hand had touched her through her dress. "What do you think you are doing?" she gasped, taking a quick step away from him, shaken.

Lloyd raked his fingers nervously through his golden hair, feeling as though he were the rogue she had already called him. This was not the time to approach Nadine in such a way. Her mother was ill. She was too vulnerable. He would not take advantage of her now.

"I'm sorry, Nadine," he murmured, gently taking her hands and looking down into her eyes. "Your mother? How does she fare?"

Nadine swallowed hard, battling her feelings for Lloyd as he mesmerized her with his intense stare. It warmed her clear through to realize that he wanted her as badly as she wanted him.

"My mother was not doing well at all, but I think the fever has broken," she said softly. "Thank you for caring."

There was a strained silence between them. Nadine lowered her eyes bashfully, aware of the reason for the silence. Lloyd's hands still clasped hers, and she felt almost dizzy with desire.

But this was not the time for such thoughts. She must return to her cabin in case her father again requested her presence at her mother's bedside.

Easing her hands from Lloyd's, Nadine lifted her eyes to his. "I really must be going," she murmured. "My mother—"

Lloyd started to reach for her, to draw her into his arms, to give her comfort, but decided against it. He was afraid that if she came any closer to him he would not be able to let her go, and he must.

"Yes, I understand," he said thickly, clasping his hands tightly behind him. "If there's anything I can do—"

"Thank you," Nadine said softly, smiling up at him. With a nervous heartbeat, she turned quickly and fled.

Lloyd doubled a fist at his side and swore under his breath. Just how long could he deny himself? It was in her eyes, in her whisper of a voice. He knew she wanted him!

He went to his horse and began stroking its flanks. "Though you've been a faithful steed, I'm still going after that brumby," he whispered. "And, by damn, not only that stallion, but also that lovely lady that just hurried from my arms."

Harry Quinn stirred uneasily in the chair beside his wife's bed at the sound of footsteps approaching from behind him. He turned and saw Sam moving quietly toward him. Oh, how he despised the sight of the man, especially at a time like this, when he was reminded of how short life could be.

Harry could not even recall how Sam had become his "partner." In the beginning, Sam had been his accountant. Harry had been the one who had the money and the wherewithal to run a successful business. But somewhere along the line, things had taken a different turn. Sam had duped Harry out of a lot of money. Harry was sure of it. Now he was barely keeping his head above water financially, and Sam was the one with the money. His money, he was sure of it.

Harry had remained civil to Sam, accepting his handouts and behaving like a man who still possessed riches to save face with his family. He had to, at least long enough to figure out just how the son of a bitch had tricked him and how to get it all back!

Harry even had to pretend to approve of Sam's desire to marry Nadine!

But when push came to shove, he'd be damned if he'd give his daughter away to such a sneaking, conniving bastard.

Harry pushed himself up from the chair and intercepted Sam's approach, taking him by the elbow and guiding him back out of the darkened room. "Mariel's not at all well, Sam," he said quietly. "I don't like the sounds of her breathing. There are traces of death rattles now. It surely won't be long."

"Does Nadine know?" Sam asked, clasping his fingers around the ship's rail as he and Harry stopped to look out to sea.

"She thinks her mother is better," Harry said, kneading his brow nervously. "But she's never heard death rattles before. When she saw her mother sleeping, she thought she was better! But she's not. She's not." He turned his eyes to Sam. "If her mother dies, Nadine will have only me."

"And me," Sam said thickly. "She'll be my wife."

Harry winced at the determination in Sam's voice, but he also recalled Nadine in Lloyd Harpster's arms. It seemed that Nadine might have plans for her future that did not include Sam. The more Harry thought about it, the more he thought that perhaps it was for the best. For it was sure that Lloyd Harpster could put Sam Parsons in his place!

"Sam, I know that's what you want," he said hoarsely. "But sometimes things don't work out exactly as we plan. And, Sam, listen well to what I have to say. Death being so close makes one think on his own death. I'm thinking of the future, when I may not be around. You'd better treat Nadine fairly! You know my dislike of attorneys. I have not made out a will because of my aversion to them. I don't want them poking their nose into my private affairs."

"Yes, I know," Sam said, giving Harry a sideways glance. "And I understand."

"What I am trying to say is, Sam, should Nadine choose not to marry you, and should I die an untimely death sometime in the near future, you'd better see that she gets part of what you cheated me out of," Harry said. He turned his eyes back to the sea. "If you don't, I'll haunt you from my grave until the day you die."

Sam's eyes lighted with fire, and his jaw tightened. He started to protest, but stopped short when a movement at the corner of his eye caught his full attention. He turned and jolted with alarm at the sight of Nadine stepping up from the companionway ladder.

His insides grew cold as she turned and paled. Their eyes met and held, and he recognized guilt in the green depths of hers. He did not have to guess where she had been, or with whom. She had had a rendezvous with that damn Australian.

Sam turned his eyes slowly away from her, seething inside, for it seemed that where Nadine Quinn was concerned, he was going to be the loser.

He could not allow that to happen.

"Harry, you'd just better see to it that Nadine does marry me," he threatened smoothly. Turning, he walked briskly away.

Chapter Five

Breathless, Nadine rushed into her cabin and slammed the door behind her. Her heart pounding, she leaned against it, still feeling Sam's icy eyes upon her. There had been so much in the way he had looked at her. It was as though she had interrupted something between Sam and her father, and it surely had to do with her, for Sam had never looked at her with such hate and lust.

"What did Father say to him?" she whispered, her breathing becoming more even as her heart slowed its beating to a more normal pace. "I ought to be thankful that Father didn't see me when Sam did. If he realized that I was alone with Lloyd again, who is to say what he might do?" But she had to wonder why Sam had not pointed her out to her father. Why had he let her pass on behind them unnoticed?

There was a knock on the door behind her and Nadine jumped away in fright and eyed the door warily. Then her gaze swept around the room. The copper tub still stood with water in it. Her clothes were strewed carelessly around. She sighed with relief. Why, surely it was only the cabin boy, coming to remove the bathtub and water.

A smile quivering on her lips, Nadine lifted the latch and flung the door open, only to stiffen when she discovered that it was Sam. His dark eyes bore down upon her as he leaned against the wall, his arms folded casually across his chest, his black suit and shock of hair hardly definable in the dark, scarcely lighted corridor.

"You!" Nadine said, putting a hand to her throat. "What do you want?"

"Why are you so alarmed to find me at your doorstep? Me, your intended," Sam taunted, smiling crookedly down at her. "Was our last private encounter all that distasteful?"

Nadine squared her shoulders and set her jaw firmly, glaring up at him. "You know that it was far less than pleasant," she hissed. "And, if you will recall, you were warned against bothering me again."

Sam looked aimlessly from side to side before turning back to Nadine with a smile of mockery. "There's no one here to stop anything I choose to do." He chuckled. "If I'm observant enough, I would wager to say that you just left your Australian friend."

He tsk-tsk'd, shaking his head. "Do you lower yourself to meeting men in the hold of a ship now? That's not at all respectable, Nadine. What's a body to think? What's a man who is ready to offer you a wedding ring, and all the security in the world that you could ever want, to think?"

"If you speak of yourself as that man who offers so much, then who cares what you think?" Nadine said dryly. Still, she felt uneasy about his having realized where she had just been.

"Nadine, did you ever think what might happen if your mother died and then your father should just suddenly up and die, also?" Sam said, edging his way past her into her cabin.

Nadine was taken aback by Sam's words. She turned and watched him, momentarily stunned by what he had said and by his crudeness. He was walking idly around the room, lifting her discarded clothes, a piece at a time. Nadine's insides turned cold as he raised her delicate underthings to his nose to take a whiff of her scent, which still clung to them.

"My father is as healthy as a horse," Nadine finally blurted, rushing to him and grabbing her camisole from his hands. "Sam, you're despicable. Leave my cabin at once. Why do you persist in bothering me? You know that no matter what you say or do I will never care for you in the way that you want."

"If the Australian had not come into your life, things would not have changed between you and I," Sam growled, going to Nadine and grabbing her by a wrist to yank her next to him. "Nadine, if not for him you would be planning to marry me."

"That's not so," Nadine said, her eyes wild, recalling just how he had overpowered her before. Lloyd had intervened then, but Lloyd would not this time. Lloyd had no reason to believe that she was not perfectly safe.

This time Sam could get away with murder, should he choose to!

Panic seized Nadine. She feared the worst. Her gaze swept around the room, stopping at the pistol that she had left lying on the table beside her bed. If she could get to the gun, she could grab it and put one good scare into him. When she thrust the barrel of the pistol into his ribs, surely he would think twice before attempting to accost her again!

"Sam, once and for all, you will leave me alone!" she snarled, grabbing a handful of his hair with her free hand and pulling for all it was worth. His yowl pierced the air, and his eyes bulged with pain as he released his hold on Nadine's wrist long enough for her to scramble to the table and pick up the pistol.

Nadine aimed the firearm with one shaking hand, steadying it with the other. "Sam, I won't hesitate to shoot if you take one step closer," she said, her voice quivering. "Now do you leave? Or do I pull the trigger?"

His dark eyes glittering, Sam placed a hand before him and began to edge toward the door. "Where did you get that thing?" he said hoarsely. "Be careful. You surely don't know the first thing about a gun. You may fire it by accident."

"If I fire it, it won't be by accident," Nadine threatened, breathing hard, not knowing if she could truly pull the trigger. He was obviously unsure himself, or he would not be moving so cautiously away from her.

Her insides grew warm with a feeling of power over him. "And who gave me the pistol? Father, Sam. Father!"

"Why in hell did he do that?" Sam growled, slowly moving his hand toward the latch on the door.

"Because he feared I might have trouble with low-down vermin on this ship on the long voyage," Nadine said, her eyes twinkling. "He never thought it would be you, did he, Sam?"

"You'll be sorry you're treating me this way," Sam said, circling his hand around the latch, his knuckles white. "If something should happen to your mother and then your father, it would be up to me to see that you were looked after. If you don't change your attitude toward me, I swear I'll see to it that you don't have even a dress to call your own."

Nadine's eyes wavered. "Of course you are lying," she said dryly. "Father will have made provisions for me. He would have seen to it that I would be taken care of, at least financially, especially now that he has chosen to take us to the godforsaken land of Australia. I would be helpless, except for—"

"Except for that damn Australian?" Sam taunted. "He's hardly got the shirt on his back. Don't think you can depend on the likes of him."

Nadine curved her free hand into a tight fist. "I will not banter with you about Lloyd Harpster," she said with annoyance. "And as for what else we were discussing, I fear not at all what you said."

"Then you don't care if your father does not have a will?" Sam went on. "You don't care that your father only moments ago told me to look after you if anything should happen to him? Do you think that I truly would under these circumstances? I hardly think so."

Nadine lowered the pistol a fraction. "Now you resort to blackmail?" she said, her voice quivering. "It won't work, Sam. You know my true feelings for you. Why do you continue to pursue me?"

Her eyes widened and her mouth dropped open. The reason was suddenly there in her mind, as though it had been planted there by the voice of God!

"Lord, I know," she gasped, taking a step backward. "You have always had what you wanted. If not fairly won, paid for. Sam, my God, that is the only reason you pursue me. Not because you love me as a man loves a woman, but only because you cannot have me. I am not a possession that can be bought and sold. So now you resort to blackmail. If that doesn't work, what next, Sam?"

"I will have you," Sam snarled, swinging the door open and turning to storm away. He was stopped dead by Harry Quinn, who was just reaching out to knock on the door.

"Harry!" Sam said in surprise, then fear. He knew that Nadine was most surely still standing there with the pistol in her hand. There would have to be explanations made that Sam did not want voiced aloud. That could ruin everything. It would be Sam who would have to force the issues that he wanted to save for later. The timing wasn't right for him to show Harry that the game was over between them—a game that thus far he had won. It had been like a game of chess, skillfully played.

"What the—?" Harry said, grabbing Sam as he barged into him. "What are you doing here, Sam?"

Harry placed his hands on Sam's shoulders and bent down to look into his face. "Sam, what's happened?" he growled, seeing the anger in his partner's eyes, hearing it in the harsh way he was breathing.

Harry's gaze then moved on past Sam, and he saw Nadine standing beside her bed, holding the pistol. "Damn," he growled. "What the hell is going on here?"

Harry moved past Sam into Nadine's cabin. "Explanations are in order," he said blandly, looking from Nadine to Sam. "Who's going to be the first to speak?" His eyes rested on Nadine, his insides twisting painfully as he saw her cower away from him as though she were afraid of him, too.

His gaze followed the pistol as she lowered it to her side. "Nadine, why the need of the pistol?" he asked, the strain evident in his voice.

"Sam? Do you tell him or do I?" Nadine said, her voice weak. She placed the pistol gingerly on the table, feeling trapped now. If she told her father about Sam, then wouldn't Sam respond with what he had surmised about her having been with Lloyd in the hold of the ship?

Perhaps it was best to let her father know the truth than for her to have to resort to sneaking around behind his back for the remainder of this voyage.

Sam forced a nervous laugh as he moved into the cabin. "Harry, it was all a big misunderstanding," he said, glancing at him sideways. "She thought I was a prowler. I gave her quite a fright, just walking in on her unannounced. I'll know to never do that again. I didn't know that she had a pistol."

Nadine's eyes widened. She looked at Sam wonderingly, almost convinced herself of his story. It did sound plausible enough. Her father appeared to believe the falsehood, for he no longer looked angry.

Nadine looked on stubbornly. She would not let Sam get away with it. This was the time to reveal just what a lout he truly was. And it would be best to reveal her feelings about Lloyd. This incident had proved that to her. She would not let Sam have reason to blackmail her again.

"I'm glad the explanations are that simple," Harry said, nervously kneading his brow. He looked from Sam to Nadine, then let his eyes linger on Nadine. "This is not the time for any more complications in our lives."

He went to Nadine and gripped her shoulders, and his eyes were dark and heavy as he peered down at her. "Nadine, I've come to tell you your mother has had a turn for the worse. I think it's best if you go to her. Now. She isn't going to last much longer."

All thoughts of anything but her mother were swept from Nadine's mind. Her knees grew weak, and her face drained of color as she teetered from the shock.

She lunged past Harry, then Sam, running, her painful sobs carrying along after her. Her heart felt as though it were tearing apart with anguish. Her mother...oh, her dear, sweet mother! She couldn't be dying! Surely she hadn't been that ill. The fever had come so quickly. Nadine had thought it would leave just as quickly.

But no. It had consumed, and was now claiming, her mother! It wasn't fair! What then if something did happen to her father?

She could not help but let Sam's words plague her.

An overwhelming sense of emptiness swept through her, but it was banished almost as quickly when she let herself remember Lloyd.

The sky was cold and pitiless. The *Lady Fortune*'s decks seemed to be set on fire by each flash of yellow lightning. They were incessant, nearly blinding. A sudden swell from the southwest gave notice of the heavy weather to come. Great marching hills of water battered the ship in thunderous crashes.

Fighting the wind that was beating against her, Nadine held the black veil to her face as she clung to the ship's rail. She continued to look down at the churning water, unable to believe that her mother's grave now lay within its dark abyss. The funeral had been immediate, as were all burials at sea. Nadine was stunned by the abruptness and by the void that now filled her life.

"Daughter, let me escort you to your cabin," Harry said, slipping an arm around Nadine's waist. He tensed as another bolt of lightning streaked straight down from the heavens into the water, followed by a great crash of thunder reverberating across the raging sea to the deck of the ship.

Clasping Nadine's waist, he hauled her away from the railing and across the slippery deck. Relieved when her cabin was reached, Harry hurried her inside. He watched Nadine as she removed the veil. She was so pale. Her lack of color was accentuated by the black silk dress that she wore, a dress taken from her mother's belongings. It had been meant to be worn for a very different occasion. It was elegant, with a scooped neckline and puffed trim that formed a lattice design from the bodice down to the nipped-in waistline. The sleeves were of black lace and matching the black lace shawl from which Nadine had taken the material to make her veil.

"It still doesn't seem real," Nadine murmured, gingerly placing the veil on her bed. She settled into a chair and stared into space. "Why Mother?"

Harry knelt before her and took her hand, patting it affectionately. "Your mother was never very strong," he said hoarsely. "When the fever hit, it was just too much for her. She couldn't fight back. Nothing could be done for her. Who will ever know exactly what did cause it? So many of the mysteries of illness are left unsolved for eternities."

The upsurge in the wind howling outside the cabin startled Harry to his feet. The ship lurched against the pounding waves. "Nadine, I must go see to the crew and make sure they take every precaution to see that the ship will fare well enough under the approaching storm," he said, drawing her up to hug her. "You stay put. Don't leave the cabin. Secure yourself against being tossed about as best you can. We may be in for quite a time in the next hour or so."

"I'll be fine," Nadine murmured, nodding as he released her and moved hurriedly toward the door.

"Will you be all right?" she asked, following him. "Father, please be careful."

"Nothing is going to happen to ol' Harry Quinn," he said with a low chuckle. He gave Nadine a lingering look and went on out the door. Hearing the whipping of the sails, he looked up and tensed. They were full and shivering in the wind.

Harry steadied himself against the great gusts of wind as he watched the crew rushing around, readying the ship for the full thrust of the storm. He began giving orders, shouting above the roar. A great rush of rain fell suddenly from the sky, turning the ocean white with spume. Lightning flashed from cloud to cloud.

Harry grabbed a rope and hung on, wishing that he had thought twice before making this voyage to Australia. It was as though the devil were aboard the ship.

Nadine fought to steady herself as the ship plunged from side to side. She braced herself against the bed and drew the black dress over her head, glad to be rid of it. For the rest of her life she would hate black. In her mind, it would always represent sadness and loss.

Wanting the dress out of her sight, she went to the trunk at the foot of her bed and opened it. Digging to the bottom of the layers of dresses and gowns, she hid the black dress beneath them.

Once again, her eyes spied the red dress that Lloyd had admired so much. She drew it to the top of the clothes and caressed its softness. Her eyes misted as she recalled that her mother had still been alive the night she had last worn it.

A knock on the door made Nadine slam the lid of the trunk with a thud. Realizing she was scarcely clothed, she rushed to her feet and drew on a robe, tying it snugly at the waist. She looked toward the door with a frown. With her in such a weakened state, this would be the perfect opportunity for Sam to taunt her. Determined not to banter with him any longer, Nadine went to the drawer in which she had deposited the pistol. Once and for all she would show Sam that she was not to be toyed with. Then she would go to her father and tell him everything about Sam and his threats.

Taking the pistol and steadying it in front of her, Nadine faced the door. "Come in," she said, her voice quaking with anger.

The door opened slowly, revealing Lloyd instead of Sam. A rush of color flamed Nadine's cheeks. She dropped the pistol to her side and smiled weakly at him.

"My God!" Lloyd exclaimed. "Who did you expect? The devil himself?"

Nadine released a shallow breath, then replaced the pistol in the drawer. "No," she murmured. "Much worse, believe me."

Lloyd closed the door and went to Nadine. He drew her around to face him. "I came because of how you must be feeling after your mother's burial, and also because of the storm. I didn't think that you should be alone," he said thickly. His gaze swept over her, seeing how pale she was and how she trembled. "I would have come sooner, but I knew that you were worried about what your father might do or say. But

I don't give a damn any longer. Surely somebody has been causing you trouble. Why else would you feel the need to protect yourself with a pistol?''

Nadine felt suddenly weightless, drained of all emotion. She eased herself into Lloyd's arms and let him enfold her within his solid embrace, relishing his closeness. "I'm so glad you came," she whispered, close to tears. "I need you, Lloyd. I need you."

"What bastard were you expecting?" Lloyd growled. "Or need I ask? It was Sam, wasn't it?"

"Yes, but I can take care of him," Nadine said, clinging to him. "It's the heartache I am now feeling that is troubling me the most. I miss my mother so, Lloyd. I feel that I let her down. I wasn't at her bed-side when she took her last breath."

"Be glad that you weren't," Lloyd said thickly, softly running his fingers through her hair. "That would haunt you much longer than the guilt you feel for not having been there."

"You speak from experience?"

"No," he said hoarsely. "I wasn't with my parents when they died. But in my nightmares I have been. I have been there, dying inside over and over again, as they took their final breaths."

"Please hold me, Lloyd," Nadine whispered. "That will lessen the burden in my heart. Oh, thank you for coming."

The tempest outside raged with increasing fury, but Nadine was no longer aware of it. She had found bliss within the gentle arms of the man she loved. He held her there until the ship stopped its swaying. He lifted her chin with a forefinger and kissed her tenderly.

"I truly must go now," he said, guiding her to her bed. "I think the storm has worn itself out. You can rest now."

"Please don't go," Nadine pleaded. "Stay with me, hold me throughout the night. Never have I needed you as badly as I do now."

"Nadine, are you sure, darling?"

The way he spoke her name, as though it belonged on his lips, sent a gentle warmth through Nadine. Though this man promised nothing but the irresistible passion of the moment, she knew that was enough, for she was melting beneath his heated gaze.

"I do love you so," Lloyd whispered, his mouth sweet and gentle as he kissed her, easing her robe from her shoulders. His hands then cupped her breasts, his thumbs circling her nipples as they hardened with pleasure.

Nadine's robe fell away from her and lay at her feet. A moan escaped from deep inside her. Lloyd's hands filled her with such wondrous desire that she could not help but give in to the rapture. It was a raging hunger that had to be fed. All sadness, all that was ugly in the world, was being swept away from her as though on a high, raging tide.

Twining her arms around Lloyd's neck, Nadine clung to him as he carried her to her bed and placed her on it. His kiss was lingering. His hands were once again on her breasts, kneading them, causing a strange, sweet sort of pain to stir between her thighs. It was pulsing, as though her heart were centered there. This was a feeling she had never experienced before. And this man, whose blue eyes had stolen her heart, was the cause.

As though he had read her thoughts, Lloyd crept his fingers up her leg to her inner thigh and touched the throbbing core of her womanhood. As he caressed her there, Nadine's head began to reel with pleasure.

"You are a vision," Lloyd whispered, showering heated kisses over her taut-nippled breasts, his fingers stroking her womanhood, readying her for the moment of ultimate pleasure.

He had no doubt that she was a virgin, for she had fought her feelings for him from the very beginning. But now the victory was near to being won. His loins ached for the moment.

"Please, don't talk," Nadine whispered, trembling as he stood away from her and quickly disrobed. His blue eyes were smiling down at her, and his sunburned hair was tousled, making him look more like a boy than a man. She dared not look down at the part of him that soon would transport her into the world of bliss. If she did, she might be too afraid to continue what she had started with him. Never before had she seen a man fully unclothed, and soon she would know the true wonder of this man.

The cabin was dimly lighted. The faint glow from the candle cast a golden glow over their bodies. Nadine leisurely ran her hands over Lloyd's wide shoulders as he leaned close to her, resting the expanse of his tanned, sleekly muscled chest on the bed beside her. She still could not believe that she was actually here with him in such an intimate way.

Touching his lips wonderingly, she felt as though she were suspended in air, floating. "I can't help but love you," she murmured, smiling up at him. "I wish that I could. But it's impossible. Your eyes, your lips, have haunted my nights."

She ran a finger over the scar on his cheek. "Lord, I don't even know you, yet I am here, wantonly sharing everything with you." She turned away. "Never before have I..."

Lloyd placed a finger on her chin, forcing her to meet the passion in his eyes. "I love you, Nadine. Let me show you just how much."

"I think you already have," Nadine purred, again twining her arms around his neck. "You've been so gentle, so wonderful. Thank you for that. Thank you."

She drew his head down. Her mouth quivered as their lips joined in a sweet, soft kiss. Her breath quickened as Lloyd gently caressed a breast. He positioned himself over her, his knee slowly parting her thighs. Her heart skipped a beat when she felt his manhood softly probing where no man had ever been before.

But his lips, his hands, kept her spellbound, as though a powerful drug had been introduced into her body, so much so that when he finally entered her in one maddening thrust, the pain was brief.

The feel of his hardness inside her, filling her so completely, the way his every thrust sent sweet messages to the rest of her, made Nadine sure she had been right to accept what he offered, the passion of the moment. Never could anything feel as peacefully wonderful as the feelings he was stirring inside her.

Abandoning herself to her feelings, she locked her legs around him. She nestled close to him and let him move against her, loving her as she had known he would, in a sweet and leisurely fashion.

When his mouth left her lips, she coiled her fingers through his hair and guided his lips to a breast, where his tongue flicked the tip until it tingled, causing a glow to spread inside her with a building heat.

Never had Lloyd felt so on fire. His hands could not keep still. He wanted to touch all of Nadine at once. Her body was like silk, and her lips were like the petals of a soft rose.

His hands swept across her slim body and around to her soft, round buttocks. He dug his fingers into her, lifting her higher, closer.

He kissed the hollow of her throat, feeling her pulse beat go wild, moving on to her lips as he felt his passion reach a fever pitch.

He breathed hard, his body stiffened, and he made the last maddening plunge. Crying out, he tremored into her as she opened to receive him.

Nadine's hands clung to Lloyd's sinewed shoulders as his thrusts inside her hastened, quickening her blood to near boiling. He pressed his hot lips against her throat, breathing hard, as she experienced the ultimate of feelings splashing through her. Everything in life was blocked out except this man and what he had taught her tonight.

* * *

"It was beautiful; *you* are beautiful." Nadine sighed, softly kissing Lloyd's perspiration-laced brow.

Lloyd lay beside her, his cheeks flushed and his hair dampened from the labors of loving her. He took her hand and kissed its palm, his eyes filled with peace. "Perhaps it's time I put your mind to rest about a few things," he said cautiously, concerned that telling her the one truth that she must know about him before reaching Australia would make her fear him.

"What things?" Nadine asked in a voice that was scarcely more than a whisper, her eyes wide.

"Truths about me that you have wanted to hear from the start," Lloyd said hoarsely, his thumb lightly caressing her flushed cheek. "You do still want to know, don't you?"

"You are ready to tell me?" she said in disbelief.

"As I see it, I *must*," he said, eyeing her carefully. "To prove to you just how much I care for you, I must."

A splendid joy swept through Nadine. She knew the intensity of his feelings for her without further confession, but she was touched by his sincerity. She drifted toward him, enfolding herself within his solid embrace.

"You have already proven so much to me," she murmured.

"But not enough," he said, drawing back a few inches to allow himself to look down into her translucent eyes. "Once you return to the world as you have known it, when you are not with me, questions about me will haunt you again. I don't want any secrets between us.''

Nadine shot him a look through her lashes. "What secrets do you need to tell me?'' she asked breathlessly, her gaze settling on the scar on his cheekbone. Was he truly going to tell her everything?

Chapter Six

"Here," Lloyd said, gathering Nadine's robe up from the floor. He placed the robe gently across her outstretched arms.

"Thank you," Nadine murmured, the full impact of what she had just shared with Lloyd settling in with bone-weakening intensity.

Turning her back to him, she hurried into her robe, hoping that he would get dressed, for the raw awareness of his nudity was stirring her insides into renewed and dangerous quiverings. Would she always need him now that she had been held so beautifully within his arms? Once they reached Australia he would most surely go his way, she hers. Yet, if he truly loved her, he would never leave her! Somehow he would see to it that they would make a life together.

Nadine's fingers trembled as she secured the robe around her waist. Then she spun around, surprised to find Lloyd dressed except for his shirt, which he had left lying on the floor. Nadine combed her fingers through her hair to straighten it, looking at him with questioning eyes.

Lloyd moved to stand directly before her. His shoulder muscles tightened and his hands doubled into tight fists as he turned so that she had a full view of his bare back. The faint light from the flickering candle cast dancing shadows on the welts and scars that crisscrossed his back.

Nadine's hands went to her throat and she gasped loudly, suddenly light-headed, when she saw his beautiful body so terribly marred. As her gaze moved from scar to scar she felt her heart pierced by the same pain that he had most surely felt when the whip that had inflicted the scars had torn into his flesh.

"Oh, Lord," she said, her voice cracking with emotion.

Almost too stunned to move, Nadine trembled as she reached toward his back. Then she dropped her hands in front of her, clasping them tightly together, wincing at the thought of touching him. It was not the scars that bothered her, it was the fear of hurting him by touching them, for nothing about Lloyd Harpster could ever be less than beautiful in her loving eyes.

While making love, she had not ventured her hands across his back. If she had felt the welts while in the midst of passion's throes, what would she have done?

Oh, Lord, she knew that if she had known that he had been abused so terribly she would have given him twice the loving, no matter what his reasons for having them.

Lloyd turned to look at her over his shoulder. "Touch them," he whispered. "It will make it easier for you to accept what I have to tell you."

Nadine shook her head, frightened now of what he had kept from her, for to have been scarred in such a way he almost had to have been a prisoner.

"Lloyd, I just don't know," she said, torn by conflicting emotions. "Perhaps it's best if you don't tell me anything. I'm not sure if I want to hear."

Lloyd turned on one heel and took her hands, softly kissing the palm of each one. "You must listen," he beseeched as he released them and turned his back to her again. "Touch the scars."

"All right. But, oh, Lloyd, how terrible for you that this happened to you. It hurts me so to know that you went through such an ordeal."

Forcing herself, Nadine lifted her fingers to a scar and touched it, stifling a sob as she felt its cold, corded hardness. She ran her finger gently down its full length, then moved to another and another.

Then she crept her arms around Lloyd and hugged him from behind, placing her cheek against him. A tear streamed down his back, silver in the candlelight.

"My love," Nadine whispered, hugging him tightly to her.

Touched by her sympathy and gentleness, Lloyd uncoiled her arms from around him and drew her around to face him. Gently he gathered her into his arms, relieved that her alarm at what she had seen had not thrown her into a rush of questions. He knew that one wrong word could cause her to turn her back on him forever.

"Don't fret so," he crooned. "These scars are totally healed except in my mind, where the memory of why they were put there, and by whom, seethes like a festering wound. One day I hope to right the wrong that was done me. Once I set my feet back on Australia's soil, my energies will be spent in finding ways to clear my name. But first much has to be done. I have a score to settle with the 'Flogging Magistrate,' Captain Grover Grenville, the man responsible for the misfortunes of many innocent people who were shipped to Australia from England."

His words were spinning in Nadine's head, confusing her. Yet he had said enough for her to know that he had surely been a convict, or why else would he be seeking a way to clear his name?

Nadine clung to him and closed her eyes. Having shared such gentle moments with him, she knew that he was not capable of performing any sort of vicious crime. She could not be that bad a judge of character.

Lloyd eased her away from him and held her gently by the arms as her eyes moved slowly upward to lock with his. "Darling, what I am about to tell you will alarm you, but, knowing you, I believe you will begin to understand me," he said thickly. "With our feelings so deep for one another, you must be told, for once Australia is reached, the chances are I won't even set foot on soil before I will be arrested."

"Arrested?" Nadine said in a harsh whisper, her heart aching with the knowledge that she had been right in her suspicions.

She slipped from his grip and stood before him, readying herself to hear anything he had to tell her. She would have to be brave. She must trust him and his account of why and how he had gotten into trouble with the law. Her gut instinct was to help him in any way she could. That was what love was all about.

"I'm ready," she said dryly. "Please tell me everything."

Nodding, Lloyd took her by an elbow, led her to the bed and motioned her to sit down. Reaching to grab his shirt, he sat down beside her. There was a moment of silence between them during which only the creaking of the ship's timbers and the slapping of the waves against the ship could be heard. Lloyd slipped into his shirt, staring into space. Nadine watched him, scarcely breathing.

"It happened several years ago," he finally said, his voice soft and cool. "In England, where I was born and raised. At that time, the laws had become so cruel that the penalty for stealing was death, or to be sent to some foreign country and forced to work many years without pay and under the lash, for some master whose only interest in his slave was to get as much work out of him as possible."

He hung his head. "Transportation became the punishment for stealing so much as a handkerchief. Transportation to Australia."

Nadine listened, aghast at what she was hearing. She had thought that life had been miserable in San

Francisco, with the constant threat of mud slides and fires, and vile men murdering and raping almost every night. In comparison to the streets of England, it had been pure heaven.

She continued to listen anxiously, wondering just what she was going to find once she arrived in Australia.

"Of course, transportation began long before that," Lloyd said, combing his fingers nervously through his hair and looking over at Nadine. "Before the American rebellion, England had sent many convicts to its American colonies. When the colonies declared themselves independent of England, no more convicts could be dumped there. The jails of England were overflowing, so the prisoners were shipped to Australia, where the riffraff of the British army soon took over."

He rose to his feet and began pacing the small cabin. "Australia was a land so far away no convict would stand a chance of getting back to England," he growled. "The prison ships that traveled from my homeland were filled with chained people lying around in their own filth. I shall never forget that long voyage."

He squatted down before Nadine, smoothing a hand over her cheeks. He saw that his disclosures had caused her to grow pale. In her eyes he saw a trace of fear. He hoped this fear was not of him, for she now knew that he had been a prisoner on one of the dreaded ships.

"Many of those who traveled on the prison ships were not desperate criminals but political prisoners, petty lawbreakers and poor people. My crimes were only that I voiced aloud my distaste for what the government was doing," he said hoarsely. "I not only voiced aloud my genuine dislike for what was happening to poor, innocent people, I recommended that many changes be made in the government. That everyone, even the poorest of poor, have the right to vote."

"And because of this you were shipped to Australia on a prison ship?" Nadine gasped, taking his hands and holding them tightly on her lap. "Lloyd, oh, Lloyd, how terrible. How unfair."

"I was not the only one to suffer because of my outspoken nature," he continued.

He eased his hands from hers and turned his eyes away as he rose to his feet and turned his back to her, his head bowed. "My parents," he said. "They lost their lives in a fire the night of my arrest." He swallowed hard, trying not to envision how they must have died.

His eyes wild with fury, he turned and looked down at Nadine. "My God, Nadine, I know the fire was purposely set. They died because of me."

His pain reached deep into Nadine's soul. She hurried to her feet and into his arms, hugging him tightly to her. "I'm so sorry," she murmured. "So very, very sorry."

"So you see?" he said, relishing her embrace, her understanding, her love. His muscled arms nestled her close. He buried his nose into the perfumed depths of her hair. "It's been hell living with the knowing, Nadine. Pure hell."

"You can't continue to blame yourself for your parents' deaths," Nadine murmured, feeling the thundering of his heartbeat against her cheek. "It wasn't your fault. You've got to believe that it wasn't your fault, or you will forever be haunted by guilt that in truth is someone else's, not yours."

Lloyd placed his fingers firmly on her shoulders and held her at arm's length. "There is one man responsible for much of the ugliness on the prison ships and in Australia," he growled. "He was in England the night of my parents' deaths. I know that he gave the orders for my arrest and that he ordered the fire set. It was he I spoke up against. Even then he was a corrupt man."

He dropped his hands and began angrily buttoning his shirt. "But Captain Grover Grenville is now permanently in Australia. I soon will be there, also. Once I return to Australia, Captain Grenville will be made to pay." His lips lifted into a slow smile.

Nadine's insides chilled at the sight of his determination. Though she believed in revenge, she did not want to think of the dangers Lloyd would face in seeking his. Her fingers could still feel the welts on his back. This time his punishment might be much more severe. He might be sentenced to death.

"Where were you imprisoned once the ship you were on reached Australia?" she asked, clasping her hands in front of her. "You received your scars there?"

"I was imprisoned in a penal establishment on the island of Tasmania. Captain Grover Grenville went on to a penal establishment in the state of Victoria, where he was promoted to inspector general. I was flogged on the prison ship and at the prison." Lloyd looked down at Nadine, his eyes two points of fire. "And the only medical treatments offered for a lashed back were buckets of seawater thrown on the raw wounds."

Nadine stifled a choked gasp. She turned her eyes away from him, not wanting to envision him being tortured in such a way. Yet the image was there, in her mind's eye. She could even hear his tormented screams.

Lloyd went to Nadine and touched a finger to her chin, urging her to look at him. "Nadine, I was released three years later for good behavior. But I hadn't forgotten Captain Grenville. I moved to the mainland near Melbourne and formed a gang to torment Grenville and those like him. They called us bushrangers because we lived in the woods. We stole from them, the rich bastards, and gave everything we stole to the poor."

"How brave." Nadine sighed, then frowned. "But darling, were you caught again and imprisoned? Did you escape? Why would you have the need to clear your name?"

Lloyd rose to his feet and resumed pacing, his hands clasped tightly behind him. "No. I wasn't imprisoned, but, yes, I was caught," he growled, scowling. "Grenville didn't want to take the chance of imprisoning me. He was afraid I would again be released on good behavior. Instead, he lashed me until I was unconscious and threw me on a ship bound for San Francisco. He said that if I ever returned he would have me arrested on trumped-up charges of murder.''

Nadine paled. She rose quickly to her feet and went to him. ''My darling,'' she softly cried, cupping his face with her hands. ''Life has been so unfair to you.''

Lloyd twined his fingers through her hair and pulled her close. ''After I reached San Francisco I was determined to return to Australia, to get Grenville and to make sure my name was cleared of any charges he may have posted against me. That's why I was gambling with your father, to book free passage back to Australia.''

He chuckled softly. ''I'm not much of a gambler,'' he said. ''It was a damn lucky draw of the cards that won me this voyage. It would never happen again in a hundred years.''

He paused, as though weighing his next words, before continuing. ''I'm hoping that most of the people of Australia have grown tired of the corrupt men who control their land and will side with me and my kind to see that things are made right.''

''Your kind?'' Nadine murmured. ''Are you speaking of your bushranger gang?''

''Yes. My gang,'' Lloyd said, his eyes awash with memories as he spoke. ''We were called bandits by some, Robin Hoods by others. We stole from the rich and gave to the poor. I shall again, if need be.''

Nadine leaned away from him, and her fingers moved to the scar on his cheek. ''This scar,'' she said, silently comparing it to those on his back. ''How—?''

''One day, when Captain Grenville was flogging my back,'' he muttered, lowering her fingers from his face, "the whip's teeth went farther than my back, around to my face."

Nadine's heart ached for him. She wanted to help him forget, but she knew that he never would, for everything was embedded too deeply in his memory. All that she could do was give him her heart, her love. Anything else had to be gotten on the day of his revenge, for that seemed to be the only thing that could make things truly right for him. Her hopes, her desires, her goals in life, seemed far less important.

Lloyd drew her into his arms and hugged her fiercely. "Damn it, Nadine, you're the only bright thing on the horizon for me," he said tightly. "Somehow I have to think that fate led me to America. It was you who beckoned."

He lowered his mouth to her lips and kissed her feverishly.

Harry Quinn stood on the top deck. He had fought and won his battle with the sea, but he had lost his wife, and now, in a sense, his daughter, as well. He had seen Lloyd Harpster go to Nadine's cabin, and she had not turned him away. If Nadine had given the Australian permission to enter, then so be it. Harry Quinn would not interfere again in matters of the heart. Even Sam Parsons would soon realize that! Sam would be dealt with as soon as possible, but first Australia must be reached, so that Nadine could have solid footing, at least for a while.

His thoughts returned to Lloyd Harpster. If the Australian took one step out of line and hurt Nadine in any way, he would pay dearly. Just as Sam Parsons would pay for having interfered with the lives of the Quinn family.

The only thing was, Sam still held the trump card. This was one game that Harry had yet to win, and his insides grew cold at the thought of losing such large stakes.

Chapter Seven

AUSTRALIA

The air was redolent with the fragrance of kelp beds at low tide. The day of their arrival in Melbourne found the *Lady Fortune* clutched in the clammy grip of a dawn shrouded in a fog so thick it was barely possible to see the ship's bow from its stern. Her black velveteen cape billowing around her in the wind, Nadine stood on deck wrapped in a world all her own, listening to the cries of unseen birds.

Her worries were not of the fog. They were of the future, of her father's inability to accept his wife's death, of Lloyd's welfare and of Sam Parsons and how he might affect her life. She had not confided in her father about Sam. Since her mother's death, he had been in a strange, brooding mood, and she hadn't wanted to trouble him about matters that seemed taken care of already, for Sam had not bothered her again—thus far.

"One hell of a way to arrive back in Melbourne," Lloyd grumbled as he stepped to Nadine's side.

Having been in such deep thought, Nadine jumped with a start. What might happen to Lloyd once the fog lifted? Now that their destination was so near, it tore at her heart to know that they would be saying goodbye. Although Lloyd had promised to arrange it so they could meet from time to time, the times between each rendezvous would be moments spent missing him and worrying about him.

Until he had this thing settled with Grenville, his life was on the line.

Nadine leaned against him as he slipped an arm around her waist. "The fog could give you the cover you need to escape through the city," she said.

She was again reminded of his status in life when she felt the handle of one of his holstered pistols press ominously into her side as he pulled her closer. She longed for the day when he would no longer be branded an outlaw.

But was it truly possible? Was this something beyond reach? Should he not even have returned? In America, he had been free. In Australia, she was the same as branded, for even loving him. Only when he won his freedom would she also be free.

"The fog is going to draw more attention to the *Lady Fortune* than had she arrived in clear weather," Lloyd said, nervously placing a hand on a holstered pistol.

The bellow of a foghorn suddenly pierced the air, causing Lloyd's grip to tighten on the gun. "The foghorn. I knew they'd have to use it. It will be audible for miles. If Captain Grenville hadn't been aware of the ship's arrival before, you can be damn sure he will now."

Nadine cringed at the thought. She looked up at Lloyd, fear creeping into her heart. "You are truly expecting to be captured, aren't you?" she murmured.

"I have always known that I'd be taking that chance by returning," Lloyd said bluntly. "Captain Grenville gave me fair warning. Though I've been gone from Australia for months, he hasn't forgotten me. Nor shall he ever."

"There must be some way that you can arrive without being seen," Nadine said. "Lower a longboat. Arrive on shore somewhere besides Melbourne."

Her hair shimmered around her shoulders as she spun around to face him. She clutched his arm anxiously. "Lloyd, that's it. That's how you can elude Captain Grenville."

Lloyd's lips lifted into a lazy smile as he looked down at Nadine. "There's no chance I'd arrive on shore alive that way, for sure."

"Why not?" Nadine asked, her innocent eyes wide. "What could happen?"

"This is a dangerous harbor," he said, turning his gaze to peer into the whiteness surrounding him. "Even now the *Lady Fortune* could be passing a ship that the lookout doesn't see. A longboat would never have a chance out there."

A loud shout from the lookout wrenched Nadine away from Lloyd. She turned in the direction of the voice, tense. Then she looked toward the water as the unseen voice was heard again.

"Port! Hard to port!" the lookout shouted.

Another voice responded, "You mean starboard?"

"No, port! Port! Quick!"

Nadine teetered as the ship jerked violently. Then her breath was stolen when she looked up and saw the *Lady Fortune* barely clear the stern of another ship that had turned directly across the *Lady Fortune*'s bow. Its wake hit the *Lady Fortune* broadside, and Nadine was thrown against the rail, the wind momentarily knocked out of her.

Lloyd swept her into his arms and held her tightly as the ship continued its game of hide-and-seek through the fog. A single short blast of the ship's horn signaled that another ship was passing the *Lady Fortune* on the port side.

There was a strained silence for a moment, and then another ship signaled from close by. In response, the *Lady Fortune* steered slightly to starboard to keep well clear.

"Will we even arrive at all?" Nadine asked, her ribs aching from having hit the rail.

"I think I see the promise of sunshine," Lloyd said, pointing toward the sky. "Yes. The fog is already starting to burn away. Soon the ship will be riding safely again."

"But you won't be safe," Nadine said sullenly. She turned and clung to him, pressing her cheek against his chest. "I am so afraid for you."

"Now let's look on the bright side of life," Lloyd said, chuckling, his breath hot on Nadine's cheek as he leaned close to her. "Let's think of the fresh water we'll soon be drinking. You know how stale the water got a few weeks back, after being carried in the wooden barrels for so long."

"It will be good not to have to add brandy or wine to the water to make it easier to swallow," Nadine agreed with a low laugh. She looked up at Lloyd, her eyes gleaming. "Yet I have come to acquire a taste for brandy that I didn't have before."

"Perhaps too much of one," Lloyd teased, his eyes dancing. "I should've made sure you only added molasses or vinegar to your water. That is more like what a genteel woman should add to make the water drinkable."

"Are you saying that I have become too fond of brandy?" Nadine asked, slipping from his arms. She shook her hair back from her shoulders. "I only teetered once or twice after drinking it."

"Land ahead!"

The lookout's voice broke through again, changing their mood. Nadine's heart skipped a beat. She looked away from Lloyd at the fog, now only a veil of white, as though it were made of a thin, transparent lace that revealed everything behind it.

Lloyd moved away from Nadine and clasped his hands on the ship's rail. Something within him mellowed as he watched the fog lifting to reveal to him the land that he had grown to love. Though many long hours of suffering had been spent in this land of wild and rugged beauty, the land itself had been a balm to his wounds. No land could be lovelier. Even now, with so much of his future left unresolved, seeing this land gave him a deep sense of immense peace.

He now knew that he had returned not just to get revenge and to clear his name but also to embrace Australia.

Nadine moved to Lloyd's side, awestruck by what the lifting fog was revealing to her. As she stood there in the stinging salt wind it gave her a strange sort of pleasure to look in every direction.

Slowly she absorbed the beauty of it all... gaunt gray mountains towering over primeval forests, cliffs climbing high above deep black tarns, mists floating in the valleys and swirling around precipitous bluffs.

With the sun now high in the sky and the fog only a memory, Nadine could see deep valleys surrounding copper hills, the colors changing from mauve to oxblood to orange, then to mustard and to pink, with the passing of the windblown clouds.

Elsewhere she could see the barren earth flashing to life in the sun, blushing in bumpy nakedness against the blue sky.

"So this is Australia?" She sighed, placing her hands on her cheeks. "I never dreamed it would be so beautiful. I had thought that it would all be barren."

"Much of Australia is," Lloyd said thickly. "But Melbourne is a place of beauty, probably the closest thing to heaven you'll ever find on earth."

Nadine moved her eyes slowly to Lloyd. "Yet the prison hulks are there," she said, her eyes wavering. "Surely nothing about them is lovely!"

"Nothing," Lloyd growled, tightening his grip on the ship's rail. "Nothing at all. But Melbourne is more of a whaling port now than a convict settlement. In earlier times the city was savage and dangerous. Now it has built up into a favorite haven for whalers, sealers and sailors of all kinds, who stop here for supplies and to make repairs."

"I'm glad to hear that," Nadine said, laughing nervously. "I had enough of savage behavior in San Francisco."

"Now, I'm not saying that you should make it a habit to go to Melbourne without some sort of escort," Lloyd said, giving her a troubled glance. "It's not a safe place for a lady, especially one as lovely as you."

An awkward silence fell between them as the ship moved closer to land. Fur seals basked on sea-lashed rocks close by, and startled cranes wheeled into the sky. On land, a kangaroo peered at the ship with its dark, questioning eyes before bounding into a thicket.

As the ship drew closer to the busy port, Nadine got her first good look at the town that would be her new home.

Melbourne sat neatly alongside the sea, framed by a marvelously fertile patchwork of dark chocolate-brown soil, bright green oats and buff-colored paddocks. Low wooden buildings with metal roofs lined the streets.

Farther away, small hamlets were scattered across the land, their white stone cottages surrounded by dense forests and mossy banks of fuchsia gone wild. It appeared friendly enough, but Nadine would never forget that somewhere there lurked an evil man, waiting to take away the man she loved.

"So we've arrived in one piece," Lloyd said, his eyes moving restlessly over the pier jutting out from the land. "It's not been all that long since I said my goodbyes. Not all that long, indeed."

His gaze slowly moved farther down the quay to two ships moored far away from any others. Rocking with the tide, they were gray and stark, like ghost ships, their masts stripped of rigging and sails. These were prison hulks. A threat to the sanity of any man who was not at peace with the law. Lloyd knew that he could very well end up there if he wasn't careful in his schemings to settle his score with Grenville.

Glancing over at Nadine, he was relieved to see that she hadn't seen the hulks, her interest piqued by something else on shore. He turned his head to follow her gaze and froze at the sight of a dozen mounted policemen waiting on the pier.

His insides churned until he recognized the officer in charge, and his lips lifted into a lazy smile.

As the ship inched closer to the pier, the sailors readied the lines. Nadine's eyes were riveted on the mounted policemen. Their bright red uniforms stood out against the dull clothing of the other men who swarmed over the dock, busy at their various tasks.

Nadine gasped as she saw one of the mounted men separate himself from the others. He sat astride a lovely white stallion, his shoulders squared, his eyes watching the approach of the *Lady Fortune*.

Oh, Lord, was that Captain Grover Grenville? Would Lloyd be swept away from her this quickly?

Would he be beneath the lash of the whip as early as this afternoon?

Nadine looked in alarm at Lloyd, who swept her into his arms and held her to him, his eyes relaying a silent message of love. His mouth found her lips in a soft, trembling kiss. Then he turned and sped away, down into the hold of the ship.

"I'm not sure if I can stand this," Nadine said, choking back a sob. She straightened her back and watched as the ship came alive with activity. The gangplank was lowered to the pier, and animals and supplies were moved ashore.

Nadine kept her eye on the man on the white stallion, for he never took his eyes from the ship and those who were leaving it. Nor did the other policemen, who sat at attention on their own horses.

"What do you think of Melbourne?"

Sam Parsons's voice made Nadine cringe as he stepped up beside her. She did not look his way, instead watching anxiously for Lloyd's departure and what might happen to him when he attempted to leave.

"Nadine, I think it's time we call a truce," Sam said, placing his hands on her shoulders and turning her to face him. "We're in a strange country. It's best to have friends to fall back on in times of trouble."

"You are not among those I would seek out," she hissed, slapping his hands away from her shoulders. "For I no longer look to you as a friend. I look to you as trouble."

"Trouble?" Sam said, throwing his head back and laughing. Then he sobered and peered icily down at

Nadine. "My dear, if your attitude doesn't change about me you'll soon be introduced to the true meaning of the word."

Nadine lifted her chin haughtily. "Sam Parsons, whatever you do will not affect me one way or the other."

The sound of a horse's hooves on the gangplank drew Nadine around. Her heartbeat quickened as she watched Lloyd lead his strawberry roan down the gangplank, walking square shouldered, his hat drawn down low over his brow, surely knowing that at any moment he might be seized.

Her gaze moved to the mounted policemen, the pit of her stomach tightening as she waited for them to make their move.

Lloyd reached the pier. As he slowly mounted his horse, his eyes met and held those of the man on the white stallion.

Nadine was taken by surprise when she saw Lloyd smile lazily and give the man a mocking half salute, then ride briskly away. He was soon lost in the crowds mingling on the streets of Melbourne.

"I can't believe it," Nadine whispered, stunned.

Then warm relief flooded her insides. She turned to Sam, triumphant, wondering who the mounted man was. Surely it wasn't Captain Grenville.

"Now what were you saying about being in Melbourne, Sam?" she said, tossing her hair back from her shoulders. "I suddenly feel wonderful about being here."

Sam looked at her questioningly, then looked back at the mounted policemen, wondering about her reaction to them. He had seen her watch them guardedly as Lloyd had left the ship. Why? Was there cause for Lloyd Harpster to be afraid of the law?

He smiled to himself. He would ask around and find out. Perhaps there were more ways than one to rid Nadine Quinn's life of that shiftless bastard.

Smiling smugly, Sam stepped closer to the rail and singled out the man on the white stallion with his eyes. "I see our message was received soon enough," he said thickly. "That must be Lieutenant Jon Upchurch awaiting the arrival of the *Lady Fortune*. I requested that someone of the local militia be here."

"Lieutenant Jon Upchurch?" Nadine said, her eyes raking over the thin red-haired soldier. She turned back to Sam. "Why would you request the presence of the British militia?" she asked stiffly, wondering if he somehow knew Lloyd's background and had planned to have him captured upon the arrival of the *Lady Fortune* in Melbourne. Yet he had not acted upset when Lloyd had not been captured.

"You know that your father and I discussed the matter of housing before our departure from San Francisco," Sam said, raking his fingers through his coal-black hair, smoothing it back where the breeze had lifted it from his brow. He twirled his mustache between his fingers. "We wrote to the militia in charge here at Melbourne, asking them to find us a suitable residence. We promised a considerable payment for their trouble. Lieutenant Jon Upchurch wrote back and told us about a fine ranch with a formal house and plush grounds. You won't have reason to ever be reminded that you are on foreign soil."

He smiled down at her, his dark eyes squinting. "You see, Nadine? Not only your father, but also I want only the best for you," he said, mockery evident in his voice.

"How considerate," Nadine said icily, still wondering why Sam had anything to do with the purchase of the house at all. There were so many questions to ask her father whenever he showed signs of being in the state of mind to answer them.

She flashed Sam a stare full of hate. "Don't ever expect me to repay you for any kindnesses given me, Sam, for you will never have the opportunity to get near me again."

"Ready to depart the ship?" Harry Quinn said, sweeping a thick arm around Nadine's waist, purposefully leading her away from Sam. Now that they had arrived in Melbourne, he would attempt most heartily to find a way to get even with Sam. He knew that it would take time, though. Sam was too clever not to know when he was being toyed with.

"I'm anxious to see the house in which we'll be taking up residence," Nadine said. "I'm so tired of being on a ship."

"I promise you that you will be settled in before you can hardly wink an eye," Harry said, feeling lighthearted and anxious to get on with the business of establishing his stagecoach line. He was happiest when he was busiest.

And he had to busy himself to forget what the sea had taken from him—his beloved wife. He had spent too much time brooding. It was time to learn how to live again.

Feeling the heat of the sun beating down on her through her black velveteen cape, Nadine swung it from around her shoulders and carried it over her arm as she moved alongside her father down the gangplank to the pier. She scarcely breathed when Jon Upchurch directed his white stallion over to her and her father and smiled down at them. She looked up at him, seeing the warmth in his dark eyes. With his long and narrow face, he wasn't a handsome man, but she could tell that he was friendly, and most surely kind. Yet the way he kept glancing in the direction that Lloyd had ridden made Nadine feel uneasy.

Setting her jaw firmly, Nadine did not return Jon Upchurch's smile. She looked icily up at him, deciding that she was wrong to think that he was a man she could like. Anyone who was a threat to Lloyd was also a threat to her.

"Sir, Lieutenant Upchurch at your service," Jon said, extending his hand to Harry Quinn from where he sat in his saddle. "You are Harry Quinn, the owner of the *Lady Fortune*?"

"Co-owner, lieutenant," Sam Parsons said, moving to take Jon Upchurch's hand before Harry had a chance to. "Harry and I are co-owners of the *Lady Fortune*. Will you personally direct us to our ranch? It is, I presume, suitable for the price paid for it?"

Nadine glanced over at her father and saw his eyes brimming with anger. She wondered what on earth was going on between him and Sam. It had begun to be noticeable only recently. Sam seemed to be taking charge.

"Suitable enough, I am sure," Jon said, giving Nadine an appraising glance. "Surely suitable enough for the lovely lady."

Nadine lifted her chin haughtily, ignoring the compliment, still seeing how Jon kept glancing in the direction of Lloyd's escape. Oh, Lord, she hoped that Lloyd had managed to travel far in this small amount of time, for it seemed that Lieutenant Upchurch was most surely going to seek him out.

"My men will show you the way. I suddenly have business elsewhere," he said, nodding toward his men and then toward a nearby horse and buggy. "Please take the horse and buggy for more comfortable traveling. You have quite a ways to go."

Nadine's heart began to thunder inside her as she watched Lieutenant Upchurch ride quickly away. It did not surprise her to see in which direction he was traveling. She had been right to fear the worst. Lieutenant Upchurch was most surely going after Lloyd.

Scarcely aware that someone was helping her up into the buggy, Nadine was numb with fear of what the next few hours would hold for Lloyd. Would he be arrested and thrown back in prison? Would he receive fresh scars on his back to add to those already received so many months ago?

Would she ever see him again?

Chapter Eight

Enormous gold-rimmed purple clouds parted to reveal a colossal marigold moon and a silvery sheen clung to the landscape, turning the darkness inside out. Lloyd had arrived at his destination in the golden light of evening and was now camped near the hut of his friend, Tipahee, an aborigine. A sparkling fire cast weaving shadows on Tipahee's nearby bark house. Lloyd gave his companion a half glance as he accepted a cake made of nardoo fern from him.

"I am glad you return," the aborigine said, nodding his head anxiously. "It's not been good with you gone."

Lloyd nodded in silence, looking up as Tipahee came and knelt down beside him, watching Lloyd with large, inscrutable eyes that saw so much. Tipahee was an aging, dwarfish little man with dark skin.

He wore sparse clothing of rough animal skins that covered only the most intimate parts of his body. His skin was leathery from sun, wind and cold, and his teeth were white and even.

"It's good to be back, Tipahee," Lloyd said, smiling at him, recalling how he and Tipahee had become loyal friends, those many years ago. Lloyd had found him wandering alone in the forest, ill with a high fever, and had taken him to his bushranger hideout and nursed him back to health. Tipahee had then vowed full allegiance to Lloyd and had become a part of the bushranger gang, working as their scout.

"Yes, it's good to be back," Lloyd said starkly, staring down into the flames, his thoughts on less pleasant things, like Captain Grover Grenville. "We need to get our gang together. Quickly. We've things to do."

As Lloyd took his last bite of the cake, Tipahee placed his hands to his shoulders. "You must free your name," the aborigine said softly. "Tipahee can help you. He listens to the wind and he knows the earth and sky. He is filled with wisdom and courage!"

"I'll need all the help I can get," Lloyd said, laughing at the Indian's seriousness.

The sound of a horse's hooves approaching drew Tipahee away. He grabbed his spear and positioned himself protectively between Lloyd and the approaching horseman. He held the spear threateningly in the air, ready to throw it.

His shoulder muscles tensing, Lloyd swung his pistol from its holster and bolted to his feet, nudging Tipahee aside and positioning himself in front of him.

"Damn, I've probably been followed," he growled, his finger tight on the trigger, his eyes alight with fire. "But why didn't they advance on me earlier?"

Lloyd turned a trained ear in the direction of the approaching horse. "It's only one man," he whispered.

Then a white horse took shape, silhouetted against the dark backdrop of night. Lloyd lowered his pistol. He smiled and gave Tipahee a reassuring glance over his shoulder.

"Lower the spear, Tipahee," he said thickly. "A friend approaches, for I know my horses sometimes better than I know the riders. And that damn white stallion has only one owner."

Flipping his pistol back into its holster, Lloyd stepped around the camp fire and placed his hands on his hips as the horse drew closer. He gave a mock salute as Jon Upchurch reined his stallion in beside him and swung himself out of the saddle.

"How's it going, mate?" Lloyd said, his eyes gleaming as Jon came to him to embrace him fondly.

"You came back," Jon said, stepping away from Lloyd and looking him up and down. "You really did come back." He patted Lloyd on the shoulder. "I knew that you would. I knew that you wouldn't let Captain Grenville get the best of you."

"He almost did," Lloyd said, haunted by the memory of the whip on his back.

"Never. He's not man enough," Jon said, clasping his hands together behind him. He looked beyond Lloyd to Tipahee. "Good evening to you, Tipahee. How are you?"

"He's barely making it, like all other aborigines before him," Lloyd said, looking weary-eyed at his Indian friend.

"Not much different than most of the population," Jon said darkly. "Captain Grenville and his followers continue to make it damn hard on everyone. It's probably not too wise that you came back. The power to pardon offenses rests solely with the lieutenant governor, and while Captain Grenville continues to poison the governor's mind, nothing can be done about clearing your name. The governor listens only to the clink of the coins Grenville hands him for cooperating."

"Well, then, I shall see to it that that changes," Lloyd growled, taking Jon by an elbow and leading him closer to the fire.

He raked his eyes over his friend, noting his thinness and the gentle strength of his shoulders under the red uniform. As always, there was an intense, sincere warmth in the depths of his dark eyes.

"You should be the one in charge here. Not Grenville," he growled.

"And I will be," Jon said smoothly. "Grenville's kind can't last forever." He clasped his fingers on Lloyd's shoulders. "Lloyd, I know the charges that Grenville plans to use against you are trumped-up charges. All of Grenville's men know it, but they are afraid of him. As long as he's alive, they'll back Grenville all the way. You've got to find a way to force Grenville into telling the truth. My hands are tied, you know."

Lloyd eased away from Jon and went down on one knee, placing wood on the fire. "Yeah, I know," he muttered. "As are most decent policemen."

Jon stooped down beside Lloyd, his rusty hair picking up the reflection of the fire. "I've sympathized with your cause all along," he said sincerely. "It's been my pleasure to be your informant from time to time. But as for opinions, I've had to keep them to myself in order to make things right for all good people when the time showed itself to me."

"And that will be soon," Lloyd said. "Captain Grenville has got to pay. I now plan to finish what I started long ago."

"That bastard still hunts that black stallion mercilessly," Jon said, his jaw tightening. Then he laughed under his breath. "Ever since Grenville captured the stallion and his mares that one time and they broke free, it's truly hard to say just who is hunting who, Grenville or the horse." He turned to Lloyd, his eyes gleaming. "Do you know that Grenville is convinced the horse is after him?"

"How's that?" Lloyd said, idly scratching his brow.

"Grenville came close to catching the brumby a second time, but the horse swung around and attacked him, crushing two of his fingers in the attack, maiming them," Jon said. "The next time around, the horse might even kill him!"

Lloyd chuckled beneath his breath. "You don't say," he drawled. "Seems I have a partner in crime."

"Could be." Jon laughed, then frowned. "But Grenville has sworn to catch and kill the stallion. Every time he sees it he sends his men after it." He laughed throatily. "So far, the stallion is smart enough to elude him."

"Just as I plan to elude Captain Grenville until I'm ready to go in for the kill," Lloyd said, rubbing his back, feeling the welts through his shirt.

He looked over at Jon. "Thank God it was you who was on the pier today when the *Lady Fortune* docked," he said softly. "Had it been Grover Grenville, I'd already have fresh welts on my back. How was it that you were there, and why didn't the mounted police come after me?"

"I was handed the letter from Sam Parsons and Harry Quinn when it arrived from America, with the names of those who would be arriving on the *Lady Fortune*," Jon said blandly. "I appointed myself the person in charge of watching for the arrival of the ship, and the one who found residence for the owners. The police under my command are those who have been loyal to me since my arrival in Melbourne. They knew not to disclose the news of your arrival to Captain Grenville."

"I appreciate your kindness," Lloyd said, nodding. "And, Jon, did you notice a lady among those who arrived? One who is so petite and lovely it steals a man's breath away?"

Jon chuckled low as he glanced over at Lloyd. "How could anyone miss such a lovely lass?" he said, raising an eyebrow. "But she did not warm up to me at all. She showed no trust of me at all in her sparkling green eyes."

"So you also noticed her eyes?" Lloyd asked, aching to hold Nadine in his arms.

"Yes, it would be hard to miss them."

There was a silent pause. Then Lloyd rose to his feet, Jon following his lead. He laid his hand on his devoted friend's shoulder. "Do me another favor, Jon?" he asked, his voice anxious.

"I'll do anything that's humanly possible, Lloyd."

"Send a message to Nadine that I'm all right," Lloyd said thickly, glancing over at Tipahee. "I know that you can't do this personally, because you would not want Captain Grenville to get word of it. But take Tipahee, show him where Nadine now makes her residence. Then he can give her the message when he sees that it is safe to do so."

Jon scratched his brow idly. "Think it'll work?" he said, raising his eyebrows questioningly. "Since she's not familiar with the aborigines, he could really scare her."

"Tipahee will know what to do," Lloyd said, giving the dusky Indian a lazy smile. "Nadine will take to him as quickly as a child takes to candy." Turning to Tipahee, Lloyd placed his arm affectionately around his shoulders. "Tipahee, there is a lady I want you to meet...."

The vast red brick house sat high on a bluff, exposed to the wind and sun. It was fronted by a veranda that shaded larger windows that opened to the sea breeze. Its weathered gray roof was topped by a fanciful widow's walk. Stone walls and hawthorn hedges heavy with red berries and sweetbrier bordered the yard.

At the one side of the house, where hills rolled off to the horizon, cattle and horses that had been

brought from America grazed peacefully. On the
other side and at the back, the forest and its mysteries stretched out to what seemed infinity.

Nadine felt like an alien in the house, which until
recently had been occupied by a British officer and his
wife. It was large and beautiful, like all the other
houses she had lived in, yet there was something im-
personal about it. It was as though she were treading
on someone else's life, someone else's privacy, for
everywhere she looked there was someone else's furniture. None of the Quinn family's private furnishings had been shipped on the *Lady Fortune*. They had
been auctioned off in San Francisco as though they
had never been loved at all!

That was almost the way she felt, too. She missed
her mother, who had always made their house a loving home.

Restless, Nadine moved into the parlor and placed
her hands over the warmth of the flames in the fireplace. The room was lavishly decorated. Deep, comfortable chairs and sofas sat before the massive
windows that provided a view of the sea. Brocade
draperies, Oriental rugs and drop-leaf and lamp tables crafted from solid maple and highly figured black
cherry veneer were part of the elegant setting. But
there was nothing familiar to call her own.

Nadine could see beyond this parlor into a hunting
room with great beamed ceilings and gun displays.
Her father was there, pacing the floor before another
fireplace, his face thrown into shadow by the dancing flames.

Though Nadine knew that her father had tried to appear more settled and cheerful since their arrival in Australia, he had not succeeded in fooling himself or her into believing things were going to get back to normal anytime soon. She had never seen her father as moody or as restless as he was now. Was he missing his wife as badly as Nadine was missing her? Or was it something else? Did it have to do with Sam? Sam had also changed, and not for the better!

"I see you've settled in all right," Sam said, moving with a light gait into the room, his coal-black hair sleeked down on his head, his mustache freshly clipped.

He went to Nadine and edged close to her, also placing his hands over the warmth of the fire. "Nadine, I have to go into Melbourne today to see to business. Your father has chosen not to go with me. But he and I will have to leave tomorrow for several days to travel up the coast to see how our new stagecoaches are coming along. You know that the order was made for the construction of the stagecoaches long before we left America. You will remain here. There are enough staff present to see to your welfare. The servants, maids and stable hands came with the sale of the property. They seem dependable enough, and they have been here for many years now, through several different families."

Nadine turned her eyes slowly to Sam, nervously smoothing her hands across the gathers of her simple cotton dress, with its puffed sleeves and low neckline. "It seems that Father is no longer in charge here," she said blandly. "Why is that, Sam?"

Sam lifted his shoulders in a casual shrug as he began walking away from her. "I guess it's because of your mother's death. He misses her. It's left him a bit unsettled. I'm forced to take over under the circumstances," he said over his shoulder. "I must leave now."

He stopped abruptly and swung around to look at Nadine with narrowed eyes. "If you get restless and have a need to go exploring, it's best that you choose not to wander too far from the premises."

A shiver raced across Nadine's flesh, and she drew closer to the fire. It was as though he wanted to keep her prisoner.

"You're not my keeper," she said, turning her back to him. She cringed when she heard him laugh sarcastically as he walked on from the room.

Glad that he was gone, Nadine glanced at her father again. He was pouring himself a glass of whiskey.

Hurrying to him, Nadine placed a hand on his arm. "Father, what is it?" she murmured. "Please know that you can tell me anything. Mother is no longer here for you to confide in. Please let me take her place. I want to help you. You seem haunted by something. Is it Mother's absence?"

Harry slammed the glass down on a table, splashing whiskey in all directions. He glared into the fire. "I'll be riding into town," he said thickly. "I guess what I need is a damn good game of poker."

A familiar twinkle entered his eye at the mention of his cardplaying. He seemed to have come to life, and his cheeks were now pink with excitement. "I'd like

to see what the city of Melbourne has to offer me,"
he said, chuckling. "Perhaps my luck'll be better than
it was the last time I played cards. I could have lost
my soul to that fella Lloyd Harpster."

Harry's smile faded. He leaned down to look into
Nadine's face, frowning. "Where in the hell did he go
after we docked at Melbourne?" he said in a growl.
"Honey, does it hurt much that he loved, then left
you?" He doubled a hand into a fist at his side.
"Maybe I'll find him in Melbourne and teach him a
thing or two about how to romance my daughter."

Nadine laughed nervously as she looked away from
her father. "I don't believe you'll be seeing Lloyd in
Melbourne," she said, leaning over to place a log on
the fire. "Nor anywhere else, for that matter."

Harry's eyes widened. He knelt down beside Nadine and urged her back up to stand before him.
"Why do you say that?" he asked, studying her
expression, seeing so much hidden there. "What do
you know about Lloyd Harpster that you're not telling me?"

Nadine's eyes lowered. "Nothing at all," she said.
She was glad when her father turned and began
walking away from her.

"I'll be in town," he growled. "You stay put, do
you hear?"

"Yes, sir," she murmured, but she already knew
what she was going to do. She was very restless, and
she longed to go exploring, no matter what Sam had
said. She had been watching the horses as they
grazed. She would choose one and go for a ride. Perhaps if she got a breath of fresh air she could sort

some things out in her mind. Perhaps getting closer to nature would ease her longings for her mother and Lloyd.

Rushing to her room, she opened her trunk and chose a travel skirt and a long-sleeved blouse. She dressed quickly, anxious for the feeling of a horse beneath her as she rode free in its saddle.

Deciding that no evil could ever lurk in such a beautiful place, Nadine rode a gentle brown gelding through a pebbled ravine that led through a vale of unfamiliar-looking trees. The soft light shone through the strange mixture of a short, stubby variety with thick leaves and the polished silver flanks of much taller plants with a myriad of slender branches topped with glittering bunches of leaves. Hundreds of tiny birds festooned the trees overhead like confetti and set up a thunderous squawking as her approach disturbed them.

Smoothing her hand across the gelding's brown neck, Nadine murmured comforting words to him. "I can understand why you're uneasy," she said. "You were on the *Lady Fortune* for too long. You haven't left your sea legs behind yet, have you? Well, you will soon. We both will."

Straightening her shoulders and holding her chin high so that her hair tumbled in fiery streamers down her back, Nadine closed her eyes as a wondrous feeling of freedom engulfed her.

The sound of twigs breaking somewhere close by made Nadine's eyes fly open with a start. Her hand went to the bulge in her saddlebag and touched the shape of her pistol, reassuring her that she had brought protection. When a dark figure carrying a spear stepped in the way of her slow-moving horse, the gelding neighed and shied.

"No!" Nadine screamed, finding herself slipping.

The fall to the earth momentarily stunned her. She slowly pushed up on one elbow, kneading her brow. "What happened?" she whispered. She looked up and found an elderly, dwarfish figure of a man staring down at her.

Her gaze darted over him, noting his flat facial features and his dark skin and hair. His sparse clothing was made of some sort of hide. His legs were lean, with little flesh on the calves. The spear that he carried was gaily decorated with strange symbols and bright colors. She knew it was not a threat to her, for he was holding it calmly at his side.

Nadine met his steady stare with one of her own, now seeing such depth, life and knowledge in his dark, brilliant eyes. She scarcely breathed when he pointed to himself with a bony finger.

"Tipahee," he said. "Tipahee."

Nadine inched up from the ground. She smoothed her fingers through her hair. "That is your name?" she asked guardedly.

"You are Nadine?" Tipahee said, having watched her since she had left the house. "You are friend of Lloyd?"

Nadine's heart skipped a beat. She put a hand to her throat, stunned. "How did you know?" she gasped.

"Lloyd friend of Tipahee. Tipahee friend of Lloyd," he said, again gesturing toward himself with his hands. "Lloyd wants you to know he is well."

Relief surged through Nadine like a wild tidal wave. "You have seen him?" she asked, her pulse racing. "Where is he? Is he far? Oh, Tipahee, will you please take me to him?"

Tipahee tilted his head, his eyes filled with doubt. Then he shrugged his shoulders. "We go," he said, taking Nadine's horse by the reins. "You ride. Tipahee walk."

Nadine was in a state of mild shock, not really believing this was truly happening. She wanted to pinch herself, to test the reality of the moment, but knew that was foolish; nothing could be more real.

She eyed Tipahee warily. Should she trust him? She would chance anything to see for herself that Lloyd was all right. Placing her foot in the stirrup, she swung herself up into the saddle, then let the aborigine be her guide.

Chapter Nine

Unnerved by the length of time it was taking to get to Lloyd, Nadine wondered if she had fallen into some sort of trap. She was frightened, and she clenched her fingers more tightly on the gelding's reins. Tipahee led the horse relentlessly onward through varying degrees of forest, plain and rock. The only thing that lightened her burden of worry was the discovery of all sorts of strange new creatures about her.

A flash of movement caught her eye, and she saw a large black-and-white bird alight from its perch, its bright coat gleaming against the foliage. A squirrel-like creature lapped nectar from the flowers of a tree, leaping and dashing from blossom to blossom and finally hurling itself from dizzying heights to another tree. Sailing on membranes between its outstretched legs, it flew as far as Nadine's eye could see.

Along a cliff, flowers clustered in rich and somber beauty and feathery green plants grew higher than one's head.

There was silence and a sense of great age as a path began to wind upward toward a high amphitheater of red rock. Directly ahead rose a huge orange wall, and overhanging it was a massive roof of sandstone. Nadine's breath was taken away when she began seeing ochre-colored paintings on the walls that stretched out before her.

But before she had a chance to actually study the drawings she saw the wide opening of a cave straight ahead, and tied beside the opening was a horse. Her heart frolicked within her chest, for it was not just any horse, it was Lloyd's beautiful strawberry roan!

"Lloyd!" she whispered, dismounting her horse before Tipahee could take her an inch farther on it. She lifted the hem of her travel skirt and began running across a pebbled path that led upward.

"Lloyd!" she shouted. "Lloyd, are you all right?"

When he stepped from the cave, his blue eyes brilliant with surprise, Nadine's footsteps faltered. Lloyd was the same man, yet not the same man at all. The clothes he now wore were more savage. His fringed shirt and breeches were made of a hide similar to his kangaroo boots.

But this savage side of Lloyd made a sensual sweetness press in on Nadine's heart when she saw how his breeches fit him so snugly, as though molded to his powerful legs and thin hips.

The fringed shirt was unbuttoned halfway to his waist, revealing his powerful chest, covered with thick blond chest hair. His muscled shoulders strained at the seams of the hide shirt.

Lloyd was momentarily speechless. He looked down at Nadine, then at Tipahee, who looked up at him with mischief in his dark eyes. He had counted on Tipahee to set things right with Nadine for him, but never had he thought that Tipahee would go this far. It had only been necessary to tell Nadine that he was all right, not to show her.

Yet he should have known that with Nadine's daring, adventurous personality, hearing about him would not be enough. She would have been the one to insist on being shown.

Seeing wonder in Lloyd's eyes instead of anger, Nadine broke into another mad run, sighing happily when she reached him and he swept her up into his arms and nestled her close.

"You shouldn't have come," Lloyd murmured. Then, as she twined her arms around his neck, he kissed her with an easy sureness.

He received her quivering lips against his as he spun around and carried her into the privacy of the cave, placing her on a blanket beside a glowing camp fire.

Still cradling her close, still kissing her, he spread her out on the blanket beneath him, touching her breasts familiarly through the cotton of her blouse.

"I had to come," Nadine whispered as his lips moved to the hollow of her throat. "I hope you aren't angry."

"Do I look angry?" Lloyd said, his eyes picking up the color of the flames as he gazed down at her. "Did you find your Australian house to your liking?"

"It's adequate, but no, I'm not happy with it."

"Tell me, why?"

She placed a hand on his smooth cheek, reveling in this stolen moment with him. "I imagine it is because now that I've found you I won't be happy anywhere without you."

She grazed a kiss across his lips. "Tell me," she murmured, "how are things for you? What are your immediate plans? Do you plan to meet with your friends—your bushranger gang?"

"Immediate plans?" Lloyd said, his eyes gleaming mischievously. "Love, they don't include anything but you. Now, later? As soon as my gang is rounded up, we will break all hell loose for Captain Grenville."

Lloyd brushed a copper strand of her hair back from her brow with his lips. "But let's not talk about my gang or Grover Grenville," he said huskily. "That you are here is—"

Nadine touched a finger to his lips. "Shh," she whispered. "I am here. Oh, I am so glad that you are free for me to come to! Had that captain—"

Lloyd eased her finger from his lips and gave her a fleeting kiss. "Shh. Let's not ruin these moments with even the mention of that bastard's name."

"I don't have long," Nadine murmured as his lips eased away, his fingers feverishly undressing her. "I did not know that I would have this far to travel to be with you."

"Your father? Sam? How did you leave without them knowing it?"

"They are both in Melbourne. Hopefully, if they return before I do they won't check my room."

She squinted and let her gaze move around her. "What on earth is this place?" she asked. The dancing shadows of the fire illuminated the same sort of paintings on the inside of the cave that she had seen on the outside. There were kangaroos, crocodiles, depictions of sorcery and ancient aboriginal fertility figures.

"Later," Lloyd whispered, removing his shirt. She now lay unashamedly nude before him. "Those paintings have been there for generations. I don't think they will slip away from us in the next few moments."

Nadine moved to her knees. "Let me do the honors," she said, her own voice foreign to her in its deep huskiness. There was not a part of her body that did not tingle with the thought of what the next moments would bring—the wondrous reunion of their bodies.

"This place. Is it your hideout?" she asked, laying his shirt aside.

"Damn it, woman, will the questions never cease?" he asked, easing her away from him. He unfastened his breeches and slipped them down the muscled expanse of his legs. "If you must know, yes, this is my hideout now. It was the best place to have a rendezvous with my men, for they all know of this cave. Tomorrow I can begin to round them up. Jon Upchurch is going to spread the word."

Nadine paled. "Jon Upchurch?" she gasped. "The man who met the ship and who took care of the arrangements for the purchase of the ranch? He left so abruptly from the pier after the arrival of the *Lady Fortune*, I feared that he had gone in pursuit of you."

"No. Not in pursuit of me. He came to me to welcome me back. He's my friend," Lloyd said, tossing his breeches aside. "Probably the best damn good friend anyone can have."

His masculine nudity almost overwhelmed Nadine. She was becoming aware of a sensual promise within her grasp, and she went limp with desire when he placed his hands on her waist and lowered her onto the blanket again.

"Except for you," he said, nibbling at her lips, his hands cupping her breasts. "Yet you are much more than a friend, aren't you?"

"Darling, I would hope so," Nadine said, shivering with rapture as Lloyd flicked his tongue over a breast. "But Lloyd," she said, her fingers combing through his thick golden mane, "he's a policeman. How is it that he is a friend? Doesn't he work in conjunction with Captain Grenville?"

"There you go again," Lloyd said, pressing her body close to his. "Questions. Have I lost my skills in making you forget everything but me while you are with me?"

"Never could I be more aware of you than now," Nadine whispered, relishing the strength and comfort of his arms, the touch of his tenderness. "Love me now, while it is possible. Who knows what tomorrow will bring?"

He covered her lips with his, his mouth moving slowly, parting hers. His hands caressed her as they moved down the length of her body. When they found the throbbing mound of her womanhood, he began to stroke her gently, wondrously.

Feeling the delicious spirals of pleasure shooting forth inside her, Nadine lifted her hips so that his fingers had full access to her pleasure point. His kiss was hot on her lips, filled with searing passion. But that was not enough. With memories of pleasure found in the most intimate of ways locked within her heart, her hands went to his buttocks and guided his hardness downward. She no longer wanted the gentleness of a caress. She wanted him. All of him. She wanted him to fill her, to touch her soul with his desire.

"Love me," Nadine whispered as she drew her lips from his. "Make everything within me take on the beautiful colors of the rainbow as before when you made love to me."

He leaned over her with burning eyes. Then, without hesitation, he entered her. He gave her his beguiling, easy smile, then again pressed his mouth down upon hers, giving her a kiss of total demand while he anchored her fiercely to him with his arms of steel.

Nadine's entire being throbbed with quickening passion as he began his eager thrusts. She twined her arms around his neck and let rapture take hold, carrying her to a plateau that knew no doubts or cares. It was a sweet, warm place of sharing, of loving, occupied only by her and the man she adored, the man she would love forever.

Lloyd felt the heat of pleasure spreading, matching her passion with his. His hands could not get enough of her creamy skin as they moved eagerly from her breasts across the flat plane of her belly to the soft curves of her thighs.

And then he molded her body closer to his, lifting her higher, urging her legs around him. His breath was coming in rasps. He placed his lips on the curve of her neck and rested them there, letting the ecstasy take hold.

Nadine felt the beginning of a tremor deep within her, building, spreading. And then the sensations seared her insides, as though everything within her were momentarily set aflame with a wondrous sort of heat. She spiraled. She floated!

Too quickly, it was over and she was lying spent within Lloyd's arms as he lay there, a recipient of his own moment of sought and found release.

When he rolled away from her and lay beside her, winded, she turned to him and curled her fingers in his hair, then outlined the perfect lines of his lips with a forefinger.

"How quickly passions are peaked between us," she murmured. "You must think me whorish to come to you and be swept away in your arms so easily. But when I'm with you it's hard not to love you so easily."

She crept around until she was atop him. She wrapped her arms around him and held him close, pressing her cheek against his chest. "Oh, how I love you," she whispered. "Life would be so empty now without you. Tell me you love me as much. Tell me you will never love another. I could not bear it."

His blue eyes melted her as he framed her face with his hands and willed her eyes to meet and hold his. "I wish it was as easy as that," he said thickly. "If it was only a woman that you had to worry about, life would be simple. But a woman is not what stands in our way. It is a man. Once I am free of his clutches, then you will see that you will have no need to fret about anyone or anything again. You will become my life. Only you."

Nadine was reminded of what her hopes and dreams had always been. Her eyes lighting up, she let hope rule the moment. She placed her hand gently on Lloyd's shoulder and urged him into a sitting position. She straddled his lap, placed her arms around his neck and leaned away from him, smiling. "I don't want to be the only thing in your life," she murmured.

"What?" Lloyd said, placing his hands at her hips. "You want something more? What?"

"A child. A house that can earn the title of home," she said in a rush of words. "I want to hear the laughter of children from room to room. I want to plant roses that I can see bloom from year to year. I want to belong. I want stability."

Lloyd was at a loss for words, for her dreams matched his own, though he had never spoken them aloud to anyone. He was from a quiet family, and he had been an only child. Though he had only known one home, it had not been a cheerful one. There had not been all that much love, even between his mother and father. They had not been skilled in voicing their love for him aloud. When they had died he had been saddened, had felt guilt over their deaths, but he had not truly missed them all that much, for never had they allowed him to become close to them.

He hungered for children of his own. He would be a father, brother and playmate all in one.

"Nadine, I promise to give you as much as life allows me to give you," he said, drawing her into his arms and nestling her close. "But first, let us get all obstacles behind us before we make too many plans for the future."

He eased her from him and moved to his feet, drawing his wallaby-hide breeches on, then his shirt. He watched as Nadine moved slowly into her own clothes, silent. Speaking of the realities of life had cast a shadow over the magic of the moment. He smoothed his hair back from his eyes and went to Nadine, buttoning her blouse for her as he looked down at her with heavy-lidded eyes.

"Don't come here like this again," he warned. "There are too many risks. Wait until I come for you."

"I shall never be sorry I came today," Nadine said stubbornly, shaking her hair till it hung, long and lustrous, down her back.

Lloyd put his hands on her shoulders. "You must promise not to come here unless I send for you," he ordered flatly. "I'm going to be busy getting my gang together. I can't wait too long before I begin my attack on Captain Grenville."

Nadine lowered her eyes. "Yes, I understand," she murmured. Her eyes shot up. "Honest, I do. And if I can help, please tell me how."

"Just go back to your house and be patient," he said, turning her around and swatting her playfully on the behind. "Pretend you don't even know I exist. It will be better that way."

He walked her out of the cave. She turned and eyed the paintings, awed by them. "Tell me about them," she said, clasping her hands together behind her. "Are these the only ones? Or are there many in Australia?"

"I am sure there are many that have yet to be discovered," Lloyd said, letting his gaze move from painting to painting. "The aborigines say that Australia was created in what they call the dreamtime, the mythical time of beginnings. It is said that the spirit figures of the dreamtime play out their lives on the sandstone walls."

Lloyd touched one of the paintings. It was in the shape of a snake. "It is said that a long snake, trimmed in white, wriggled forth from the dreamtime when the ancestors made all things. But mostly you will see painted hands. The hands are in a sense memorials to death."

Nadine's gaze moved to Tipahee, who had come out of the shadows. She watched him move to the paintings and touch the snake, then a grouping of hands. He turned and smiled at Nadine. It was a smile that reached deep into her core.

"Damn!" Lloyd gasped.

Lloyd's voice drew Nadine from what seemed almost a trance. She looked toward him with a jerk, then followed the line of his vision. She took a step backward, stunned by the loveliness of a horse out-

lined on the horizon, high on a cliff. Its body was
sleek and black, its long mane and sweeping tail gor-
geous!

"Is that the wild stallion you have mentioned?"
Nadine said in a low voice, stirred deeply by its com-
manding presence. A shiver coursed through her
when she saw him strut back and forth, as though
teasing those watching. She had vowed to hate black
for the rest of her life, but this horse was black, and
she could never hate him.

"That's him," Lloyd said, his shoulder muscles
flexing as he clenched his fists at his sides. "God, I
want him. And one day I'll have him." He turned his
gaze to Nadine, having yet to tell her that once he
captured the horse it would be hers.

Nadine was caught up in a different sort of spell.
She could feel the horse's eyes on her now. "Should
you even want to capture him?" she murmured.
"He's so free, Lloyd. Should you want to control
him, as though he were only a thing?"

Lloyd snaked his arm around Nadine's waist. "If
I tame him to love him, what could be wrong with
that?" he asked, burrowing his nose into the depths
of her hair. "Just the same as I've tamed you."

Nadine giggled. "As I recall, there was nothing to
tame about me once I was in your arms," she said
softly. "Darling, I was yours from the very beginning. You know that."

The stallion neighed and shook its mane nervously. When another horse neighed somewhere close
by, and then another, Lloyd yanked quickly away
from Nadine, his eyes filled with fire.

"What is it?" Nadine gasped, then paled when several riders appeared suddenly at the foot of the path that led up to the cave.

"Captain Grenville," Lloyd growled.

Nadine's eyes widened and she felt her knees weakening when she saw a face that she recognized. "Sam," she said, paling even more. "Sam Parsons."

"Seems you were followed, my love," Lloyd said, drawing her protectively next to him, though he had no true way of protecting her, for his pistols lay within the cave.

Tipahee scrambled to cover as the horses approached in single file, Captain Grenville at the lead, his pistol drawn.

"So you've returned for more lashings, have you?" Captain Grenville said, his lips barely visible through the thickness of his brown beard and mustache. He was burly and beady eyed, his hair worn thick to the collar of his red uniform.

"Well, Harpster, I'm here to see that you get worse'n that," Grover Grenville said, holding his left hand behind him so that Lloyd could not see and laugh at his two maimed fingers.

Tears pooled in Nadine's eyes. She cowered next to Lloyd. "Oh, Lloyd, what have I done?" she whispered harshly. "I led them straight to you. I'm so sorry."

"It seems your father's partner duped you, love," Lloyd growled. "And you played right into his hands."

He turned her to face him. "But don't you fret, Nadine," he said reassuringly. "It would've happened sooner or later. I, myself, didn't believe it would be long before Grenville and I would meet again."

"I shall never forgive myself," Nadine cried, desperately holding him. "No matter what you say, I will never forgive myself."

"What a beautiful picture," Sam Parsons said, sidling his horse next to Captain Grenville's. "Nadine, what would your father say if he knew you were here? Perhaps I might just have to tell him, unless you—"

"Unless nothing," Nadine hissed, stepping away from Lloyd. She placed her hands on her hips. "Sam, you are despicable. One day you're going to pay for all of this."

"Go get your horse," Sam said icily. "I'm going to take you home."

"Never," Nadine cried. "I shall go where Lloyd goes. Even if it's to prison."

Sam quickly dismounted and grabbed Nadine and began walking her away from Lloyd. Lloyd lunged for Sam and wrestled him to the ground. "You son of a bitch, I should've killed you when I had the chance," he growled. He drew back a fist, but Nadine's screams drew his head around just as the butt of Captain Grenville's pistol came down on it with a loud, cracking thud.

Sobbing, Nadine fell to her knees and cradled Lloyd's head in her lap. His eyes were closed, and blood was streaming from the wound. She looked up at Sam through tear-filled eyes. "I should have known that you were making it too easy for me to leave and come to Lloyd," she cried. "How could I have been so stupid?"

"Come on," Sam said, jerking her to her feet and causing Lloyd's head to fall to the earth with a loud thump. "I'm taking you home."

Nadine stumbled alongside him, his fingers digging into the flesh of her arm. As she looked over her shoulder, Captain Grenville dragged Lloyd to his horse, then draped him over it as though he were nothing more than a sack of potatoes.

She turned her eyes away, filled with pain. A loud neighing then drew her eyes upward. She rubbed them free of tears, looking with longing at the magnificent black stallion. She cringed when she heard Captain Grenville cursing the horse and vowing to one day also take him as he had taken Lloyd.

Her body jerked as Sam grabbed her by the waist and lifted her up onto the gelding. She held her chin stubbornly high, vowing revenge. But first she had to find some way to help Lloyd escape.

Remembering Tipahee, she looked over her shoulder, catching a glimpse of him lurking behind a boulder. Wasn't it also his fault that Lloyd had been captured? If he hadn't brought Nadine to him, the others wouldn't have followed. He most certainly would feel the same guilt that she was feeling. He would surely find a way to help Lloyd escape the clutches of Captain Grenville.

She must find a way to assist him. When her father and Sam left for those several days, she could be with Tipahee. Yet how could she let him know that she wanted to assist him, even if only in a small way? She hung her head sadly. As she saw it, there was no hope whatsoever.

Chapter Ten

The wind whipped Nadine's hair from her shoulders as she paced like a caged animal back and forth across the porch of the house. Sam had brought her home and had left only moments ago with Nadine's father for their planned venture up the coast. Nadine knew not to trust him. He might be having her watched. But there was no way she could do anything to help Lloyd escape anyway. She had no idea where Captain Grenville had taken him.

"Sam must think that without Lloyd to go to I have no purpose for leaving the premises," she argued to herself. "Why would he otherwise behave so smugly about leaving me alone?"

It grated on her nerves to know that Sam had gone to the authorities and upon discovering that Lloyd Harpster was a wanted man had happily informed Captain Grenville about Lloyd's return to Melbourne. The worst was she had fallen into his trap. It must have been easy to have her watched, knowing that somehow she would find a way back into the arms of the man she loved.

"I did just what he expected," she said, her eyes gleaming with anger.

"And now Sam thinks that with Lloyd imprisoned I will have no choice but to turn to him for companionship," Nadine rasped. "How could he be so stupid as to believe I would ever love him, especially after what he has done?"

The sun was a bright crimson disk against the horizon as it rose higher in the sky. The hour was early, and the air still carried a tinge of chill in it. Nadine hugged herself, the skirt of her daintily patterned cotton dress rustling against a layer of lacy petticoats as she made another turn on the porch.

She stopped suddenly when she saw movement where the outer fringes of the forest met the flat stretch of lawn at the front of the house.

Running to the porch railing, she clasped her fingers around it and peered more closely into the forest, her pulse racing. She gasped when she saw Tipahee step from the thicket, Lloyd's strawberry roan following behind him. She rushed from the porch and across the lawn to meet the dwarfish aborigine. Her hair flying, the hem of her dress threatening to trip her, Nadine ran until she was standing breathless before Tipahee, her eyes wide with fear.

"Tipahee, please don't tell me that something more has happened to Lloyd," she said in a rush of words, grabbing the Indian by the arm. "You have his horse!"

Her gaze swept over the roan, seeing Lloyd's pistols draped across the saddle. She placed a hand to her throat. "You even have his pistols."

Her fingers tightened around Tipahee's bony arm. "Why, Tipahee, why?"

Tipahee handed the reins to Nadine. "Tipahee watched for evil man who took you away from Lloyd to leave today," he said, his dark eyes filled with anger. "Tipahee come to take you away for good. You no want to live with evil man. You come with Tipahee. You ride on Lloyd's horse. You keep his guns while Tipahee goes to get Lloyd from prison hulk."

Nadine's head was spinning, trying to grasp everything that Tipahee was saying to her. Lloyd was on a prison ship. Tipahee had come to take her away. He had seen Sam's roughness to her.

"Tipahee, thank you for being so kind," she blurted, her eyes anxious. "But, Tipahee, I must go with you to help with Lloyd's escape. Please let me go with you."

Tipahee took a startled step backward. "White woman know how to shoot?" he said, nodding toward Lloyd's pistols. "White woman brave?"

Nadine laughed nervously, wondering herself about the answer to both these questions. Was she brave, or simply naive, to believe that she was capable of actually going up against odds that could cost her and Lloyd their lives? Could she, in the face of actual danger, kill a man, or perhaps many men?

This was not the time to question her decision to do what she felt must be done. She owed it to Lloyd. Tipahee most surely felt the same way about his own debt to his friend, since they shared the responsibility for Lloyd's capture.

"Are you saying that I can come with you?" Nadine asked, swallowed almost whole by the thundering beats of her anxious heart.

Tipahee shrugged. "Tipahee not familiar with white women's ways," he said blandly. "If white woman wants to come, white woman come."

He took a step toward Nadine. "But white woman must take care of white woman," he said thickly. "Tipahee care for himself." He cast his eyes downward. "And Lloyd."

"I understand," Nadine said, paling at the thought of being on her own in this battle of the heart. She looked anxiously over her shoulder at the house. Thank God her father and Sam were planning to be gone for several days. She wouldn't even be missed.

Then she turned back to Tipahee. "You wait here," she said softly. "I must go and change. I won't be long."

Tipahee nodded, then eased down to the ground and crossed his legs and arms to wait. Nadine rushed back to the house, her insides quaking with fear.

Close to the prison hulks, steep heights and gullies choked with scrub looked down upon a foaming sea. Giant trees grew on the hillsides. The wood was heavy. The convicts had to fell this valuable timber and carry it down to the sea.

Fetters weighing twelve pounds were riveted around Lloyd's ankles and linked by a chain. Chained together with sixty other men, he was helping to carry a huge tree down a crooked, rocky path. He swayed under the heavy weight as he struggled over the uneven ground. He was soaked to the skin from the slow-falling rain, but he didn't falter, for Captain Grenville stood watching, whip in hand, waiting for a reason to whip the shirt right off his back.

And if one man got a lashing, they all would.

Chained together, it was as though they were one soul, one breath, one heartbeat.

He moaned under his breath from the weight of the tree. His muscles were crying out with pain as he pushed himself beyond his capabilities. He willed one foot ahead of the other, all the while thinking of escape. Thinking of escape was the only way to remain sane while imprisoned in the hellish hulks. He depended on his friends. He knew that they would find a way to set him free.

The memory of Sam Parsons arriving with Captain Grenville at the aborigine's cave gave his insides cause to recoil. The way Sam had made Nadine leave with him made his blood boil. What had he forced her to do after Lloyd had been rendered unconscious? What was her fate now?

He must find a way to escape and to seek vengeance now on two men. He must escape for Nadine.

Moving relentlessly onward, he was glad when the sea was reached. Heaving as though one arm, the men sent the huge tree crashing to the ground, then kicked it until it rolled into the water along with the others they had placed there.

Then, through the wet, thorny thickets, he and the chained men climbed to the forest again. Another tree was chopped and its limbs lopped off, and the pattern was repeated until night fell around them in a cloak of darkness.

Almost dragging, his mind a blank from the long day of gruelingly hard work without even a bite to eat to give him strength, Lloyd moved with the others away from the forest, down a steep grade toward the gloomy edifice of a ship. With heads ducked they walked up a gangplank onto a stench-filled deck and stood in line as one by one the chains were unfastened and they were led downward into the hold to individual cells.

Lloyd entered his own dark, narrow cell and flung himself on the floor, panting hard, while around him rose the nightly music, the sound of the lash and the screams of the victims.

"Time for your last meal," a voice said from the corridor in a familiar mocking tone. "Like I said, the lash ain't good enough for you this time, Harpster. After gettin' a good day's work outta you I'm going to show you what happens to those criminals who don't learn lessons all that easily."

Lloyd forced himself up from the floor. Though every inch of his body rebelled, he would not cower at Captain Grenville's feet. He would die first.

His blue eyes pale, dark circles beneath them, his golden hair wet and tangled, Lloyd straightened his back and then his shoulders, drawing his wet, ripped shirt together in front of him. As Captain Grenville stepped into the cell carrying a bowl of flour and water cooked into a thin gruel, his dark eyes were dancing with amusement. His beard was flecked with grease.

Lloyd set his jaw firmly, then spit at the captain's feet. "Keep your damn garbage," he growled. "It's probably floating with bugs anyhow."

"Like I said, this is your last meal." Captain Grenville chuckled, placing the bowl at his feet. "I'm going to take you where you'll wish you were dead. I'm taking you to my private island of torture. Misery Island, the rock reserved for men whom the jail did not subdue."

Captain Grenville bent and spoke directly into Lloyd's face. "On this tiny island, cells have been scooped out of the rock," he said dryly. "Here a doomed man is left for days and weeks to scream himself hoarse with only the seabirds to hear. Many a prisoner destined for Misery Island kills himself first. Does that sound tempting, Harpster? Want to save me the pleasure? You see, once I remove you from Misery Island, you will be hanged. It will be over." He snapped his fingers. "Just like that."

Captain Grenville chuckled as he straightened his back and glared at Lloyd. "Your friends won't know where to find you to help you escape," he said darkly. "No one but I will know where you are. I will take you there personally."

Lloyd's insides turned cold, yet he held a grain of hope within his heart. Jon Upchurch. He had ways of finding out everything, since he was also of the British militia stationed in Melbourne. If Jon could find out, then Tipahee could rescue him by canoe.

If Tipahee wasn't smashed against devilish rocks while attempting the rescue.

Lloyd eyed the dreaded gruel. The mere sight of it made his stomach turn, but he knew that he had no choice but to eat it. Now that he knew his destination, he needed food of any sort to give him strength. Once he was left in isolation on Misery Island, he would be shackled to the rock without food for days.

His pulse raced as fear forced its way inside his heart. He sank his fingers into the gruel and eased some up to his mouth, shuddering....

With spear in hand, Tipahee led Nadine through the forest. Soon they would reach Lloyd's bushranger gang. Surely by now Jon had contacted enough of them that they could storm the prison hulks. There was no doubt that Lloyd would be set free. Everyone knew that Captain Grenville would stop at nothing now that he had Lloyd back in his clutches. Lloyd was going to be an example set for others. But she and Tipahee would stop him.

Nadine squirmed uneasily in the saddle, her backside numb from sitting so long. She smoothed her windblown travel skirt back down to cover her knees, the hem resting just above her brown calf-length leather boots. She undid another button of her white long-sleeved blouse, blowing down its front to momentarily cool her perspiration-laced cleavage. The hair at her brow and the nape of her neck was damp from the soaring humidity.

She looked nervously upward at the slanting rays of golden sunlight that shone through the foliage of the trees. Soon it would be dark. Though she would welcome the cooler temperatures that night would bring, a feeling of dread swept through her at the thought of spending a night in the forest.

She had grown used to the wondrous beauty of orchids shaped like birds under the towering canopy of the hardwood forest, and to the flaming eucalyptus that appeared like apparitions out of the dusky shrubs. She looked slowly about her. Tipahee had just led the strawberry roan into a swamplike area of an incredibly dense tea-tree forest. In so many places the trees stood as thick as bristles in a brush. Tall, slender trunks grew so close together that no man could ever think to worm his way through them.

It was eerie, fascinating, haunting, verging on the unreal, and this sudden change in the vegetation made her very uneasy.

Shackled, Lloyd hovered in his cell scooped out of rock. The tide was full, the moon not yet risen. The seawater rushed at Misery Island in long rollers out of the darkness, continually spewing icy spray across Lloyd's shivering body. The cold was so intense that it seemed as if he were shriveling up into nothing. His wrists and ankles were aching and bleeding where the steel bands locked around them ate away at his flesh each time he tried to move.

Even if he could manage to get out of the hole in which he had been placed, there was still the danger that he might topple into the sea, where the poisonous sea nettles and sharks would quickly finish him off.

Alone on this rock of death, Lloyd was reminded of the prisoners who had drawn lots to decide who was to be murdered to escape this sort of damnation, who would be the murderer and who the witnesses.

He now understood why they would go to such lengths not to be given the sentence of Misery Island.

Would he, also, have drawn lots if given the chance?

He tried to will himself to study the stars. It could have been a wondrous, memorable night if shared with the woman he loved. The Southern Cross blazed overhead like a great brooch on a velvet canopy. In this southern land, Orion and Pegasus hung upside down in the sky. He marveled at the splash of the Milky Way stretching far and wide in the heavens.

Too soon his eyes fell and he stared southward into the unrelieved blackness of the sea, as if something palpable and compelling held him. In truth, it was as though he were looking into the face of death.

Nadine settled in for the night by a blazing camp fire, her face shadowed by its flickering glow as she looked down into the flames. A great green turtle had been killed for the evening meal. Hot stones had been pushed into its interior through a hole under the throat, and the hole had then been blocked by a bunch of grass. When the turtle's lower shell had been cut away by Tipahee, it had released a cloud of fragrant steam from within.

Nadine's stomach was now comfortably full. The taste had been heavenly, more delicious than any roast duck or chicken she had ever eaten at an elegant dining table.

She and Tipahee had moved beyond the densest forest and were camping on a flat plane of land where they could see in all directions around them. To the east, the moon was now clearing the horizon, large and bright. Against its stagelike illumination a long line of stately pelicans flew past. A large red kangaroo bounded into the shadows and disappeared.

Drawing the warmth of her black velveteen cape around her shoulders, Nadine peered over at Tipahee. It alarmed her that they had just a short while ago made a detour before stopping for the night so that Tipahee could search for and then gather pituri, a native narcotic plant that aborigines chewed.

She watched as he took another bite of the plant. When he was drugged, would his gentle politeness turn into something ugly and threatening?

Never had Nadine felt so alone.

"Soon it will be *moomba* time," Tipahee said, his dark eyes twinkling as he looked over at Nadine.

"Moomba?" Nadine murmured, eyeing him questioningly, recalling some of the lighter moments when they had been traveling, when Tipahee had spoken in broken *Pitjantjatjara* English, making her laugh softly at his antics, for he was normally quite well versed in English.

"What is *moomba*?" she asked, glad to break the silence that had fallen between them.

Tipahee laughed softly. "It is an aboriginal word meaning 'let's all get together and have fun,'" he said, slipping another piece of pituri into his mouth and under his tongue. "When we rescue Lloyd it will be a time for much *moomba*!

"Captain Grenville is *rama rama*," Tipahee growled.

"Rama rama?" Nadine said, shivering when a splash of cold air blew in from the depths of the nearby forest. "Explain the meaning of that to me, also, Tipahee." She hoped to keep his mind occupied. She was worried about the glassiness of his eyes, which was most surely caused by the dreaded plant.

"Crazy person," Tipahee said, giggling like a child. "Tipahee calls Captain Grenville crazy person."

Then his eyes narrowed and his body tensed. He grabbed his spear and moved quickly to his feet, looking in the direction of the sound of an approaching horse.

Nadine's insides grew numb with fear. Her own pistol lay close beside her, but she reached for Lloyd's pistols because they would appear more threatening. Her hand trembled as she withdrew one from its holster. Then she sighed with relief when the rider came into sight and she saw that it was a man she now understood was a friend.

"Lieutenant Upchurch!" she said, exhaling shakily. She laid the gun aside and rose to her feet to meet the white stallion's approach, curious as to why Jon was there.

Jon stared down at Nadine in surprise. "Nadine?" he gasped. "You are traveling with Tipahee?"

"Lieutenant, please," Nadine pleaded. "What about Lloyd?"

In his neat red uniform, Jon dismounted and moved to place his hands over the fire. Nadine saw immediately that his dark eyes were troubled and that his brow was creased with worry. Oh, Lord, did he have news about Lloyd that she did not want to hear?

"Lieutenant, why have you come?" Nadine persisted, moving to Jon's side. She clasped her fingers tightly together behind her, trying to stop their trembling. "What news have you brought?"

Tipahee dropped his spear to the ground and went to stand solemnly at Jon's side, his dwarfish stature even more pronounced next to the taller man.

"You spread news? We are meeting in assigned place close to the prison hulks?" Tipahee asked. "Is it all set, Jon?"

"Everything has changed," Jon grumbled. "Everything."

Nadine placed a hand on her brow, feeling suddenly light-headed. Just as she had feared, the news was anything but good. Her heart ached and her knees were weak, yet she squared her shoulders and lifted her chin stubbornly.

"Tell us what has changed," she said dryly. "Is Lloyd all right?"

"He may or may not be," Jon said, giving Nadine a troubled glance. "Only time will tell how the damn isolation will affect him."

"Isolation?" Nadine gasped.

Jon's eyes wavered as he looked from Nadine to Tipahee. "Through my investigations I found that he has been taken to Grenville's private prison island. Most men go insane when doomed to that version of hell."

A bitterness rose up in Nadine's throat. She turned her head away, willing the tears not to flood her eyes. Captain Grenville had promised the worst sort of punishment for the man she loved. Apparently he had kept his word.

"At least it will be easier to rescue him," Jon said, trying to reassure her. "Captain Grenville thinks no one knows Lloyd is there other than those who are under his direct command, and therefore there are no guards posted on the rock. There is only rock and the holes cut into it that are used for one-man cells."

"No," Nadine said, a queasy sort of sickness grabbing her, making her teeter.

Jon turned to Tipahee. He placed his hands gently on the Indian's gaunt shoulders. "I managed to spread the word of the change to Lloyd's gang. They are waiting for your arrival. I will lead you to the rendezvous point. A canoe will be readied for you."

He turned away from Tipahee, looking darkly at Nadine. "One small canoe will be less noticeable," he said thickly. "In case Captain Grenville has posted guards on the land that I don't know about."

"What are the chances that we will find Lloyd alive and well?" Nadine asked, her voice strained.

Jon ran his fingers nervously through his thick crop of rusty hair. "I'm not sure. It depends on just how tough he is, and how he can stand up to the cold. You see, Nadine, he will be shackled there, on those cold rocks, lashed by the sea."

Nadine's insides were gripped by a sudden cold clamminess. She lowered her eyes, closing them tight, not wanting to envision the man she loved suffering so.

Jon slipped his hand inside his right front breeches pocket and withdrew a small, rusty key. He slapped it into Tipahee's hand. "One key is shaped to fit all leg and wrist irons," he said dryly. "Thank God there are several keys. Take this one, Tipahee. Use it well."

Chapter Eleven

The sea mirrored the cold gray sky. Long swells of water were grinding in a foamy white lather against the bark canoe forging through the rough water. Tipahee was drawing his paddle at a steady pace through the water, and Nadine sat in front of him, shivering from the cold and from the rain that was falling in a fine, driving mist. She huddled beneath her wet cape, clasping it securely around her neck with one hand, holding on for dear life to the edge of the canoe with the other. The crude vessel lay low in the water and flexed dangerously with every swell.

Through the darkness, Nadine caught her first glimpse of the prison rock jutting black and sinister from the water just ahead. It was like a shadow of a cloud, it was so vague, yet it was real enough, with its forbidding dark edges reaching out into the sea.

Fear grabbed at Nadine's heart when she saw its stark isolation. Her eyes searched frantically for signs of life, but the only movement she could see was the lashing of the waves against it, spewing sprays of water as high as the rock stood.

"Lloyd, oh, Lloyd," Nadine said with a choked sob, remembering that Jon had said that Lloyd would be shackled without protection on the rock. As cold as she was with her rain-soaked clothes, she did not want to think about how cold Lloyd must be.

Daylight was just now creeping over the tossing waters. She and Tipahee had received the news of Lloyd's misfortune from Jon Upchurch early last evening, and they had left immediately. Even so, it had taken too many hours to get to the rendezvous point where the bushrangers and the canoe had been waiting.

As the minutes, then the hours, had ticked away, she had known in her heart that each minute was added suffering for Lloyd.

Now Tipahee's every thrust of the paddle through the churning water brought them closer to the place of lonely confinement, the canoe pitching jerkily. There were only minutes until they would reach the base of the rock. Hopefully, soon they would have Lloyd safely back in the warmth of Tipahee's hut.

Thankful that Captain Grenville had at least not thought it necessary for Lloyd to be guarded while imprisoned on the rock, Nadine took a folded blanket from beneath her. She had placed the blanket there in an attempt to keep it dry, wanting to have something dry to place around Lloyd for his return to land.

Thrusting it quickly beneath her cape, she held on to it as she watched the rock draw closer, showing its true size now that they were within moments of landing. It rose some fifty feet above the sea level and was about forty yards long and eight yards wide.

Nadine looked at the slant of the side of the rock and at the seaweed that clung to it, all wet and slimy. Panic seized her. How could they get onto the rock without slipping into the sea?

Her answer was suddenly before her eyes as Tipahee guided the canoe to the edge of the crude steps carved into its side. Her pulse racing, she watched Tipahee tie a rope to an iron ring set in the stone and scramble from the canoe onto the first step leading upward.

Her heart skipped a beat when Tipahee gave her a studious stare, then turned and began climbing the slippery steps without her. He had argued against her traveling with him because of the danger, but had finally acquiesced when she had pointed out that she would keep Lloyd warm by holding him within her arms until they had returned safely to land.

But what now? Did he plan to rescue Lloyd alone? Did he not want her along?

Tossing her burdensome cape aside, she placed the folded blanket beneath her arm and climbed from the canoe. Her heart felt as though it had plummeted to her feet when water lapped at her boots, causing them to slip on the wet, seaweed-covered step.

But a determination born of love for a man made her begin to move steadily upward, testing each foot-step on each rock, all the while looking anxiously from side to side. Where was he? Had Captain Grenville returned for him?

The sea breeze whipped her rain-soaked hair around her, and the rain was cold and driving against her face. Nadine held the blanket closer to her chest with one hand, steadying herself on the ledge of rock with the other.

Pausing to wipe the hair from her eyes, she turned and looked over her shoulder. Her breath caught in her throat when a crevice opened to her left and she saw a set of leg irons with bony remains lying awkwardly within them.

"Oh, no!" she gasped, fighting the light-headedness that was sweeping through her, knowing that this could be Lloyd's fate if he wasn't found. "We must find Lloyd."

Nadine's head snapped around as she heard Tipahee shouting in his language.

Nadine heard the desperation in his voice. With weak knees and fast-beating heart she pushed relentlessly upward, then paled and swallowed hard when she finally saw Lloyd.

Tears welled up in Nadine's eyes as she moved them rapidly over the man she loved. She placed a hand over her mouth to stifle a sob. He was clothed in rags, his body blue from exposure to the cold winds and the continual sprays of water that bathed him with their icy fingers.

Nadine crept closer, remorse sweeping through her when she saw how small Lloyd looked lying there in a hole cut out of the rock. Her insides ached when she saw his wrists and ankles, raw from the tight steel bands. His eyes were closed, his breathing uneven.

Nadine fell to her knees at his side. Crying, she ran her fingers over his hair, which was dark with grime and dirt and clung to his head like wet leaves. She unfolded the blanket and laid it across his body, smoothing it over him.

"Lloyd," she sobbed, taking one of his icy hands in her own. She looked at the lips that had taught her the wonders of a kiss. They were purple from the intense cold. "Oh, my love, what has he done to you?"

Lloyd lay somewhere on the edges of consciousness. His whole body ached from the cold and hunger.

Yet there was something arousing him. It was the voices reaching into his consciousness. It was the warmth of hands touching him. And then there was one voice that reached his heart, separate from the other. Nadine. How was she there? Wasn't he in hell? Nadine would not be in hell with him.

Suddenly he no longer felt the cold press of the leg irons. How had they been removed? Who had set him free? His lips began to move, and his eyelids fluttered as he tried to open them. No. It wasn't shadows. It was Tipahee and . . .

"Lloyd," Nadine gasped when she saw him trying to open his eyes. She leaned over him, covering his cold body with hers. She hugged him to her, her tears wetting the blanket that lay snugly against his chest. "My darling, my darling."

Lloyd licked his lips. He forced his eyes to focus. He looked down and saw the wet strands of Nadine's hair that swept across him, close beneath his chin. He lifted a trembling, cold hand and touched her hair.

"Nadine," he said, his voice weak. "Tipahee?"

Lloyd smiled up at Tipahee and then at Nadine, who was now cradling his head on her lap. "How did you find me?" he asked hoarsely.

"Jon Upchurch," Nadine said, tears pooling in her eyes again.

Tears formed at the edges of Lloyd's eyes. He swallowed a lump that was building in his throat. "Yes, I should've known," he said, nodding. "He hasn't let me down yet."

He smiled at Tipahee. "Nor have you."

He looked at Nadine and cupped her chin in his hand. "Nor have you, either," he said thickly. Then he closed his eyes wearily. "God, I'm sleepy. So sleepy."

Nadine looked quickly up at Tipahee. "We must get him away from this place and to the warmth of your hut," she said in a rush of words.

Her eyes were drawn to the discarded leg and wrist irons, and she shivered fiercely at the sight of Lloyd's blood.

Easing Lloyd's head from her lap, she lifted the irons from the rock and hurled them angrily into the sea. "What will you do next, Captain Grenville?" she shouted. "Whatever it is, you will not succeed."

Then she eyed Lloyd warily and thought of the slippery steps that led downward, then of Tipahee and how frail he was. Could they get Lloyd to the canoe?

Determined, Nadine went to one side of Lloyd and placed one of his arms around her shoulders. "Hurry, Tipahee," she shouted. "Place Lloyd's other arm around your shoulder. We'll get him to the canoe together!''

The blanket hanging loosely around Lloyd, Nadine struggled as she began descending the stairs with his arm heavy around her neck and shoulder. She steadied herself along the way by leaning against the solid wall of rock beside her. When the canoe was reached, she helped Lloyd into it, climbed in herself and settled down beside him on the floor.

Cradling him close, she spread the blanket more snugly about him. Looking up at the heavens, she cursed the falling rain. The gray skies continued for as far as she could see.

Lloyd's head lowered on his chest, and he leaned back peacefully against Nadine as the canoe headed steadily for land.

Nadine sat stiffly beside Lloyd, who lay sleeping on woven screw-pine mats beside the fire in Tipahee's bark hut. She was trying to keep her eyes open. It had been two nights since she had slept.

Trying to keep her hands busy, she smoothed Lloyd's blanket down along his body, glad to see that natural color had returned to his cheeks and that his lips were no longer purple.

While he slept she had gently washed the mud and grime from his body and hair. When he had momentarily awakened she had spoon-fed him opossum broth.

Feeling the need to stretch herself, Nadine rose shakily to her feet. Clutching a blanket around her shoulders, she moved to the entrance flap and, easing it back, looked outside. She and Lloyd had been given the full privacy of the hut until he was well.

Outside, a camp fire sputtered in the softly falling rain. Several men dressed in wallaby-hide clothes and kangaroo-hide boots circled the fire, loaded pistols and rifles at their sides. They were the bushrangers that Lloyd had spoken of so often. The gang was comprised of soldiers and people with government jobs who had escaped Captain Grenville's evil clutches. These men had a network of informers and were able to hear about troop movements almost as soon as they began.

But Captain Grover Grenville was most skilled at eluding them. There was not one man among them who did not wish to see him dead.

Nadine's gaze shifted. Her insides warmed. Sitting beneath a lean-to of kangaroo hide close beside his hut, Tipahee was smoking a stemless pipe, drawing on the stub of the bowl.

Looking quickly over her shoulder as Lloyd cried out in his sleep, she crept back to him and lay down beside him beneath the blanket, fitting the curve of her body into his side. "It's all right," she crooned softly, caressing his cheek with her fingertips. "You're safe now."

She snuggled closer to him, their bodies becoming one. "Lloyd, you're safe. Thank God you're safe."

She placed her cheek on his heaving chest, unable to fight sleep any longer. She felt too good to let herself drift off. Thoughts of her father and Sam Parsons flitted vaguely through her mind. Somehow it did not matter that they might return home before her. All that mattered was that Lloyd was all right and that she was here with him.

Sighing, she let herself move into the twilight of sleep. Yet the slumber held no peace, for her dreams became nightmares of the rock in the middle of the sea.

Captain Grover Grenville sat straight backed in the longboat, sneering as he looked toward the bold black rock jutting out of the water just ahead. Lashed by the sea, Misery Island could look no more sinister than at this moment. He turned an ear in the direction of the rock, hoping to hear the cries of Lloyd Harpster, who was surely close to being driven mad by his isolation and by the cold and hunger that accompanied it.

"Row harder!" he commanded his men, who moved the oars relentlessly through the heavy waves. "I want to get this over with and get back on solid ground, where I can warm my blood with brandy."

His face was hardened into an expression of grim determination, and droplets of rain clung to his beard and mustache. Though damp, his thick brown hair blew wildly in the wind, and his cheeks were scarlet from the cold. His lame fingers ached from the damp coldness, making him curse the stallion.

"Damn, get me to that rock!" he shouted, raising a fist into the air. He leaned against the rain, mumbling obscenities to himself, his dark eyes on fire with the anticipation of seeing his prisoner cower and beg to be released.

Captain Grenville chuckled under his breath. Lloyd Harpster would surely now welcome the noose.

The rock reached and the longboat steadied, Grenville climbed from the boat and marched determinedly up the steps, cursing when his feet slipped on the wet seaweed that clung to the rock. He laughed hoarsely as he passed bones and skulls of those men who had not learned their lessons. He had taught them what hell was before they died.

Squinting, he looked up to where the rock leveled off, to the cell that held the man he hated within its cold confines. He was anxious to see the wet body of his longtime enemy. He was anxious to see the blood that most surely covered his wrists and ankles, for Grover Grenville had purposely placed irons on him that were too small so that they would pinch the flesh each time he moved.

As the captain drew close enough to the hole in the rock to see inside, his footsteps faltered. It was empty!

"No!" he gasped, blood rushing to his brain. Dizzy, he steadied himself on a ledge of stone and moved cautiously forward, never taking his eyes off the vacant carved-out cell.

"How?" he stormed, raising a fist into the air. "Who would know? How would they know?"

His forehead creased with a frown. He looked around for the discarded leg and wrist irons but found nothing. Because of the cursed rain, not even a trace of Lloyd Harpster's blood was left to at least prove that the man had suffered.

Then his eyes lightened and a broad smile fluttered across his face. "By God, the man must have squirmed and fallen into the sea,'' he said, looking down at the dark abyss of water below him.

He kneaded his brow. ''That's surely what happened, or the leg irons would've been left behind. No one would have dared escape with their ankles and wrists shackled, for one tip of the vessel and they would be gone.''

Smiling, feeling jubilant that he was finally rid of the man who had plagued him since they had first become acquainted, long before the voyage on the slave ship that had brought them both to Australia's shores, Grenville went back to the longboat.

''Take me home,'' he said, nodding. He again bent against the falling rain, clamping a hand over his aching, bent fingers. He was suddenly not all that happy. Something deep within him cautioned him against believing that Lloyd Harpster could be dead. His sort did not die so easily.

''No,'' he said, laughing boisterously. ''He's dead. I know that damn bastard is dead. Now, when I capture that wild stallion, I'll have both major scores of my life settled.''

Harry Quinn paced the porch of the great brick house, peering through the slowly falling rain. He was cold, not only physically but mentally. Nadine had not been home when he had returned, yet he had not disclosed the fact to Sam. Harry had planned to take Nadine into his confidence upon their return, but Nadine had not been there to confide in.

"Where the hell is she?" he said, fussing to himself. "Could it be that Lloyd fella? Damn! What if she is with him?"

The last he had heard, Lloyd had been captured and sent to the prison hulks. That at least had been the word in the pub earlier this evening, when he had been trying his luck again with the cards. He had also learned that Harpster was more than a gambler, he was an outlaw. An outlaw who had been courting his daughter.

Sam watched Harry through the window. He kneaded his brow feverishly, having himself checked and seen that Nadine wasn't in her room. She could be with only one person! But how? Lloyd Harpster was in the clutches of Captain Grenville.

Uneasy, Sam rushed outside and stood beside Harry. "I think she's lost, don't you?" he said blandly. "You know her restless nature. She's surely strayed too far in the forest."

Harry gave Sam a troubled sidelong glance. There was no way he could trust the bastard, but something had to be done about Nadine's disappearance. And he would not want Sam to be involved in the search. More and more, Sam had become a threat to him.

Harry now knew that the records of the business transactions that had rendered him penniless could be found in the ledgers that Sam had locked away somewhere. Sam had used his brains to his advantage. He knew quite well the art of cheating an old man out of his money.

"Yes, my daughter seems to have become restless just one time too many," Harry said, his eyes narrowing. "I'm going to go and find her. You stay behind. Our stagecoaches should be arriving soon. One of us should be here to receive them."

He turned on a heel and went to his study and placed his gun belt around his waist, hoping that he wouldn't be too late for his daughter. He had already let her down in ways she wasn't even aware of.

Chapter Twelve

Nadine stirred in her sleep as hands moved over her breasts, across her stomach and then between her thighs, caressing, oh, so gently. She heard someone whispering her name, drawing her fully awake to look up into eyes so blue she felt as though she might drown in them. Perhaps she already had, for the sensations Lloyd's hands were evoking inside her made her feel as though she were floating.

"Morning," Lloyd said, winking down at her from where he knelt above her. "Are you going to sleep your life away?"

Nadine raised herself up on one elbow, rubbing her eyes in disbelief. "Are you truly so well that you are capable of joking?" she gasped, smiling wickedly up at him. "Even well enough to—"

"To make love to you?" he asked, lowering his mouth to her lips and brushing them teasingly with a kiss.

"Yes, to make love," Nadine said, trembling anew as his mouth awakened the memory of past kisses and promised more for the future.

She twined her arms around his neck and clung to him fiercely, wanting never to let go. "I had doubted that we would ever be together again, much less make love."

"It's not easy to rid Australia of Lloyd Harpster," he said in a low growl, his fingers setting Nadine on fire as he continued caressing her. "Nor will you ever be rid of me easily."

Nadine's breath caught in her throat as he lowered his lips to a tight-peaked nipple and swirled his tongue over it. "Oh, Lord, I would never want that." She sighed. "But are you sure you are strong enough?"

"Darling, you are what I need to build my strength," he said, his mouth coming down over hers in a wondrous kiss. His hands swept over her body. She moaned softly against his lips and surrendered to the torrent of rapture that was washing over her.

Lifting her hips, she received his hardness inside her, and her blood began to race. Locking her legs around him, she matched his thrusts with movements of her own, receiving him more deeply inside her. His kisses were wild and hungry, and his hands were setting fires across her body. Her breasts strained against his chest. She wanted to feel all of him, take all of him, relish the moment of togetherness.

His mouth forced her lips apart. His tongue plunged inside her mouth, awakening Nadine to a new sensation that made her feel as though she were being turned inside out by the onslaught of passion.

She wove her fingers through his golden hair and drew his mouth closer. She moved her hips rhythmically, drawing him farther inside her as she savored the heat of his hardness pleasuring her.

His mouth left her lips and slipped down, fastening gently on her breast, where he suckled as his teeth teased the nipple. Then he pressed his lips to the hollow of her throat, his fingers digging into the flesh of her buttocks as he lifted her higher, his thrusts now wild and demanding.

"Oh, Nadine, how I need you...want you..." Lloyd whispered huskily, breathing hard. "You are my life."

Nadine brushed a finger over his lips. "I am yours, forever," she whispered, gently kissing his perspiration-laced brow.

She closed her eyes ecstatically as she felt the rush of warmth spreading inside her as though a tightened coil had been released. She moaned softly, moving her head back and forth as she felt the pleasure mounting. She cried out against Lloyd's lips as he again feverishly kissed her.

As Lloyd stroked her satiny breasts he felt the red-hot embers of pleasure scorching his insides. All those hellish hours on the rock had been spent thinking of moments like this. Those thoughts had kept him sane. The memory of his woman and the promise of moments with her had helped him forget the cut of the steel bracelets, the cold of the rain and wind and the constant splash of the sea upon his body.

The thought of Nadine's body, warm against his, the thought of the fire of her kiss, had kept his heart pumping heatedly through his veins and his mind clear.

Now there was no pretense. She was there, and his aching loneliness was gone forever. Though his body still ached from the torture, loving her was erasing painful memories from his mind. She was his cure for everything.

Lloyd let himself get lost in the curling heat that was growing in his lower body. He nestled her close, relishing the feel of Nadine's breasts pressed into his chest, the touch of her brushing against him as his thrusts reached an almost maddening peak. His lips trembled against hers as his body hardened and tightened in sought-for release.

Then the pleasurable tremor began at his toes and moved like a violent storm upward, cresting and exploding.

He was filled with peace.

With her fingers, Nadine combed Lloyd's damp hair back from his brow, swimming in an aftermath of languorous sweetness, for when his body had feverishly tremored, so had hers. They were still in tune with one another in every way.

She lifted his hand and studied the rawness of his wrist. Her lips moved softly across the scabs, from front to back. "Damn that man," she whispered harshly. "First he scars your back, now your wrists and ankles."

Lloyd eased his wrist away and rubbed its rawness, frowning. "At least my back was spared this time," he muttered. "The bastard felt the prison rock was worse than the lash." He shuddered. "He was right. That place is surely what hell is like."

Nadine eased into his arms and clung to him, her cheek pressed against his chest. "I feel so responsible," she cried softly. "Had I not so carelessly led Captain Grenville to you, you would not have had to suffer so."

Lloyd twined his fingers through her copper hair and drew her up to face him. "Never speak of it again," he said grimly. "What's past is past. The future is what weighs heavy on my mind now." He nodded toward the hut's entrance flap. "My men? Are they all here?"

"Yes. Jon spread the word. They are here."

"Then you must leave."

Nadine's insides rippled uneasily. Her mind was suddenly catapulted back into the real world. Surely her father hadn't been gone all this time. Several days had passed. She felt as though she had just slept two of them away within Lloyd's arms, yet she knew that in truth it had only been a day and a night. Her stomach attested to how long it had been since she had eaten. It growled unmercifully!

Then she scowled up at Lloyd. Having almost lost him made her realize that she did not want to leave him, to have to wonder again about his welfare. Though there were many bushrangers awaiting him, ready to ride with him against Captain Grenville and his injustices, there was no guarantee that Lloyd would come through it all alive.

"I don't want to leave," Nadine said in a soft whine, again easing into the sweet haven of his arms. "Must I, truly? I want to go with you. I have proven that I am capable of taking care of myself. I would be no bother to you. Truly I wouldn't.''

Lloyd chuckled. Again he urged her face upward so that his eyes could look into hers. "From the very beginning you have tried over and over again to convince me that you are capable of taking care of yourself," he said, his eyes gleaming. "And you have proven it, time and time again. But, my darling, this is different. Though your part in rescuing me was dangerous, and you shouldn't have done it, there are many more dangers involved in what I have planned. I will not put you through any of the awkward, dangerous moments that lie ahead. You must return to your father. Stay with him a while longer. When I have taken revenge and cleared my name, I will come for you.''

"I shall not rest until then," Nadine said softly. "My heart will be so empty.''

"As will my arms." Lloyd sighed, again holding her close. "As will my arms.''

"Are you well enough to travel with your men?" Nadine asked. "You were so weak when we brought you here. Your wounds are still raw. Shouldn't you stay here a while longer until you have fully regained your strength?''

"It's too dangerous to wait," Lloyd said, kissing the delicate taper of her neck. "As soon as Captain Grenville discovers my escape, all hell will break loose. I must make it hell for him first.''

He urged Nadine away from him, his eyes wavering. "Now get dressed, and as soon as you get something to eat, you must head for home," he said thickly. "Tipahee will make sure that you get there safe and sound."

Nadine let her gaze roam over him, studying him as though for the first time. Then tears gathered in her eyes. "That place is not home," she murmured. "When you and I live together as man and wife, only then will I be home."

"And that time will come," Lloyd said, smoothing her silken hair back from her eyes. "I promise, love. I promise."

"I will live for that day," she whispered, placing a hand on his cheek. "Oh, Lloyd, please be careful."

"You don't have to worry about me." Lloyd laughed hoarsely, urging Nadine to her feet and slapping her naked behind playfully.

Nadine turned on her heel and stared down at him, her lips quivering into a smile. She wiped the tears from her eyes. She knew she could not tell him of her fear of what lay ahead.

Tipahee led Nadine through the dense forest, his hands wound tightly around her horse's reins. Nadine sat on a handsome gray mare borrowed from a bushranger. She sat square shouldered, watching the loveliness of the setting around her, yet filled with dread. She feared what her father would say when he discovered where she had been, with whom and why. Once he knew that Lloyd was an outlaw, and that she had risked her life to save him, he might even force her back on the *Lady Fortune* and return her to America.

"He just can't," she whispered. "He must be made to understand. I must even tell him about Sam, that he is worthless and can't be trusted. The partnership must be dissolved. Immediately."

A noise off to one side, beneath the floating canopy of ghostly peppercorn trees, drew Nadine around. Every nerve in her body grew tense until she caught sight of two milk-white plumed egrets. Sighing heavily with relief, she watched, entranced, as they approached each other, the plumes rising like lacy veils. Undaunted by their audience, the birds behaved as though actors on a stage. In an instant of incredible beauty the two egrets touched each other tenderly. Chest to chest, they momentarily entwined their necks, then parted, only to repeat the scene again.

As Nadine watched the ceremony the birds suddenly lurched and flew away. Her gaze swept around her, trying to place the sound of an approaching horse from somewhere close by. Her heart skipped a beat as she heard her name being called.

"Father?" she whispered, meeting Tipahee's eyes as he turned and looked at her, bringing the horse to a sudden halt.

Nadine felt the heat rise to her cheeks as her father suddenly came into view on his cream-colored horse. His eyes were fierce with anger and his jaw set as he reined in beside Nadine.

"Damn," he said with a growl, nervously running his fingers through his hair, looking from Nadine to Tipahee and back. "Daughter, you've got some explaining to do." He gestured with a sweep of a hand toward Tipahee. "Who is he and where have you been? What prompted you to leave without a word as to where you were going? Don't you know the dangers?"

For a moment, Nadine was at a loss for words, not knowing where to start with her explanations. She smiled awkwardly down at Tipahee, then swung herself out of the saddle, grabbing her saddlebag. "I'm on a borrowed horse," she murmured. "Can I ride the rest of the way with you? Tipahee will return the horse to its rightful owner."

"Tipahee?" Harry spit, his eyes narrowing as he looked down at the elderly aborigine. Then he noticed the horse. "Whose horse? Or do I have to ask? You've been with Lloyd Harpster, haven't you?"

Nadine's eyes lowered for a moment, then rose again bravely. "Yes, I've been with him," she blurted. "I had to go to him. He had been imprisoned, and I could not just stand by and do nothing."

"Good Lord," Harry gasped, paling. "I'm not sure I want to hear more."

He took Nadine's saddlebag and secured it in front of him, then reached a hand to Nadine and helped her up. "Come on. Let's get you home. You look as though you've been run over by a team of horses."

Nadine laughed nervously as she placed her arm around his waist. Turning to Tipahee, she said, "Please see that nothing happens to Lloyd. And thank you. I shall always remember your kindness."

Tipahee smiled and nodded, turning the horse in the direction of the camp. Nadine hugged her body against her father's as he wheeled his horse around and began working his way through the dense forest.

"Now tell me exactly what this is all about," he demanded. "Then I'll determine whether or not you return to America tomorrow."

Nadine grew cold inside at the thought but was not intimidated by his words. She was old enough to take care of herself, and her father was no longer going to be the one to choose her destiny.

Now that there was Lloyd, everything in her life had changed.

The horse was now traveling across a vast limestone plateau riddled with holes. Mysteriously, pale green wardweed grew to the north of the trail, while bluebush covered the land to the south.

Nadine was relieved to have answered all of her father's questions. Thus far he had not responded in any way to what she had said, but she knew she could expect an explosion once they reached the house.

Now it was her turn to question him and to tell him about Sam Parsons. It should not be all that hard, since her father now knew that Sam had set the law on Lloyd—and why. It seemed her father had a lot to cope with now.

"Father, on your trip..." she said, shaking her perspiration-dampened hair from her face. The breeze felt wonderful as it slipped down the front of her blouse. "What did you accomplish?"

"The stagecoaches are done and should be arriving soon," Harry said, his shoulders slumped. He was tired from the long ride. "They're going to be something new for Australia. They're going to be drawn by the most beautiful matching horses money can buy. A person can't help but feel grand and important when he rides in a coach like that.''

He turned to give Nadine a glance. "How does that sound? Grand enough?''

"Sounds thrilling,'' Nadine said, but her tone of voice belied her words. There was a coolness about it that her father picked up quite readily.

"Huh!'' Harry spit. "You don't sound all that thrilled. What's troubling you, Daughter? We've plenty of time to talk. Let's get it all out now.''

"It's about Sam Parsons—'' Nadine began, but her words locked in her throat as one of the palomino's hooves caught in a hole, causing it to lurch forward.

In a flash, Nadine watched as her father was wrenched away and thrown over the horse's head.

Screaming as she was jerked sideways, Nadine felt the horse collapse beneath her and was herself hurled to the ground. A hazy blackness grabbed hold of her when she felt the pain of impact and her head hit the ground with a strange popping noise.

The maniacal cries of a kookaburra bird broke through Nadine's consciousness. Its startling peals of loud laughter from somewhere close by echoed around her throbbing head. Her arms were covered with mosquito bites, and ants and other insects were crawling all over her.

Rubbing her brow, Nadine leaned up on one elbow with a wince. It even hurt to open her eyes. "What happened?'' she whispered, aching so badly that she could hardly keep from breaking into tears.

She scooted up into a sitting position, jumping with alarm when a black cockatoo burst out of the scrub and a wild pig charged off through the bush. She moaned, her gaze drawn to the horse. It was groaning in its own pain, its leg broken. Panic rose inside her as she recalled what had happened. Her knees weak and her whole body trembling with pain, she moved up from the ground and looked desperately around her. Her eyes wavered and she gasped as her gaze found her father lying in an awkward sort of heap just ahead.

"Oh, no," she cried softly, stumbling over and falling to her knees beside him. She looked him over carefully, relieved to see that he was still breathing. Her fingers went to his head and searched through his scalp where his head had hit the ground. When she pulled her hand away from him, it was covered with blood. She shook her head frantically back and forth in disbelief.

"Father, please, please don't die," she whimpered. She covered his body with hers, hugging him desperately to her. "Had you not come searching for me, this would not have happened."

The horse's heavy breathing drew Nadine's head up. Her gaze went to the beautiful cream-colored horse. She bit her lower lip as tears flowed down her cheeks.

"Even you?" she whispered.

Knowing she must put the horse out of its misery, she went to the horse and removed the saddle and saddlebags.

Sobbing, she looked down at her father's pistols. With trembling fingers she reached for one and slipped it from the holster. With wobbly knees she rose up from the ground and stood over the beautiful horse, who rolled his eyes and looked at her. Nadine stifled another sob as she aimed the pistol.

Her body jerked as the gun discharged, and she turned her head away as the horse's body jolted from the impact, then shuddered into death's stillness.

The gun heavy at her side, Nadine returned to her father and slumped down on the ground beside him. She tossed the pistol away and crept her arms around him. Hugging him to her, she wept softly. Without the horse, how was she going to get her father home? Was he going to die?

A noise from somewhere close by startled her. She lifted her head and wiped the tears from her face when she found Tipahee standing there, looking down at her with his wide, dark eyes, still holding the reins of the bushranger's horse.

"Tipahee?" Nadine gasped, combing her fingers nervously through her hair.

"Tipahee follow you, not far behind," he said, glancing over at the horse. "Tipahee hear gunfire."

"Thank the Lord," Nadine said, swallowing another sob. She rushed to her feet and gestured toward her father. "He's injured, Tipahee. Please help me. We must get him home."

Nodding, Tipahee led his horse up close to where Nadine's father lay. Together they strained and groaned until they had him lying across the saddle and secured with rope. Nadine reached for the pistol, which still smelled of spent gunpowder, and thrust it in her father's saddlebag. Solemnly she placed his saddlebag and her own on the horse beside him.

Her head throbbing from her own fall, Nadine walked quietly beside the horse on one side, while Tipahee walked on the other. Darkness fell. They walked through streams, up banks and across stretches of open fields under the stars.

Soon, through a break in the trees, Nadine saw lamplight shining from the windows of the great brick house. She was so tired that she felt faint. She struggled to put one foot before the other. But she had the insight to remember that Tipahee must not be seen by Sam Parsons, or Tipahee would join the hunted along with Lloyd!

Nadine stumbled around the horse and put her weary hands on Tipahee's shoulders. "You must not go any farther," she murmured. "It wouldn't be safe. I can take Father the rest of the way alone. Please return to Lloyd, Tipahee, and see to his safety at all times."

She hugged him affectionately, then went back to the horse and, grabbing its reins, moved from the forest.

Chapter Thirteen

Nadine sat at her father's bedside, watching for signs of a return to consciousness. He had not even fluttered an eyelash since she had gotten him back to the ranch the previous night. Sam had been kind enough to go and get a doctor from Melbourne to see to their needs. Besides her throbbing head and the mass of yellowing contusions on various parts of her body, she had checked out all right. But her father seemed to have suffered a skull fracture. Only time would tell if he would recover.

Wringing out a damp cloth, Nadine laid it across his brow, just below the bandage placed there by the doctor. Her movement caused her to wince. She ached from head to toe, and the slightest turn of her head caused it to throb unmercifully.

"Must everyone suffer because of your love of that outlaw?"

Nadine groaned at Sam's voice and pushed herself up from her chair. Reeling from the pain, she closed her eyes for a moment to steady herself and then determinedly opened them again.

Though last evening Sam had not accused her of having been with Lloyd, she knew now that he must have guessed that Lloyd was still alive. Did he also know that she had been a part of Lloyd's escape from Misery Island? If so, how would he use this information against her? Though her father had not approved, he already knew everything about Lloyd and her part in his escape. Sam could no longer threaten her with blackmail.

She glanced down at her father. He had known. Would he still, when he regained consciousness?

Turning her attention back to Sam, she placed a hand on his elbow, ushering him from the room. "This isn't the time or the place to argue," she said in a harsh whisper, the skirt of her dress rustling as she guided him into the sun-splashed parlor. "Father is quite ill. He doesn't need to be disturbed by our bantering."

Once in the parlor, she dropped her hand and turned to face him. "Now that we are away from my father's room, say anything you wish," she snapped angrily, forgetting the pain. "What were you saying? Something about suffering?"

"You know exactly what I said," Sam said, grabbing her by the wrists, his eyes shining with anger. "Must everyone suffer because of your love of that outlaw? Your father lies somewhere between life and death and, by God, I feel as though I'm in no better shape than he. Damn it, Nadine, I can give you everything that your outlaw never could. How could you love such a man? You were brought up to expect better than the likes of him."

It took all the willpower Nadine could muster not to cry out with the pain he was inflicting on her wrists. She began to tremble with building anger.

Her gaze raked over Sam. Then she laughed sarcastically. "Look at you in your handsome dark suit, with white ruffles at your wrists and collar," she said mockingly.

She faced him with a set stare. "Do you think you are more a gentleman than Lloyd Harpster just because you dress the part? You are nothing at all compared to the man I love."

"But he is an outlaw," Sam said, releasing her wrists, his face shadowed with hurt. "How could you compare me with a roguish outlaw?"

Nadine stepped closer and spoke up into his face. "If the truth were known, I would wager that you have done more wrong in your lifetime than most criminals who are imprisoned. Something is terribly wrong between you and Father. Something that would more than likely get you sent to prison in America should anyone fully investigate your underhanded activities!"

She spun around and marched to the window to look down at the sea, where the sunlight glittered like sparkling diamonds. "Please don't bore me with talk of Lloyd being a criminal," she snapped, hugging herself as a chill coursed through her. "He is only branded a criminal because of injustices done to him."

Sam went to Nadine, grabbed her by the shoulders and spun her around to face him. "Nadine, I don't care to talk any more of Lloyd Harpster and what his lot in life is, or of your accusations against me," he said roughly. "None of this has anything to do with how I feel about you."

His hands rose gently to her cheeks. He lowered his mouth and brushed a tender kiss across her lips. "God, Nadine, I love you. I've always loved you. I can hardly stand it, I love you so much."

Nadine was stunned by the gentleness, soft words and tender kiss. Momentarily speechless, she looked up into his eyes, bewildered. She had never seen this side of him before. Perhaps if she had at the beginning, her feelings might have been different. As it was, she had learned only to despise even the merest touch from him.

Shaking herself from her momentary reverie, Nadine stepped away. She rubbed her mouth feverishly with the back of her hand, trying to remove the taste of his kiss.

"Please, don't touch me. Never attempt to kiss me again," she said softly, still shaken. "You say that you love me. But you don't know *how* to love."

Sam raked his fingers nervously through his dark hair, his dark eyes haunted. "Damn it, Nadine," he said harshly. "Must I beg?"

A shudder coursed through her at the idea of Sam groveling at her feet. She did not want to pity him, for there was too much about him that pointed to dishonesty toward her father.

"Please don't do this," she cried, turning her eyes away.

The sound of horses arriving outside broke the strain in the room. Nadine sighed heavily with relief at her stroke of luck, for as Sam rushed to the window and looked outside, his mind was suddenly elsewhere.

Sam gasped, his eyes lighting up. He swung around and smiled widely at Nadine. "They've arrived." He let out a loud whoop and rushed from the room.

Nadine went to the window and looked out. Her eyes widened when she saw the reason for Sam's excitement. Four colorful stagecoaches drawn by beautiful horses stood in a straight line in the drive, awaiting inspection.

"No," Nadine said harshly. "Not now. It's not fair. Father would want to witness the arrival of his new stagecoaches. He would be so proud."

Her eyes were dancing angrily as she stamped from the room and on outside to the drive. With the wind whipping her auburn hair around her face and shoulders, Nadine moved around the stagecoaches.

Though every inch of her ached, she continued her inspection, letting her gaze move over each of the coaches and the horses that pulled them. Her pulse raced at the sight of them.

Her father had personally drawn up the plans for them and sent them to Australia before anyone knew of his plans to move there with his business and family. It was his idea to have the coaches painted gaily and hung on leather straps so that the coaches would sway gently back and forth instead of being tossed around when the wheels hit holes and ruts in the road.

The white horses attached to each of the coaches were beautifully matched and groomed, as her father had wished. Gay blue rosettes decorated their polished harnesses.

"Don't they take your breath away, Nadine?" Sam asked, stepping to her side and proudly squaring his shoulders. "They will be taking their first run tomorrow. It should be a proud day for the both of us."

Nadine frowned up at him. "It should be a proud day for Father," she snapped, turning to give her approval to the men who had brought the coaches. As she started to walk toward the house, a lone rider appeared, coming up the drive.

Nadine cupped a hand over her eyes, shielding them from the blinding rays of the sun, as she studied the approaching horseman. He was dressed in wallaby-hide clothes, hat and boots and armed with great silver pistols holstered at each of his hips. As he drew closer, she could see that his face was covered with a mass of pitted scars.

He gave Nadine the shivers, for he looked less than friendly as he frowned down at her. She gave Sam a nervous glance as he greeted the approaching horseman with a handshake.

"Who is that?" Nadine whispered to herself as she turned with a swish of petticoat and skirt and went back inside the house.

Once inside, she paused at the living room window, feeling an icy coldness sweep through her when the stranger caught her watching him. His eyes were the same cold silver as his pistols.

Nadine swung away from the window and cowered against the wall, her eyes wide with fear. This man was surely a gunman. What did he want here and what did Sam have to do with it?

Nadine rushed on to her father's room, momentarily forgetting the stranger when she found her father awake and smiling at her as she approached the bed.

"Nadine, you look as though you've just seen a ghost," Harry said in a shaky whisper.

Nadine knelt beside her father's bed. She took his hand from beneath the blankets and hugged it to her chest. "Thank God you're all right," she whispered, swallowing the urge to cry.

She looked toward the window, remembering the lovely stagecoaches, and smiled down at her father. "Father, I've the best news."

Lloyd's strawberry roan pawed nervously at the ground. Lloyd ran his hand down its sleek neck, comforting it. His gaze was locked in front of him on Captain Grenville's quaint two-story stone cottage, which was nestled beneath a thick grove of trees.

Flowers filled the window boxes, and smoke spiraled peacefully from a great stone chimney at one side of the house. Captain Grenville's prize cattle stood grazing in the surrounding fields.

Lloyd and his gang had watched the captain leave and were now ready to raid his home. The livestock, food and wine would be taken and passed on to the needy farmers in the countryside close to Melbourne. This was just the beginning of the torments planned for the evil captain.

"I think we've waited long enough, don't you, Lloyd?" Gary Rice asked, inching his horse close to Lloyd's. "It's been a long time coming, I'd say."

Lloyd smiled his lazy, self-assured smile at his bushranger friend, who had ridden with him until the day Lloyd had been forced onto a ship bound for San Francisco. During Lloyd's absence, Gary, like the rest of the gang, had been fighting the injustices of the rich and the police.

"How many nights have you spent dreaming of this?" Lloyd asked, chuckling.

"A fair number of them," Gary retorted.

Gary was a tall, thin man who sported a thick crop of red hair. He was dressed similarly to the others, and the pistols at his side were supplemented by a rifle strapped to his saddle.

"Once we leave the bastard's house there'll be no doubt in his mind that you're still alive," Gary said, laughing boisterously. "He'll come looking for you, that's for damn sure."

"Let him come," Lloyd said with a growl, looking over his men, confident now that they had joined forces again. "This time he'll be the loser."

He placed a hand on Gary's shoulder. "Pass the word again that no one is to be harmed today," he said calmly. "Just frightened. That will carry the message to Grenville that it is him we're after."

Gary nodded. He leaned his head close to the next bushranger. Like a ripple on the water, the message moved from man to man.

Lloyd raised his hand in a signal and thundered out of the thicket with the others following close behind.

Pulling up to the front of the house, he drew his pistol and ran up the steps and across the porch and crashed through the door into the foyer. His entrance was met with screams and shouts as the servants scattered in all directions.

Lloyd gave orders to his men as they came through the door. The servants were rounded up and taken to the cellar to be tied and gagged. A massive display of wine lined one whole wall of the cellar. Lloyd gave Gary a smile over his shoulder.

"Shall we?" he asked with a chuckle.

"Yeah," Gary said, lumbering over to the racked bottles. He withdrew one bottle after the other, studying the dates. "But I think we should taste it before passing it on to the others. It might not be any good."

He yanked the cork from one of the bottles with his teeth and guzzled it down in deep gulps, his eyes gleaming as he lowered the bottle from his lips. "It's not bad," he said, hiccuping loudly, the wine red on his lips.

Laughing, he threw the empty bottle across the room, where it shattered at the feet of the wide-eyed servants.

Then he chose another bottle and set it aside. "Your turn," he said with a mocking half bow toward Lloyd. "Take your pick, Lloyd. For our troubles we should save a couple of bottles for ourselves. It will make it sweet and nice when your lady friend comes to call again."

Lloyd's blue eyes twinkled. He grabbed two bottles and set them aside before returning to eagerly hand over the rest to his men, who carried them out to the waiting saddlebags.

When the last of the wine supply was gone, Lloyd gave the gaping servants a wink, grabbed his chosen bottles of wine and tore back upstairs. His gaze swept around him as he marched from room to room, seeing how the man that he had hated for so long lived. He grumbled to himself when he saw the expensive paintings, the gold and silver, the plush, rich velveteen furnishings and the carved tables.

Lloyd continued through the house, directing his gang to take what they could carry and make a mess of the rest of it. The bushrangers turned over tables and rolled up the Oriental carpets, flinging them over their shoulders, creating havoc in their wake. By the time they were through with Grenville's house, there was not one thing in its proper place, and a good deal of his possessions were on the backs of their horses.

Nadine gently lifted her father's head while easing a teacup of water to his parched lips. Her heart was filled with hope that her father would be all right. "The stagecoaches are absolutely wonderful," she said, wincing when he choked a little on the water. "You will be so very proud, Father. Even the special horses were brought today. I can hardly wait until you can see for yourself."

Harry eased his lips from the cup and closed his eyes, panting. "Daughter, no more water," he said thickly. "Let me just rest. I need rest."

Nadine nodded anxiously, laying the cup on the table beside the bed. "Do you want me to leave?" she asked in a shaky whisper, wondering if she had let herself hope for the best too soon. "Or would you rather I stay and sit at your bedside?"

Harry motioned toward a chair. "Sit. Sit," he said, opening his eyes and smiling weakly up at her. "Tell me, how are you today? You took quite a blow yourself, didn't you?"

Nadine eased herself down onto a chair and clasped her hands tightly in her lap. "Yes," she said softly. "But I will heal soon. Nothing to worry about."

Harry's face took on a pinched expression as he lowered his eyes. "And my horse?" he asked quietly. "What of him?"

Nadine's insides tightened as she relived the moment the pistol had gone off and the way the horse's body had reacted to the impact of the bullet. She bit her lower lip and cleared her throat nervously. "Father, the horse's leg was broken in the fall," she murmured. "I had to—"

Harry reached out and patted her knee. "Shh," he said reassuringly. "I know what must be done to a horse whose leg is broken."

"I'm so sorry about all of this, Father," Nadine blurted out, near tears. "But I can't say that I should have done anything any differently. I had to go to Lloyd. He needed me. I would go to him again. You'll just have to accept my feelings for him. I would do anything to help him. Anything."

Harry's guts twisted when he realized the depth of his daughter's love for the outlaw. It would have been simple, had he been well, to place her bodily back on the *Lady Fortune* and return her to America, but things were never that simple, it seemed. He was not even capable of walking across the room, much less dragging his daughter away from the man she loved.

There was also the problem with Sam. What could be done about the embezzlement? He needed proof, he needed the ledgers...but he was barely able to sit, let alone fight for what was his.

He stared up at Nadine and realized that she was the only answer. She must find the ledgers. She must find the proof he needed to point an accusing finger at Sam Parsons, so that he wouldn't get away with it.

"Nadine, there's so much I need to tell you," he blurted. "At present, it seems that all the cards are stacked against us."

"What?" Nadine said, confused by his statement. "What are you talking about?"

"Sam Parsons," Harry said, his eyes flashing angrily. "Nadine, there's so much about him that you don't know. I haven't told you before because I thought I could make things right, but I think that perhaps I've waited too long."

"Father, what things?" Nadine asked, having suspected so much for so long.

"You know that I took Sam in as my partner because of his brains," Harry said, breathing hard as the talking taxed his limited strength. "Well, Daughter, he used his brains all right. He used them to embezzle money from me. Damn it, Nadine, he had a way of fixing the books in his favor. I'm almost penniless. Thank God, for once it can't be blamed on my love of gambling."

He kneaded his brow. "In a sense it was a gamble, though, wasn't it, bringing a perfect stranger into the business, trusting him."

Nadine paled. Her mouth was dry. "Why didn't you say something earlier?" she gasped. "How long have you known?"

"For a while now," Harry said, his voice strained. "But I had to hang on and try to trick the son of a bitch somehow, give him a dose of his own medicine. He even played along with me, made it look to you and your mother as though everything were all right, all along just waiting for the right moment to kick me out of the business."

"And where did I come into the picture?" Nadine asked. "Why did he play with my feelings and emotions?"

"I truly think he loves you, or he would have called my hand long ago. He didn't only because he still held out some hope of one day having you as a wife," Harry said, turning his eyes away. "I had to pretend that I wanted you to marry him. It was part of my scheme to play the waiting game until I could find a way to get even with him, to get back my portion of the business."

Nadine recalled how sincere Sam had sounded only a short while ago when he had told her that he loved her. He had been sincere, but that was beside the point. What could she do now to help her father?

"What can I do?"

"You must find the ledgers. There are two of them."

"Do you mean he's hidden them from you?"

"You're damn right he has. They are all the proof we need to go to the authorities."

"Where do you think they are?"

"I don't have the slightest notion. That's for you to find out, Nadine."

Harry shuddered and closed his eyes. "I've worn myself out," he said weakly. "I must go to sleep. Let's talk some more tomorrow."

Nadine scooted up from her chair and fixed the blanket more snugly beneath his chin, kissing him softly on the brow. "Yes, tomorrow," she whispered. "I'm leaving for now. But I'll be back soon to check on you."

Harry nodded and turned onto his side, away from her.

Nadine was no longer aware of her own throbbing pain. All she could think of was Sam and how he had cheated her father out of what was rightfully his. Sam must be made to return it.

She rushed from the room with a determined gait. "I won't beat around the bush," she vowed. "I'm going to ask point-blank where those ledgers are, and if he doesn't tell me I'll tear apart every inch of this place until I find them!"

When Nadine reached the door to Sam's office, it was closed. She stopped when she heard voices coming from within. She edged toward the door and leaned an ear close. Her knees weakened and her face drained of color when she heard the orders that Sam was giving his visitor. Nadine had to surmise that the stranger with the silver pistols and the icy, unfriendly stare was still with Sam, and what they were saying turned her heart to stone.

"I don't like paying in advance like this," Sam said flatly. "But if that's the way you have to have it, so be it. You damn well better bring back proof that Lloyd Harpster is dead. He's been nothing but trouble, and I'm paying you a lot of money to get him out of the picture."

"It's as good as done," the man said with a low chuckle. "But I'll not return with the proof. I disassociate myself with those I do business for after the business is done. Take it or leave it. That's the way I work."

"All right," Sam said with a growl. "Just do it. And do it soon. My lady isn't going to cooperate as long as that outlaw is around to interfere."

Nadine's knees almost crumbled beneath her. She placed her hands over her mouth, horrified by what she had just heard. Sam had paid a bounty hunter to kill Lloyd.

"Lloyd! He must be warned!" she whispered, looking frantically down the corridor at her father's closed bedroom door. "But what about Father and the ledgers?"

With fear tugging at her heart, Nadine rushed to her father's office and frantically wrote him a note. Entering his bedroom, she placed it on the table beside his bed.

"Please try and understand," she whispered, looking down at her sleeping father. "I'll try not to be gone long. But I must find Lloyd and warn him."

Swinging around, she crept from the bedroom. Once out in the hall, she rushed to her room and hurriedly thrust a change of clothes into her saddlebags.

After she had also placed her pistol in her saddlebag, she went and gazed from the window at the beckoning forest, filled with dread. Danger lurked around her on all sides.

Chapter Fourteen

Chilled to the bone and frightened that she might have somehow lost her way, Nadine moved relentlessly onward. The heavens of the Southern Hemisphere were pressing down on the land around her like a glittering skullcap, and her hair whipped around her shoulders in the night breeze. Huddling beneath the fullness of her cape, Nadine peered ahead, searching for signs of camp fires, but seeing none.

Her head half bowed with fatigue, she nudged the horse's flanks with the heels of her boots, sending it into a gallop. She traveled beneath a double canopy of tree ferns that towered above her and great eucalyptus trees that soared over the ferns, their stringy bark peeling off in long fronds and swaying ghostlike in the wind.

A loud howl came from somewhere close by, and Nadine's head rose with a snap. Reaching a hand back to reassure herself that her pistol was still in the saddlebag, she continued on, determined to find and warn the man she loved.

"What is Father going to think when he awakens and finds my note?" she whispered to herself, aching at the thought of how it would hurt him to realize that she had chosen to warn Lloyd, rather than stay behind and search for the ledgers.

She had been torn between two loyalties, and her loyalty to the man she hoped would one day be the father of her children had won.

Nadine lifted her eyes to the stars. "Please help Father to understand," she prayed softly. "Let him realize that I will return and make things right for him."

Sam stared at Nadine's closed bedroom door, one hand nervously pulling on his chin. He had not seen her since they had inspected the coaches. She had not even eaten supper. Had his behavior disturbed her that much? Should he tell her now who was the wealthier of the two partners, and the more powerful? He could ruin her father in a moment, if he chose.

He would not admit any wrongdoing, but somehow he had to make her understand that she herself would never be hurt by his scheming to make himself rich. In a sense, he had done it for her. A husband's wealth was much more important than a father's.

Once Lloyd Harpster was dead, she would have all the reasons in the world to marry him. She would have no choice.

Deciding not to push his luck too far by disturbing her, Sam moved on to Harry's door. Placing a hand on the knob, he gently eased the door open, squinting as he looked into the darkness with surprise. Had Nadine meant to leave her father lying in total darkness?

Sam would have thought that Nadine would have left a candle burning, to give her father light should he awaken.

"Harry?" Sam whispered, moving quietly into the room.

When there was no response, he went to the bed and peered down at the sleeping man. Harry seemed to be resting peacefully enough. His breathing was even, and his body seemed totally relaxed.

The glow of candlelight from the corridor filtered into the room, casting a rivulet of light onto the folded piece of paper on the nightstand.

Slowly his hand went to the paper and snatched it from the table. Holding it in the light, he unfolded it, growing cold inside as he read Nadine's neat handwriting.

"No!" he whispered harshly, his eyes two points of hate as he read and reread the note intended for her father. "This time she may have gone too far!"

He slapped the note back down on the table and hurried from the room. "Damn it, Nadine," he cursed. "Your obsession for that man is going to get you killed."

He would not go after her. He was tired of reaching for something that he now knew was way beyond reach. He had a more pressing problem to deal with. In her note, Nadine had mentioned that she would find the ledgers upon her return.

Setting his jaw and doubling his hands into tight fists, Sam voiced his anger to the empty hallway. "I'll be damned if I'll let her!" he snarled.

Going to his bedroom, he dug deeply into a trunk hidden at the back of his closet and withdrew two ledgers. With a determined gait he strode outside, where he proceeded to set fire to random pages of the journals. She'd find no evidence against him!

Straightening his back, he looked down and smiled as he watched the flames eat away at the proof of his embezzlement.

Nadine emitted a sigh of joyous relief when she saw orange light, which could only mean a camp fire just ahead. She had begun to lose all hope that she was traveling in the right direction.

Then she was again swept with doubt, wondering if there would even be someone at Tipahee's bark hut to take her to Lloyd's new hideout. Since Captain Grenville had captured Lloyd at the cave, Lloyd and his gang would certainly not be there.

She flicked the horse's reins and nudged him into a steady gallop as she neared the camp fire. Her eyes widened at the sight of several other bark huts that had been placed close to Tipahee's. As she came nearer, she recognized several of Lloyd's gang sitting close to the fire.

Suddenly, Nadine found herself surrounded by men armed with long-barreled pistols aimed directly at her. She brought her horse to a shuddering halt.

Smiles flickered among the dark faces as they recognized her and lowered their pistols.

"My word," Nadine exclaimed, laughing awkwardly. "You gave me such a fright."

Gary Rice moved from the circle of men and went to Nadine, grabbing hold of her horse's bridle. "Ma'am, it ain't safe to come upon a camp of bushrangers without first giving some sort of notice," he said, leading the horse on into the camp. "It's a sure enough way to get your head blown clean off your shoulders."

When Gary had secured the horse and helped her to the ground, Nadine looked desperately from hut to hut. "Where's Lloyd?" she asked anxiously, imploring with her eyes. "I must talk to him. Now."

"Don't you ever listen to anyone's advice about riding alone in the wilds of Australia?" came Lloyd's inquiry from behind her.

Nadine whirled around, her cape tangling about her legs as she stopped to stare up at his handsome bronzed face. "Lloyd, don't even think of scolding me for coming," she said, grabbing his arm. "I had to."

She paused and took a nervous breath. "I overheard Sam talking to a bounty hunter. They exchanged money. He was paid to find and kill you. You must go into better hiding than this."

She let her gaze wander over the crude huts and the weapons propped up against them. Tipahee was sitting in front of his hut, smoking his stemless pipe. She smiled at him before looking up into Lloyd's eyes again.

"Did you hear me?" she asked, exasperated by his failure to react to the threat that she had risked her life

to warn him about. "Are you just going to stand
there? Lloyd, that was the most dangerous-looking
man I've ever seen. I imagine he does his job quite
well."

Lloyd placed his arm around her waist and pulled
her away from the rest of the men toward a hut separated from the others. As they entered, she noticed
that a pleasant fire burned in the fire pit in the center
of the floor.

Nadine welcomed the rush of warmth she felt from
the fire. She did not object when Lloyd unfastened
her cape and eased it away from her shoulders. The
warmth felt wonderful after her hard ride.

"You look frozen clean to the bone, love," Lloyd
said, easing her down before the fire. He knelt and
placed several more pieces of wood on the flames and
sat down beside her, silently studying her.

Nadine removed her gloves and held her hands
close to the fire, giving Lloyd a puzzled look. "I don't
understand you," she said softly. "I come to warn
you about someone coming after you and you just sit
there. Shouldn't you even warn your men to be on the
lookout? He could be arriving at any moment. I'm
sure he's close behind me."

Lloyd reached for one of the bottles of wine stolen
from Captain Grenville's cellar. He removed the cork
and offered the bottle to Nadine. "I'm afraid I don't
have fancy glasses to offer," he said, his eyes gleaming. "Take a drink, it'll warm your insides."

Shocked at Lloyd's casual attitude, Nadine took
the bottle, hoping that some wine would help her lose
the chill from the long journey on horseback.

"Thanks," she murmured, eyeing the bottle. "Where on earth did you get it?"

Lloyd leaned back on one elbow, smiling lazily at her. He stretched his long, lean legs out in front of him. "It's been a rewarding day, my dear." He chuckled, recalling the destruction of Captain Grenville's house. "Now, if you had come to warn me about Captain Grenville I'd have taken more notice, for you see, he has much to be upset about."

Nadine pulled her hair back from her face and smiled mischievously. "Are you trying to tell me you stole this wine from Captain Grenville?" she asked, laughing softly.

"It was taken from his premises," Lloyd said, reaching for another bottle of wine and removing the cork with his teeth. "I think this calls for a celebration. Don't you?"

Nadine straightened her shoulders, and her eyes grew wide. She crossed her legs, smoothing her skirt more comfortably about her. "You went to his house?" she gasped. "You actually went into his house?"

Lloyd gulped down a deep swallow of wine and rested the bottle against his thigh. "While he was gone, we tore his place apart and stole his food, livestock and wine and distributed it to the small farmers nearby."

Nadine's eyes twinkled. "My own Robin Hood," she said with a sigh. Then her shoulders shook as she burst into a fit of laughter. "I wish I could have been there," she said, choking with laughter. "What fun it must have been."

Lloyd placed a hand on the bottle and eased it to her lips. "Take a drink," he said thickly. "Share the spoils of war with me, my love."

Nadine smiled over the bottle at him and took a sip of wine, enjoying the warmth it spread as it flowed down her throat and into her stomach.

"Another," Lloyd said, encouraging her to tip the bottle to her mouth again.

Nadine pushed the bottle away from her lips. "This is not a good time to try and get me drunk," she said, frowning. "That bounty hunter could arrive any minute. Aren't you the least bit alarmed about him?"

"Should I be?"

"I would think so."

"I don't frighten all that easily, love."

"Perhaps you should."

Lloyd replaced the cork in the bottle and put both bottles against the far wall of the hut. "I've better things to do than worry about hired killers," he said huskily, his lips brushing teasingly against hers. "Since you've gone to all the trouble of coming here to see me, you must be rewarded in some little way. Now I wonder what sort of reward you might ask for?"

Nadine jerked away from him and rose to her feet, trembling. She placed her hands on her hips and glared down at him. "What's gotten into you?" she snapped angrily. "I didn't come all this way just to be made fun of! If I had known you wouldn't take me seriously, I would have stayed behind with my father. He needs me more than you ever will, especially now!"

Lloyd rose to his feet. "Damn it," he cursed remorsefully, raking his fingers through his golden hair. "Forgive me, Nadine. I should have asked how your father was. Tipahee told me that he got quite a bang on the head."

"Not just a bang," Nadine responded. "It was a skull fracture. He's lucky to be alive."

She covered her mouth with her hand, stifling a sob. "And so are you," she murmured. "Perhaps you won't be this time tomorrow if you don't pay attention to what I've told you. This isn't the time for games *or* making love."

Lloyd turned and glared into the flames of the fire. "Did Sam pay him well?" he said blandly.

"I'm sure he did, or the man wouldn't have agreed to do it. And you still refuse to warn your men about him."

Nadine's insides grew cold at the sound of an approaching horse outside the hut. She gasped and looked toward the closed entrance flap, then back at Lloyd. "What if it's him?" she whispered harshly. "Oh, Lloyd, you've waited too long. He'll probably kill several of your men before getting to you."

"We'll see," Lloyd said, drawing her within his arms. "You just stand beside me. I'll protect you."

Nadine shook her head in despair. "I don't understand you," she said, trembling against his rock-hard body.

Her eyes searched the inside of the hut until she found his holstered pistols resting on the floor behind them. "You don't even have your pistols on. How can you protect *anyone*?"

Nadine tensed, realizing that the hoofbeats had stopped, yet no gunfire had been exchanged. Perhaps she had been wrong to believe it was the bounty hunter?

Then her pulse quickened when she heard a new voice added to the others outside. She had only heard the voice once in her lifetime, but that had been enough to make her remember it for an eternity.

It was the bounty hunter's low rumble of a voice. And he was talking in a friendly manner, even *laughing*, as he mixed with the bushrangers outside Lloyd's hut.

"What the—?" Nadine whispered, giving Lloyd a questioning glance. "That's him. I know that's him. Lloyd, it's a trap."

"Come. Let me introduce you to one of my oldest friends," Lloyd said, sweeping Nadine out of the hut and face-to-face with the man with the cold silver eyes. "Nadine, meet Joseph Wright, one of the most admired convicts ever to flee the clutches of Captain Grover Grenville."

Joseph glared at Nadine. "What's this all about, Lloyd?" he muttered. "I saw this lady at Sam Parsons's place. Are they related?"

Lloyd drew Nadine in front of him, closer to Joseph. "Not in the least," he said, smiling. "And I aim to keep it that way. Joseph, meet my future bride. She's come all the way out here to warn me about a bounty hunter who's been paid to find and kill me. How much did you get for the dirty deed, my friend?"

Joseph laughed as he withdrew a leather bag from inside his saddlebag and slapped it into Lloyd's hand. "Damned if he didn't pay me the entire sum. I don't think he liked my looks."

Lloyd grinned, testing the weight of the coins in the bag. "How are you going to do it, Joseph?" he drawled. "Guns, rope or knife?"

Joseph kneaded his chin with one large hand. "Rope is least messy," he said, laughing boisterously and clasping an arm fondly around Lloyd's shoulder. "I sure could use a glass of something strong. Got any available?"

"Would wine from Captain Grenville's personal cellar be good enough for you?" Lloyd said, eyeing his friend with a gleam in his eyes. "My lady and I have already tasted it. It's quite good. Isn't it, Nadine?"

Nadine smiled softly at the two of them. "It will do," she murmured, enjoying their obvious camaraderie.

The first thing Grenville noticed on his return home was the absence of many of his prized cows. Something was wrong, he thought, and he rushed inside the house, moving quickly through it, seeing the destruction of his paintings, the footprints all over his expensive carpets, and his charred vases lying on the hearth of the fireplace.

He looked angrily around, wondering where his servants had been while someone had destroyed everything that was precious to him.

"Where is everybody?" he shouted.

Flinging open the cellar door, he moved cautiously down the stairs, the steps creaking beneath his weight.

"God, no," Captain Grenville said, his insides knotting. "No!"

There was just enough light seeping in through the grime on the two small windows at the foot of the stairs to reveal the absence of his wine supply. Everything had been carted away.

His footsteps faltered when he got to the bottom step. Huddled together, bound and gagged, at the far side of the cellar, were all his servants. None seemed harmed. They had just been rendered helpless!

In a raging fury, Grover stomped across the cellar through a puddle of wine and glass and jerked a gag from the mouth of one of his female servants, then untied her.

"Who did this?" he shouted, flailing a hand in the air. "Who?"

When she didn't respond but instead cowered against the wall as Grover Grenville glared down at her, he raised a hand and slapped her hard across the face. "I demand obedience!" he ranted as blood began to trickle from the servant's nose. "Now speak up or I'll set the lash to you."

"Bushrangers, sir," the woman cried, wiping her nose frantically.

"Bushrangers?" Grover said, paling. His eyes narrowed. "Describe them to me."

As several descriptions were given, one fitting Lloyd Harpster, Grover Grenville emitted a loud growl. He rushed back upstairs, leaving the servant to release the others.

"He's not dead," he snarled. "Damn it, Lloyd Harpster is still alive! How? Who helped him escape?"

He hurried to his room and slung off his coarse, dark shirt and flung it on the bed.

"Only one person would humiliate me in *this* way," he choked. "And I'm going to get him!"

In his rage his one thought was of Harpster. He must capture him, and he wanted him alive. The only way he could think to do that was Nadine.

He went to the window and threw it open with a jerk. "And to do that I'll have to get someone else first," he said, inhaling the sweet fragrance of the fresh air whipping in from outside. "That lady who he is most fond of. Then he'll come to me!"

Chuckling, he changed into clean clothes and brushed his beard and hair, then buckled a heavy gun belt around his waist. His eyes were two dark pits of hate.

"I won't go asking for her civil like," he said with a chuckle. "I'm going to go post myself close to her house and take her. Then, when Lloyd Harpster hears about it, let him come for her. I'll be ready!"

He took one last look at the ruins of his house, shuddered, then hurried outside and bounced into his saddle. Sneering, he rode into the forest. Nadine Quinn was as good as his.

Chapter Fifteen

Feeling giddy and warm from the wine, Nadine stretched herself out beside the fire pit on a mat and listened to Lloyd say his farewells to his friends. The heat from the fire seemed too much for her. She sluggishly loosened her blouse until it lay partially open and soothingly combed her fingers through her hair, until it lay around her like a red silk halo. Stretching lazily, she closed her eyes with a sigh and let herself drift off into a momentary sleep.

Her eyes fluttered open as she felt two hands softly framing her face. She trembled at the sight of Lloyd's deep blue eyes and lazy smile. Her hands rose to his face and urged his lips closer, and her insides began to melt as his fingers cupped her breast through her blouse, softly kneading.

"Oh, love," he whispered, bringing his mouth down upon hers in a frantic, feverish kiss. His hands trembled as he removed her clothes, his body aching for her.

He brushed the last of her clothes away as though possessed. He could not move his hands over the rest of her body fast enough.

Nadine's senses ignited beneath his searching hands and feverish kisses. She drew a ragged breath and touched her fingers to his fringed shirt, sliding it up and over his head.

"I feel so drunk," she said, laughing softly as she tossed the shirt aside. Her gaze swept over the expanse of his chest. She leaned up and teasingly nipped his nipples with her teeth while her hand drifted down, searching for his aroused manhood.

"Is it the wine, or are you the cause of my giddiness?" she whispered shakily.

Lloyd sucked in his breath and closed his eyes, enjoying the touch of her hand molding his hardness through his fringed breeches. "Whatever it is, you're doing everything right," he said huskily.

His stomach twitched as Nadine crept her hand beneath his breeches, encircling him with her fingers. "Damn it, woman, you are driving me to madness!"

"Good." Nadine giggled. "Then that makes two of us."

She brazenly began slipping his breeches down with one hand while tormenting him with the other, the mere touch of him sending messages of rapture to her heart. She had never before touched a man in such a way. The throbbing hardness in her hand, its silken smoothness, made sweet currents of warmth sweep through her.

It seemed that while she was with him in this way all the mysteries of him were being unveiled for her. She could tell that what she was doing was right, for Lloyd's breath was coming in short gasps and his body was trembling.

Not able to take much more, Lloyd placed a hand over hers and eased it away from his pulsing manhood, his eyes dark with heated passion.

"Enough," he said huskily. "Let's not hurry things along so quickly...."

His words trailed off. He gasped lightly as his gaze swept over her. He placed his fingers on her shoulders and moved her closer to the light of the fire, his insides growing cold at the sight of the mass of contusions on various parts of her body.

"My God, what happened?" he asked, his eyes almost wild. His fingers softly touched the contusion on her hip.

"When Father fell and was injured, so was I, but only slightly," Nadine murmured. The wine had not only made her warm and giddy inside but had also eased the ache of her bruises.

She looked up at Lloyd, seeing pain in the depth of his eyes as he looked down at her injuries. She laughed softly and placed a hand on his cheek. "Darling, they are only bruises. Please don't upset yourself."

"Only bruises?" he said thickly, his hands tracing from her ankle up to her shoulder. "My God, woman, every inch of you must be hurting."

"Well, I am feeling some pain," she teased, eyeing him wickedly as she splayed her fingers across his muscled chest. "But only the sort eased by your kisses and gentle loving."

"Let me kiss away the pain everywhere," Lloyd whispered.

Nadine gasped as Lloyd lowered his mouth to her breast and pulled a nipple between his lips. Releasing it, he began kissing a sweet, sensuous path downward, leaving a trail of fire behind him.

And when he crept lower and brushed a gentle kiss between her thighs, his tongue grazing the part of her that throbbed unmercifully with want, she closed her eyes and sighed. While his fingers held her hips gently, lifting her closer to his mouth, Nadine curled her fingers through his hair and drew his lips totally to her.

As he pleasured her in this new way, she moved her hips with the same rhythm as his thrusting tongue, aware only of the heat spreading within her.

Lloyd eased his lips away, then caressed her damp valley with his fingers as he positioned himself over her. In one thrust his hardness was inside her. He lowered his mouth to her lips and touched hers in a lingering kiss, enfolding her in his arms as he began his easy strokes.

The warmth that encased his manhood sent sparks of passion through him, causing his body to tremble. He drew her closer, relishing the feel of her breasts crushed against his chest and her legs locked around his hips. He savored the press of her lips against his, warm and soft, yet so demanding.

Nadine's hands clung to Lloyd's sinewy shoulders, riding with him, stroke by stroke. His mouth, searing hers, kissing her with such fire, was leaving her breathless. She moaned throatily as happiness bubbled from deep within, then soared with joy as the ultimate pleasure was unleashed inside her.

She clung to him, kissing him wildly as her body quaked and shivered with ecstasy.

Lloyd plunged more deeply within her with maddening thrusts as his whole body exploded with pleasure of bone-weakening intensity.

Sighing, Lloyd eased his perspiring body from Nadine's and lay beside her, moving his fingers softly over the tantalizing fullness of her breasts and across her slim waist to her silken thighs.

"Did I hurt you?" he asked huskily, his insides still throbbing from love's aftermath. "I'm afraid I forgot about your bruises."

"So did I," Nadine murmured, curling her fingers in his hair and guiding his lips to her breast. She cuddled him close as his tongue flicked a taut nipple, trembling as his fingers caressed her between her thighs. "I don't think I could last a second time."

Lloyd leaned on one elbow and with a low chuckle looked at her with passion-heavy eyes. "I doubt if I could, either," he said thickly.

He kissed her tenderly. "Yet, perhaps...?" he whispered teasingly.

Nadine did not answer him. Having found Lloyd safe, she was lost in worry about her father. She must find the ledgers as she had promised. He was depending upon her. How could she have let herself forget about her father's troubles? Suddenly she felt totally selfish.

Scooting away from Lloyd, she grabbed her clothes up from the earthen floor. "I must return home," she said hoarsely. "I've been gone far too long. My father will be frantic. Even if I leave now, I won't be home until morning."

Lloyd was stunned by her abruptness. He watched her as she frantically pulled on her clothes. "Stay until morning, love," he said. "What can be so important that you must leave now?"

Nadine tossed her tangled hair back from her shoulders as she slipped into her blouse, gazing down with longing at Lloyd. She did not want to leave him, ever, but duty to her father called.

"My father's future is at stake," she said in a rush of words. "Sam has embezzled most all of my father's money. I must do what I can to prove it."

Lloyd rose to his feet. He drew on his fringed breeches. "What do you plan to do?" he questioned.

"There are supposed to be two ledgers, one with the correct entries, the other with manipulated figures," she said flatly. "I will find them both, if I have to tear apart the entire house."

"With Sam standing by watching you and doing nothing?" Lloyd asked. "He will stop at nothing to get what he wants, we are both witness to that. If you should get in his way, who knows what he might do?"

Nadine squared her shoulders stubbornly. "I can take care—"

Lloyd placed a finger on her lip, laughing throatily. "I know." He chuckled. "You can take care of yourself."

"Well, I can," Nadine said softly, smiling seductively up at him.

Lloyd smoothed her hair back from her face and kissed her softly. "I'm sorry. This is one time I guess you'll have to find the evidence by yourself. I would like nothing better than to help you, but until this business with Grenville is finished, my hands are tied. Tipahee will go along with you to make sure you get home safe. The forest can be treacherous at night."

He drew her into his arms and looked down at her tenderly. "Promise that you won't do anything foolish," he said hoarsely. "If you don't, I can't let you go."

"I promise," she said, hugging him tightly.

Nadine's head bobbed as she rode, slump-shouldered, while Tipahee guided her horse through the dark forest. Never had she been as tired. Perhaps it *had* been foolish to try to return home without first getting some badly needed sleep, but she was driven on by thoughts of her father alone in the house with Sam.

Groaning, Nadine squirmed in the saddle, rubbing her aching behind. Her eyes brightened as she saw the first light of dawn breaking through the foliage in the east. The birds in the trees began to stir in the early light of the new day.

Nadine looked down at Tipahee, her guide and protector. In the future, there would be no reason for anyone but Lloyd to look after her. He would be with her at all times.

Recognizing the now-familiar trees and flowering vines of the forest adjoining her father's ranch, she sighed with relief. Soon she would be in bed, asleep. The confrontation with Sam could wait until morning, when she was revived and fresh. Then she would find the ledgers. . . .

Captain Grenville fought to keep awake as he sat on his horse, hidden behind a thick stand of brush near the Quinn home. The noise of an approaching horse made him straighten up in the saddle and inch his horse ahead. He was taken aback when he recognized the rider. All night, he had been watching the windows of the house for a glimpse of Nadine and, by damn, here she was, at first break of dawn, riding straight into his arms. Smiling smugly, he watched her draw closer.

His smile faded at the sight of Tipahee by her side. Resting his hand on a pistol, he began to inch his way from his hiding place.

A rustling of leaves and the neighing of a nearby horse jarred Nadine from her stupor. Her eyes narrowed as she quickly searched the surrounding forest. Her spine stiffened with fear when Captain Grenville suddenly wheeled his horse into view from behind a thick stand of brush, blocking the way.

"You—" Nadine whispered harshly, paling.

Tipahee lifted his spear, but before he could throw it, Nadine's horse sidled against him in fright, throwing off his aim. Swinging a pistol from a holster, Grenville took advantage of the split second to draw and fire at the aborigine. There was a blast of gunfire as Tipahee dropped his spear and crumpled to the ground.

The stench of gunpowder burned Nadine's nostrils. Her stomach lurched at the sight of blood seeping from Tipahee's left shoulder. She was frozen to the saddle, too stunned to scream.

Captain Grenville rode close to her horse and, grabbing her roughly, pulled her onto his. He sat behind her, holding her in place against his bulbous body.

Before Nadine could regain her voice or even her breath, the evil captain had wheeled his horse around and was riding hard into the depths of the forest.

"Tipahee," Nadine finally managed to whisper.

She looked back over her shoulder, but she was too far away to see him. Her heart ached.

If he died, she would be the cause.

Sam's words came back to haunt her. Everyone seemed to suffer because of her love for Lloyd.

She tried to wriggle free of the captain's embrace, but her struggles seemed only to amuse him. Lowering her head, she stifled a sob behind her hands and went limp in his arms.

Harry's heart leaped at the sound of gunfire. Once he had awakened and read Nadine's note, he had not slept a wink. Stumbling, he rose from the bed and went to the window, jerking the sheer white curtain aside. His breath caught in his throat as he looked toward the forest in time to see Nadine snatched from her horse and dragged onto another.

"God, no," he gasped in helpless frustration, his knees weakening as his hand clawed the windowpane. "Nadine! Daughter! Oh, God, no!"

Numbness swept through him as he watched the horse carrying Nadine thunder away into the darkness of the forest. Harry lumbered across the room. Each footstep caused his bandaged head to throb unmercifully. But he would let nothing stop him from going after his daughter. No damn bandaged head! No weak knees! No. Nothing!

He reached for his breeches, which hung neatly over the back of a chair, and slipped into them. Struggling, he finished dressing and buckled his gun belt around his waist, groaning at the weight of the pistols in his weakened state.

He steadied himself against the bed as he pulled on his boots. Then he walked, swaying, from the room and down the long corridor. He staggered outside to Nadine's saddled horse, which was grazing contentedly on the back lawn. Easing himself up into the saddle, he rode to the edge of the forest. His gut twisted when he saw a pool of blood on the ground. Fear for Nadine dizzied him. That was surely her blood.

Tears pooled in his eyes as he rode quickly away, saying a silent prayer for his daughter.

Nadine was close to unconsciousness with fatigue when Captain Grenville reined in beside his white cottage. Dismounting, he pulled her roughly from the horse and carried her into the house and up a steep flight of stairs. Throwing her on a bed, he tied her hands and feet. Overcome, Nadine closed her eyes and let sleep rescue her from the misery of the moment.

Captain Grenville chuckled as he gazed at the sleeping beauty. His eyes roamed over her young body, over the tantalizing cleavage of her breasts where her shirt had come unbuttoned. Her lips were parted, and her eyelashes clung to her pink cheeks.

He could not help himself as he lifted her skirt and touched her slim white thighs. His blood quickened, for never had he felt skin as soft as hers against his large, coarse fingers.

The burning in his loins plagued him, but he would have his fun with her later. First he must ride to Melbourne and round up his men to stand guard outside the house. This time, when Lloyd Harpster came calling, he would be greeted in a most fashionable way.

He smoothed his hand one last time along the silken whiteness of Nadine's thigh, unable to take his eyes off her heaving breasts.

With a growl, he reminded himself of what must be done before he could seek his pleasure. Tearing himself away from her, he willed one foot before the other until he was away from the temptation tied to his bed. Then he went outside and mounted his horse. His head bent low against the wind, he rode away. When he returned with his men, Nadine Quinn would find out just what being pleasured by a man was all about!

Perhaps he would let *all* his men take turns with her while Lloyd Harpster watched, helpless.

Captain Grover Grenville laughed throatily.

* * *

Harry Quinn fought against the dizziness that was sweeping through him. He held his throbbing head with one hand, the other shaking as it held the horse's reins limply. He had not caught sight of Nadine since he had seen her swept up onto a horse by a man. He had followed in the same direction, but in his weakened state he had not been able to ride as quickly. The blood he had seen on the ground tormented him. He wondered if it was Nadine's. If she was injured, how badly? Oh, God, was she even already dead? Who had taken her? It had not been Lloyd Harpster. Lloyd was taller and much thinner than the one who had abducted Nadine.

Riding relentlessly onward, fighting the urge to faint, Harry slumped over and clung to the horse's neck. When he had chosen and purchased this lovely white stallion, it had been for a much different purpose. It was supposed to be reined to a gaily designed stagecoach, carrying passengers....

Unable to fight the weakness any longer, a hazy sort of blackness reaching into his consciousness, Harry released his hold on the reins and slipped from the horse. When he landed on the ground he groaned, then slipped into total unconsciousness....

Lloyd, riding alongside Gary, the gang following close behind, inhaled the sweet fragrance of this new day. It was to be another day of torment for Captain Grenville. They were going to go to his house and burn it this time, after running the rest of his livestock off and stealing his food supply again. They expected to be met by mounted policemen guarding the house. If Captain Grenville was smart, he would have placed guards to protect his house, livestock and himself from Lloyd Harpster's wrath!

"Lovely day, isn't it?" Lloyd said, smiling over at Gary. "It's damn good to be alive."

"It's always damn good to be alive, mate," Gary shouted, laughing boisterously. "But I bet soon there'll be one bloke who'll wish he wasn't."

Lloyd's brow creased into a frown. "How many do you think we'll have to fight off before we set the bastard's house afire?" he asked. "We could be outnumbered, you know."

"Never," Gary exclaimed. "Now that the gang's all together again, no one can stop us!"

Lloyd nodded, smiling. Then he drew his reins in tightly, stopping his strawberry roan, when he saw a riderless horse just ahead.

"Oh, God, no!" he gasped. "That's the horse Nadine was traveling on. If something has happened to her..."

Urging his horse forward, he came alongside the stray. It wasn't until he reached for its bridle that he spied Harry Quinn lying unconscious a few feet away.

"Good Lord," Lloyd whispered. Dismounting, he knelt down beside the older man, easing his head up from the ground. "Quinn, what's happened? Where's Nadine? How in the hell did you get out here?" He shook Harry by the shoulders. "Damn it, Quinn, wake up. Where's Nadine?"

Lloyd's voice reached Harry. It was vague, but real enough to make him stir. He forced his eyelashes open. Blue eyes were wild as they stared down at him. He smiled weakly, glad that, yes, it *was* Lloyd Harpster. Never had he been so glad to see anyone in his life. Lloyd Harpster would go for Nadine and, by God, he'd *find* her!

"Nadine," Harry whispered harshly, licking his parched lips. "Someone abducted her. She may even be shot. I heard the gunfire and I saw him take her, but I couldn't keep up with them."

Lloyd could hardly contain his rage. "Did you see who abducted her?" he said in a low hiss.

"He was large," Harry rasped. "That's all I can tell you." He grabbed Lloyd frantically by the arm. "She may be shot. There was a lot of blood."

Lloyd stared numbly down at Harry for a moment before rising to his feet and shouting out orders to his men. "Get him on his horse and take him to our hideout!" he said. "The rest of you, follow me to Grenville's place. I think we've more to do today besides stealing and burning!"

Lloyd swung himself up into his saddle. He said a quiet prayer as he rode in the direction of Captain Grenville's white cottage. What if Grenville hadn't taken Nadine there? Where else in this land of hidden valleys could she be? What if Grenville wasn't the one who had abducted her? Who else might have taken her? It couldn't have been Sam Parsons. Harry would have recognized him.

Chapter Sixteen

The bushrangers surrounded Grenville's white cottage. Lloyd's eyes were alight with rage as he rode up to the house, pistol drawn and ready. He had expected guards to be posted around the house, but there didn't appear to be any.

His gaze swept from window to window, and he wondered if he was stepping into a carefully planned trap. Were there policemen after all, their horses carefully concealed somewhere in the forest, ready to slay him the moment he set foot inside the house?

Reining in beside the porch, Lloyd quickly dismounted and crept stealthily up the steps in a half crouch. Everything was quiet. Taking one last look around him, he stepped up onto the porch and dashed across it to the front wall of the house. He was breathing hard. His eyes were on the doorknob. Should he use it, or *kick* the damn door down?

"Whichever way is the quickest," he growled, swinging around and lunging madly toward the door. Holding his pistol steady with one hand, he grabbed the doorknob with the other and turned it, then angrily swung the door open and stepped boldly inside.

He smiled lazily as the servants scattered, running outside to safety. If Nadine had been brought here, the sadistic captain would probably have taken her upstairs to his bedroom.

Lloyd groaned and took a mad dash for the steps, taking them two at a time until he was on the second-floor landing. His footsteps could not carry him fast enough.

He threw the door open with a loud bang. Nadine lay on the bed, bound at the ankles and wrists. Her eyes were closed, and he couldn't tell if she was asleep or unconscious.

Stifling a sob, he ran across the room and leaned down over her.

"Nadine, darling," he murmured softly. Returning his pistol to its holster, he cupped her cheeks with gentle hands. "Darling, wake up. Tell me you're all right."

Nadine stirred and her eyes fluttered open as she fully wakened. "Lloyd," she gasped. Then her eyes filled with tears. "Thank the Lord, you've come." She looked toward the door, wild-eyed. "You must hurry. He'll be back. And when he does, he'll kill you!"

Lloyd pulled a knife from his boot and cut the ropes at her wrists. "You weren't harmed?" he asked hoarsely, smoothing her skirt down over her legs.

"Only my pride," Nadine said, her eyes clouding with more tears as he moved to her ankles, releasing them with one stroke. She rubbed her wrists, wincing with pain. Still, she knew, these ropes were nothing compared to the irons that had ripped Lloyd's flesh. "I was almost home when he—"

Her words froze on her tongue as she remembered exactly what had happened. "Tipahee!" she whispered harshly. "How is Tipahee?"

Throwing the ropes aside, Lloyd helped Nadine up into a sitting position. "What happened to Tipahee?" he asked guardedly. His gaze swept over her. There were no signs of the blood her father had spoken of.

Nadine crept into Lloyd's arms, clinging to him fiercely. "Oh, Lloyd," she sobbed. "Tipahee was shot. Captain Grenville shot him and left him there to die."

Lloyd's face paled at the news. "How badly was he wounded?" he asked.

"I don't know," Nadine cried. "There was so much blood."

Lloyd pulled her snugly against him and comforted her. "There, there," he crooned, running his fingers through her hair. "We'll find Tipahee. He'll be all right. He's made it this far, and he says he's going to live to be a hundred."

"But he was bleeding—"

"Shh," Lloyd murmured. "I'll send someone to search for him."

"He was shot close to the ranch," Nadine said, pulling away from Lloyd so that she could look up into his eyes. "Send someone there."

Lloyd's brow furrowed as he tried to sort out what had happened. Nadine's father had found Tipahee's blood, thinking it was hers, which had to mean that Tipahee had managed to leave the area of the attack. If Tipahee had been strong enough to travel, to take himself that far, surely he would be found alive.

Then Lloyd realized that Nadine had to be told about her father, about where and how he had been found. But he did not think it wise to worry her at such a time as this. There was enough to worry about. They had to get out of there quickly or risk getting caught. When Lloyd met up with Captain Grenville again, he did not want Nadine around to witness what he planned to do to him.

"My men will find Tipahee all right," he reassured her. Grabbing a blanket from the bed, he wrapped it around Nadine's shoulders and swept her into his arms. "I think we'd best think of our hides for now. Let's get the hell out of here."

Nadine clung to his neck, her cheek resting on his chest, as he carried her across the room, his eyes gleaming at the thought of Grenville's expression when he found her gone. Better yet, he was still going to burn the house down. Let the bastard think that he had lost more than a house in the fire. He could think that Nadine had gone up with the flames!

Clutching Nadine possessively to his chest, Lloyd carried her from the room, down the stairs and outside.

Lifting her up onto his horse, he gave her a wink. "Wait right here, love. We're not quite through with Captain Grenville yet."

Clutching the blanket around her shoulders with one hand, Nadine steadied herself in the saddle and watched, wide-eyed, as Lloyd moved among his men, giving instructions. Her mouth dropped open when several men emerged from one of the outbuildings with lighted torches and positioned themselves around the house. Lloyd questioned the servants, making sure no one was left inside.

Nadine watched, spellbound, as the torches were thrown through the windows and onto the roof. Soon the glass in the windows shattered from the heat and flames poured from the broken panes. Smoke billowed from the roof where the flames shot forth into the sky.

Lloyd ran to his horse and swung himself into the saddle behind Nadine. Sweeping an arm around her waist, he grabbed the reins with his free hand. He watched the fire for a moment, then wheeled his horse around and rode away from the fiery inferno, laughing.

Captain Grenville leaned low over his horse, his thoughts on Nadine. Perhaps he should have taken her somewhere else before going into town after men? With Lloyd Harpster running around free, who was to tell where he might show up again? Surely he would be expecting the scene of his latest crime to be heavily guarded.

Smiling, he told himself that Nadine was safe enough there, but the smell of smoke filtering through the thick vegetation behind him made him turn his head in alarm. He brought his horse to a stop, looking heavenward. Through the foliage he caught sight of billows of smoke and the splash of orange against the sky.

"Damn!" he growled, wheeling his horse around and heading back toward his house.

The moon hung like a great silver ball in the sky as Lloyd eased Nadine from his horse and carried her into his hut. "I'm so tired," Nadine said with a sigh, curling up on a mat beside the fire. "Will things ever be normal again?"

Closing her eyes, she welcomed the blanket Lloyd spread over her, and his sweet kiss on her cheek. "I'm going to check on things," he murmured, wondering about her father.

Slipping away from her, Lloyd left his hut and joined his men at the outdoor fire. He accepted a tin cup of coffee from the bushranger who had brought Harry Quinn to the hideout. "How's Quinn doing?" he asked, staring down into the fire, wondering if Captain Grenville had yet discovered that his house had been destroyed by fire.

"He's resting just fine," the bushranger said, hands on his holstered pistols. He gave Lloyd a sideways glance with cool gray eyes. "I see you found her. She didn't look as though she'd been shot, but Quinn keeps talking about the blood he saw. *Whose* blood?"

Lloyd kneaded his brow. "Tipahee's," he said with a growl. "The damn captain shot him."

"Is he dead?"

Lloyd shrugged uneasily. "Gary and a few of the others have gone to find him," he said, taking another long drink of coffee and enjoying the warmth as it spilled down the back of his throat. "We should know soon."

The thunder of horse's hooves disturbed the quiet of the camp. Lloyd tossed the remainder of his coffee from the cup and threw the cup to the ground. At his shout the men ran for cover, pistols drawn. Lloyd hovered close beside the door of his hut, ready to shoot anyone who attempted to get past him.

When he caught sight of the lead rider as they came into view, he lowered his pistol and returned it to its holster. He moved forward to meet the riders on foot. "Any signs of Tipahee?" he asked guardedly, already knowing the answer, for Tipahee was not among those who had arrived.

"I wish I could say yes," Gary answered, swinging himself out of the saddle. "But there were no signs of him anywhere. It doesn't look good."

Lloyd thought for a moment. "I'm going to go check on Quinn. Then let's ride out again and search some more."

A faint voice from close by caught Lloyd's ear, and he turned just in time to see Tipahee stumble out of the forest. "My God," Lloyd gasped. He ran to the small man and swung him up into his arms. Laying him down next to the fire, Lloyd yelled for one of the men to bring him water.

Lloyd carefully inspected Tipahee's wound. The bullet had gone clean through his shoulder. That was a good sign. He'd gotten lucky. As he looked closer, he could see some other substance dried into the blood.

Tipahee had doctored himself well. The herbs he had found in the forest and applied to the wound were already helping it to heal.

"I'll be fine," Tipahee said, smiling weakly up at Lloyd.

"Nadine," he gasped, looking desperately up at Lloyd and grabbing his arm. "What has happened to her?"

"She's here," Lloyd said, placing a hand over Tipahee's to soothe him. "She's fine. Just fine."

Tipahee nodded. "Good. Good." He closed his eyes. "Sleep. Must get sleep."

"You will," Lloyd promised, "I'll take you to your hut." Sweeping the slight form of Tipahee back into his arms, he carried him to his hut and placed him on the pallet on the floor. He covered him with a blanket and made sure the fire in his fire pit was glowing warmly before he moved on to check on Harry Quinn.

"Quinn, there's nothing to worry about," Lloyd said, kneeling down beside Harry in the hut that he had been taken to. "Nadine is safe with me. No one will threaten her again. I give you my word."

Harry looked up at Lloyd, near tears. He reached for Lloyd's arm and held on to it, trembling. "I was wrong about you, I'm damn sorry for that."

Lloyd smiled his lazy smile at Harry and slipped his hand from his arm. "We'll see just how you feel about me when I become your son-in-law," he said with a wink.

Harry peered up at Lloyd and licked his parched lips. He reached a hand to his head and scratched the flesh where the bandage was itching him. "Now I'm not objecting to any of that," he said, pinching his face into a frown. "But I think you've forgotten someone."

"Oh?" Lloyd said, raking his fingers nervously through his hair.

"Sam Parsons," Harry said with a low growl. "He's not the sort to turn your back on. But I think you already know that, don't you?"

"Seems that I do," Lloyd muttered. "Don't worry. There are ways to take care of him."

"I've not figured any way myself," Harry lamented. "I hope you have better luck."

Lloyd got to his feet. "I won at cards with you and I'll win with Parsons," he drawled. "Just watch the game unfold before your eyes."

He turned and eyed Harry with a glint in his eye. "Nadine mentioned you received your new stagecoaches," he said, smiling. "Do you think they'll be taking runs, even in your absence?"

"In my absence Sam'll feel like a king, handing out orders right and left," Harry said with a growl, propping himself up on one elbow. He winced with pain and lowered his head again. "The stagecoaches will be on the road tomorrow."

"Since you're not fit for traveling just yet, you can stay on here for a while," Lloyd said, looking over the drab hut. "It's not the best hotel, but it'll do."

Lloyd strode to the entrance flap, raising it with a sweep of his arm. "Sam will wish you and Nadine were both back by the time I get through with him," he said, chuckling. "Don't you worry. I'll make sure no damage is done to your stagecoaches. It's Sam I'm after.''

Harry groaned, trying to raise his head again. "Damn it, Harpster," he said in a harsh whisper. "What are you up to?"

Lloyd laughed softly and stepped from the hut.

Inside his own hut, he found Nadine still peacefully asleep. Filled with a tender warmth, he removed his gun belt, shirt and breeches and scooted down beside her beneath the blanket. Snuggling next to her, he thought of how he would make things right for his woman and her father. Sam would beg before it was over.

Drawing Nadine close to him, he drifted into a restful sleep, relishing this quiet moment with the woman he loved.

Chapter Seventeen

The fire cast a golden glow on Nadine's face. Her stomach comfortably filled with fruit, and refreshed by a sponge bath, she stretched her arms over her head and yawned.

Her arms fluttered back down to her sides when Lloyd came to her and began slipping her shirt away from her shoulders.

"So, you are that anxious to make love, are you?" she teased, looking at him with a mischievous grin. She trembled when his hands crept up and cupped both her breasts.

"Only if you will allow me to," Lloyd said huskily, kneading her breasts, the touch of their softness pressed against his fingers building his desire.

"It is a most wicked thing that you propose, sir," Nadine said with false seriousness. "Dare I even consider such wanton behavior with such a rogue as you?"

"Rogue? You call me a rogue?" Lloyd said, drawing her around to face him. His lips swept to the nipple of her breast as he showered heated kisses downward, across her abdomen, causing her to twitch.

Nadine wove her fingers through his golden hair, her eyes closed. "Darling, if you continue what you are doing, I won't even remember the meaning of the word rogue." She laughed softly. "Nor will I remember your name."

Lloyd rose up away from her, his eyes twinkling. "Now, love, we can't have that," he said, placing kisses across Nadine's glowing cheek.

"You just relax," he said softly. "You will have to keep control of yourself, for I plan to touch you all over." He brushed a kiss against her lips. "First with my hands and then my lips."

Nadine trembled, enjoying the sweet moment of lovemaking. Now that she knew her father was safely out of Sam's clutches and on the road to recovery, it would give her intense pleasure to torment Sam into returning to her father what was rightfully his. In the end, Sam's confession would be more proof than the ledgers.

"Everything will work out, won't it?" she asked, closing her eyes to shut out everything but the rapture building inside her as Lloyd continued his wondrous manipulations of her body. "You will finally be set free of your troubled past?" She held her head back so that her hair tumbled in a silken auburn cascade across her shoulders.

"Never fear. Destiny is ours for the taking," Lloyd said, brushing her hair aside so that his tongue could sweep down her spine, leaving a smoldering path in its wake. "Everything will soon be ours."

"You still agree to let me ride with you?" Nadine questioned, her eyelids fluttering open as Lloyd eased her down onto the soft mat beneath her.

"You have proven time and time again what you are capable of," he said, unfastening her skirt and slipping it slowly from her hips. "You deserve to share the moment of triumph with me."

His fingers lingered for a moment before pulling down her undergarments to reveal the soft, downy patch of hair between her thighs. "But you will have to travel with me dressed as a man."

He splayed a hand across the wondrous mound that held such promise within its depths. "You are more woman than any I have ever known, love, so it won't be easy to fool anyone."

Nadine rose up on one elbow. "Then I won't even try," she said determinedly, trying to fight the euphoria that was overcoming her as his hand stroked her. "I brought a pair of breeches, but I shall wear a skirt. The clothes are in my saddlebag."

"It's outside on the horse we brought into camp with your father," Lloyd said. "I'll get it for you later."

"I never want to hide the fact that I am a woman," Nadine said stubbornly. "I am proud of being a woman. I will prove to a few at least that not all women spend their time in the kitchen, laboring for men."

Lloyd chuckled. Placing a finger on her chin and directing her to face him, he bent down very close to her. "Are you saying you won't cook my meals once we are married?'' he asked softly. ''Nor our children's?''

''Marriage? Children?'' Nadine said in a whisper. She threw herself into his arms, burying her face in his chest as she fought back tears of joy. ''Oh, Lloyd, can it truly be possible that we will marry and have children?''

Lloyd cradled her close. ''Everything will be yours,'' he whispered. ''Everything. But only if you promise to spend every moment of your day in the kitchen,'' he teased.

Tears gathered in Nadine's eyes, and she looked up at him adoringly. ''Even that,'' she murmured, sniffling back a sob. ''I would do anything to spend an eternity with you.''

Kissing the scar on his cheekbone, she took hold of the fringed hem of his shirt and inched it up over his chest, past his shoulders and off. Combing her fingers through his blond chest hair, she captured one dark nipple with her lips.

Her hand felt the thundering of his heartbeat, and she knew that foreplay was no longer needed. All that remained were the sweet, passionate moments of reaching the ultimate pleasure.

''Enough,'' Lloyd said, unable to stand the torment she was creating inside him.

Deftly removing the rest of their clothes, he eased himself over her and found her open and ready for him. He plunged deep inside her, where she was velvety-warm and tight against his manhood. His body quivered. He groaned against her parted lips. He searched and found a breast and caressed it. Their bodies rhythmically rocked and swayed together as though one.

Nadine moaned softly into his mouth, his bold thrusts reaching clean into her soul with something magical . . . something almost *indefinable*, it was so beautiful. She searched his body with her hands, no longer bashful as she had been that first night with him. This morning, while the birds crooned their own various love songs outside in the trees, she was free to delve into all of his mysteries. Her hands searched and touched, fondled and explored. When his hardness momentarily left her, she touched it and gloried at its velvet softness.

She moved her hand on him, feeling him tremble from the pleasure, then relinquished him to his own desired way of getting his sought-for release.

When he entered her again, she stifled a sob of joy against his shoulder, glorying at how magnificently he filled her, setting her afire. She held her head back and sighed, melting as his mouth again bore down upon her lips, devouring, consuming.

His kiss deepened, his hunger building the ultimate of sensations within her. There was not one part of her body that did not tingle with a raging heat. Her breasts strained against his hands and she locked her legs around him, welcoming the quickening desire within her as she discovered once again the moment of ultimate pleasure.

Lloyd eased his lips from Nadine's mouth and voiced a husky groan against her creamy throat as his body momentarily stiffened, then moved again with fiery thrusts. He clung to her, crushing his body into hers as the bliss claimed him, heart, mind and soul, and his warm wetness spilled inside her as Nadine felt a peak of passion to match his own. Sighing, he kissed her gently on her heaving breasts.

Wet tendrils of her auburn hair lay against Lloyd's shoulder as Nadine moved her hands over his back. Easing from his arms, she moved to her knees and gently began to kiss his scars.

"You may be scarred for life," she murmured, "but I will always be here to kiss away the pain."

Lloyd was stirred by her gentleness and understanding. He turned, placing his hands on her waist and lifting her above him so that her hair spilled around them and her breasts lay against his chest.

"When I am with you, everything is right in the world," he said softly, his eyes filled with love for her. "Had I not gambled with your father that day—"

Nadine placed a finger to his lips. "Shh," she whispered. "You did. And you won."

"I won everything that day," he said with a steady stare. "You are everything to me. My breath, my life."

Nadine's eyes filled with tears of joy. She eased herself down upon him, feeling at peace with herself. Yet there were still battles to be fought and won.

"Damn that Sam Parsons," she snapped, her eyes flashing angrily as she drew back to look at Lloyd. "If not for him, everything would be different in my father's life. I hope that what you have planned for him works. He's not that easy to persuade about anything."

"He just hasn't been persuaded by Lloyd Harpster yet," Lloyd said, his eyes gleaming. He lifted Nadine away from him and rose to his feet, drawing on his breeches. "And we can't forget Captain Grenville, either. We have to be doubly careful. He and his mounted police will surely be on the alert, waiting for us to make a wrong move."

Nadine watched carefully as Lloyd scooped ashes from the cooled fire into a leather bag. "Whatever is that for?"

"Ashes are the only disguise worn during a raid," he said with a chuckle. "Bushrangers always place ash on their faces." Seeing her shudder at the thought, he continued. "Even you, since you've chosen to be a part of the gang."

Nadine laughed softly. "I will certainly be a lovely sight," she said, eyeing the ashes. "Will you get my saddlebag so that I can change into fresh clothes?"

"It's as good as done," Lloyd said, walking toward the entrance flap. He gave Nadine a slow wink and left her to her thoughts and her fears of the upcoming hours. Though the plan was to find the stagecoaches and scare the passengers, it seemed as though she would be committing the deed against her father, for in truth the stagecoaches were his.

Lloyd had assured her that his gang had received word from their spies as to the route the coaches would take. Nadine only hoped they had not underestimated the cunning of their enemies.

Nadine followed Lloyd's strawberry roan, riding the white stallion. As they neared the cave, they passed through a region where conical anthills stood in groups like stones in some strange graveyard.

Drawing her own horse to a halt, she noticed a group of horses on a bluff in the distance. The sight was breathtaking.

Lloyd reined in beside Nadine and turned to look. His pulse raced as he recognized the black stallion strutting around the mares on the bluff.

When the horse reared and shook its proud head, goose bumps crawled along Lloyd's flesh. The stallion's challenging whinny echoed across the valley.

Lloyd turned to Nadine and smiled. It was only right that the magnificent horse and his beautiful woman should meet.

Nadine's heart beat soundly as she watched the stallion gallop away, the mares following. She turned her eyes slowly to Lloyd and blushed, feeling she, too, had been put under the spell of a handsome male.

The fleeting moment was tossed aside as Lloyd shouted to his men and thundered on ahead. Nadine followed, her hair flying in the wind. She had chosen to wear her fawn-colored breeches after all. They would give her more freedom of movement during the long ride. Her pistol lay within reach, just inside her saddlebag. She was ready for whatever adventure lay ahead.

Chapter Eighteen

The sky could have been no bluer, had it been painted by an artist. The sun shone brightly on the flowering bushes and trees, delighting Nadine's senses with brilliant colors and a parade of splendid shapes and surfaces.

Her boots resting snugly in the stirrups, Nadine held on to her horse's reins with gloved hands, tensely watching for the first signs of the stagecoach to appear around a bend in the winding road.

There would be no doubt in the minds of the passengers on the coach that a woman rode with the bushrangers. Not only were Nadine's breeches skintight, she also wore a loose white blouse that was open at the throat, and her hair was loose and flowing down her back.

She wanted Sam to know she was a part of his harassment. He would not gloat for much longer. The business would not be handed over without a fight. That he had made no visible effort to see if she and her father were all right proved just how little they both meant to him. Her father was worth more to him dead, and if he could not have her for his own purposes, he did not seem to want her at all. She might be dead, for all he knew.

"He will soon learn just how alive I am," Nadine whispered to herself.

Lloyd sidled his horse closer to Nadine's. "Did you say something, love?" he asked. His lips quivered in an effort not to smile. He wanted to tease her about how comical she looked with ashes spread across her face.

"I was just thinking about Sam," she murmured, looking at Lloyd's golden hair and his outfit, fringed at the sleeves of his shirt and down the sides of the breeches. He wore his usual boots and holstered pistols, and though his face was hidden behind the ash, she could still smell his familiar scent, and it made her want to lean over and kiss him.

Remembering their audience of bushrangers awaiting the arrival of the stage, she ignored the impulse.

"Sam will be receiving the message loud and clear quite soon," Lloyd said, placing his hands on his holstered pistols. "One way or the other."

"You don't have to get involved, you know," Nadine said, uncertainty in her eyes. "This could delay your own pardon. If so, I would feel so responsible." She lowered her eyes. "I already have the weight of so many mishaps on my shoulders. I don't think I could bear another."

"Nadine, you don't give yourself credit for all the good you do," Lloyd said, his words trailing off at the sound of approaching horses. Slipping a pistol from its holster, he nodded to his gang, giving Nadine a glance. "You do know the dangers?" he asked.

"Yes," she murmured, swallowing the growing lump of fear in her throat. "I must be a part of this. I owe it to my father."

"No one is supposed to be hurt," Lloyd said reassuringly. "But there could be someone aboard the coach who is armed. You stay on the outer edges of the gang."

Nadine lifted her chin stubbornly. "I want to ride side by side with you," she stated flatly.

Lloyd groaned as he watched Nadine ease her pistol from the saddlebag. Shrugging his shoulders at her stubbornness, he concentrated on the task ahead of them.

Nadine's pulse raced as she watched the stagecoach make its appearance around the bend in the road. Hung on its leather straps, the coach glided along the road as though on clouds instead of wheels. Everything had been done according to her father's plans. The drivers had come from America, lured to Australia by the incentive of wages in advance.

Drawn by those beautiful matched stallions and gaily painted, the coach traveled proudly along the road.

Nadine could not help but thrill to see the coach in motion, flying the company's flag, the proud coachman decked out in his suit of red, reins and whip in his hands, displaying a magnificent air of confidence.

Nadine squirmed uneasily in her saddle when the white stallion on which she sat began pawing nervously at the ground and whinnying. She patted the horse's sleek neck, trying to settle him down. Somewhere along the road, three other stagecoaches were making their first trips, carrying mail to the countryside or happy people and precious gold to the towns.

"Let's go!" Lloyd shouted, shooting his pistol in the air. He thundered off, Nadine close beside him and the others following.

Nadine felt the pounding of her heart as she realized exactly what she was involved in. The passengers on the coach were looking frantically from the windows.

She must keep reminding herself that it was Sam she was doing this to, not the people. Once he was exposed, the people would surely trust the stagecoach line again.

She did not wince as Lloyd fired over the head of the coachman, ordering him to stop. The stagecoach screeched to a halt, the horses neighing nervously.

Nadine drew alongside Lloyd, close to the coach door, while Gary urged the driver down to the ground. She met the steady stare of the passengers forced from the coach. The two women were clothed in fancy velveteen dresses and bonnets, while their haughty male companions sported fancy, crisp suits with high-topped hats and shining boots. Nadine almost laughed when they gasped at her shameful attire.

"If everyone does as they are told, no one will be harmed," Lloyd said, dismounting. "I'm afraid the rest of your journey will have to be made by foot. Sorry for the inconvenience."

He went to the coachman and gave him a slow smile. "As for you, you'll have one horse to get you back to Sam Parsons," he said calmly. "Give him a message. Tell him that this stagecoach and horses have been given back to their rightful owner, and if he dares to come looking for them, he will pay for his crimes."

Holstering his pistol, he continued with his message. "Tell him this is only the first time he'll be hearing from Lloyd Harpster." He chuckled, glancing over at Nadine. "And tell him Nadine Quinn sends her condolences."

Moving close to Nadine's horse, Lloyd placed his hands on her waist and lifted her down. "What are you doing?" she asked softly.

"You won't be needing a horse," he replied, handing her reins to the waiting coachman.

"If he so much as says one word to the authorities," Lloyd warned, "Sam Parsons is the same as dead. Give him that message, too!"

"Yes, sir," the coachman gulped, his dark eyes wide with fright. He glanced over at Nadine as he mounted the horse and rode away.

"And now, lady, you are going to get the grandest ride of your life," Lloyd said, leading her to the stagecoach. He swept an arm out and bowed low in front of her. "Shall we go and surprise your father?"

Nadine was speechless as he helped her up into the coach. "You planned this all along, didn't you?" she murmured.

"Yes. Today one stagecoach, tomorrow another, until there are none left," Lloyd said, closing the door. "Now, you sit as proud as a princess while I take you to your father."

Tears formed in Nadine's eyes as she settled back in the plush velveteen seat. Satin tassels hung on the velveteen shades at the windows, and delicate gold wall sconces were set into the walls.

When the coach began to sway gently in rhythm with the horses' hooves, Nadine's face blossomed into a radiant smile and tears ran in a silver path down her ash-covered face. The ride was everything that her father had wanted it to be.

It was like floating on a cloud.

The sound of nearing hoofbeats drew Harry up from his mat before the fire. Creeping to the entrance flap, he flung it aside and peered out. At the sight of one of his stagecoaches in the distance, drawn by twelve white stallions, his heart skipped a beat.

"Damn," he gasped, hurrying outside to take a better look. He shook his head, choked with emotion, when he saw Lloyd Harpster perched proudly on the coachman's seat, whip in hand, leading the horses, and Nadine leaning from the window waving frantically at him.

"My God, I can't believe it," Harry said, walking toward the approaching horses, then mustering up enough strength to begin running, returning Nadine's wave. "Daughter! Nadine!"

Lloyd drew up beside Harry and winked down at him. "I didn't tell you this was a part of the plan, did

I?'' he said, jumping down beside him. He turned and eyed his booty. "Now that I've stolen them, I just might decide to keep them. It's a grand way of traveling, Quinn."

Harry wiped a tear from his eye. Overcome with emotion, he grabbed Lloyd and gave him a hug. "Thank you," he said throatily before stepping away, embarrassed. "Harpster, you never cease to amaze me. What do you have up your sleeve next?"

Lloyd moved to the coach and swept Nadine into his arms, hugging her to him. "Well, now," he said, his eyes twinkling. "As I see it, one stagecoach isn't enough. Tomorrow I'll bring you a second, and the next day a third. Then Sam will have to make his move."

Harry frowned. "It won't be a decent one," he said with a growl.

"He knows better than to try anything less than coming to give you back what is legally yours," Lloyd said, chuckling softly. "He won't dare go to the law. He's broken too many laws himself. He'd be placing a noose around his own neck."

As Lloyd finished speaking Jon Upchurch stepped out of the shadows of the camp fire, where he had been waiting for his return. Jon scratched his forehead idly, raising his eyebrows as he neared the stagecoach. "What have we here?" he asked, running a hand down the flank of one of the handsome stallions.

Lloyd turned with a start, unaware that Jon had been there. "Jon?" he said thickly, nervously glancing at him and the stolen horses and stagecoach. "How long have you been waiting?"

"Not long," Jon murmured, moving his gaze slowly to Lloyd. "I just had to come and see how things were going with you." He nodded toward the stolen property. "What is this doing here?"

Lloyd placed an arm around Jon's shoulders and led him away from the others. "It's this way, Jon," he said dryly. "And I hope you'll not interfere."

"Lloyd—" Jon began, but Lloyd interrupted him.

"Jon, you must trust me on this. We are dealing with a man who sees himself as above the law. The only way to deal with him is to give him a taste of his own medicine."

"And just who would this evil man be?" Jon asked with curiosity.

"Harry Quinn's partner, Sam Parsons."

Nadine hugged her father tightly as they inspected the coach together. "Father, soon everything will be right again," she whispered. "Mother is gone, but everything else will be returned to you."

Harry touched a finger to Nadine's chin. "Everything but you," he said hoarsely.

"Just because I will be married doesn't mean that a part of me won't always be yours," Nadine said, smiling devotedly up at him. "And you will gain more than you are losing. In the future you will have grandchildren to call your own."

Nadine had never seen such a radiant look on her father's face. "You really want that, don't you?" she asked. Easing into his arms, she welcomed his warm embrace.

"So do I," she murmured. "So do I."

Sam Parsons rose from behind his desk and went to stare from his window. Outside, several mounted policemen waited for Captain Grenville to join them. If he hadn't been the one to inform Grenville of Lloyd's return to Melbourne he would have had reason to fear the police, for he had been less than honest with his partner. As it was, Grenville now came to him, seeking help. Spinning around, he faced the captain with a sour frown.

"That bastard is alive?" he said with a smirk. "You're sure it was him who took Nadine and burned your house down?"

"I have proof enough, all right," Grover Grenville growled.

Sam moved restlessly across the room, watching the pattern of the rug beneath his feet. "The servants identified him?"

Grenville placed his palms on Sam's desk and leaned forward on them, scowling. "After the truth was forced out of them," he growled. "You're sure Nadine didn't return home? If I chose to tear this damn house apart, I wouldn't find her?"

Sam paled at the venom in Grover's voice. Toying nervously with the tip of his mustache, he sat down behind his desk and slouched down in his chair. "Neither Nadine or her father are here," he said flatly. "I'm sure they have both taken residence with that damn outlaw. Nadine because she has been foolish enough to fall in love with him, and Harry because he's a coward and has given up fighting for what is his.''

"So when I find Lloyd I find her?" Grover said, his eyes gleaming.

"Seems that way," Sam said, moving his eyes slowly upward to challenge Grover with a set stare. "Now, if your business here is finished?"

The sound of thundering hoofbeats drew Sam quickly back to his feet. Regretting having ever come to this godforsaken country, he went to the window. He grew cold inside as he watched the arrival of his coachman on a single white stallion. Reining in to the hitching post, he tied the horse in front of the house and took the front steps two at a time. His eyes were wild with fear, and his red uniform was filmed with dust.

"What the—?" Sam said, turning on his heel as the coachman scurried into the office, breathless.

Sam went to the man and grabbed him by the shoulders, shaking him. "What's happened?" he growled. "Where is the stage?"

His insides coiled tightly as he listened to the coachman describe exactly what had happened and who was responsible.

Dropping his hands awkwardly to his sides, Sam took a shaky step backward. He gave Grover a nervous glance and slumped down into his chair again, finding it hard to think, much less speak.

Grover leaned his full weight on the desk again and brought his face down close to Sam's. "So, they *are* in cahoots," he growled. "Nadine and Lloyd Harpster. Are you ready to do something about it, Parsons? To join forces with me and my mounted police?"

"To do what?" Sam asked, his voice weak.

"The coachman has informed us that Lloyd and his gang plan to steal another stagecoach tomorrow," Grover said, giving the coachman a sideways glance before returning to look at Sam. "Let's all be there to surprise them. What do you say?"

"An ambush?" Sam asked blandly.

Grover chuckled. "Something like that," he confirmed, his cheeks glowing with excitement.

Sam looked toward the window, deep in thought. "Nadine will most surely be with them again," he said, feeling a need to put her in her place for having rejected him. He smiled awkwardly up at Grover. "Yes, an ambush sounds like a good idea, Captain Grenville. A very good idea."

The two men shook hands, sealing the bargain.

Chapter Nineteen

A flash of lightning zigzagged across the early-morning sky, followed by a great burst of thunder. Nadine felt the rumbling of the ground beneath her where she sat cross-legged beside the fire pit, watching the entrance flap. Dressed in her breeches and white blouse, she took a final, lingering stroke with her brush through her hair. She had an ominous foreboding about what was planned for the day.

Turning her gaze away from the entrance flap, Nadine looked anxiously over at Lloyd as he positioned his gun belt around his waist and buckled it. As though in slow motion, she looked from one large pistol to the other. An involuntary shiver raced across her flesh as she recalled the first time she had seen them. She had wondered then whether he was an outlaw, and she had been right.

But he was not the sort of outlaw that she had thought him to be. He had been branded for all the wrong reasons. And those reasons could be erased by a mere piece of paper with a signature on it.

Unless things went wrong today.

Nadine tossed her hairbrush aside and scurried to her feet. With an anxious heart she ran to Lloyd and clutched his arm. "Please reconsider, darling," she said in a rush of words. "Sam Parsons isn't worth it. Nobody is."

She lowered her eyes. "Perhaps not even my father," she murmured, almost choking on the words.

She quickly raised her eyes again. "No. Not even he, if it means losing you again."

She threw herself into his arms and hugged him tightly to her. "Oh, Lloyd, let Jon Upchurch settle this thing with Sam. It could be done that way. Sam has broken the law. Whether it was here or in America, he has broken the law."

Lloyd ran his fingers through her lustrous long hair and eased her away from him. Looking down into her eyes, he winced at the pain and worry he saw in their green depths.

"People like Sam Parsons would never pay at the hand of the law, love," he said. "He would wriggle out of this like a snake crawls away and into the thicket. For your father's sake, for yours, we must put the fear of God in him once and for all, or it will never end."

He set his jaw firmly. "Don't you know that if he was arrested it would only delay your father's return to the ranch and his business? It could take months for the red tape to be ironed out and to prove that the embezzlement even took place."

He leaned closer to her face. "And they can't even arrest him without proof."

"But Jon..." Nadine said in a soft voice, feeling any hope of Lloyd reversing his decision to attack the stagecoach waning.

"Lieutenant Jon Upchurch's hands are tied," Lloyd growled. "Remember Grenville? Until he's taken out of the picture, he's in power. Jon is only second-in-command."

He jerked away from her and sat down, slipping into his kangaroo-hide boots. "No, I've asked Jon not to interfere. It's best that way," he said dryly. "We must get a confession out of Sam in our own way. Please understand, Nadine."

He looked up at her, his eyes cold. "There is no other way," he said flatly. "Are you with me, love?"

Nadine turned away from him, not liking this cold side of him. She shook her head and clenched her hands into tight fists at her sides. Would it never end?

A great crash of thunder turned Nadine around again, her heart racing, as though she were an extension of the storm. She gasped when she found Lloyd there, so close. She blinked the tears from her eyes and moved into his arms.

"I guess we must do what needs to be done for all concerned," she murmured, clinging to him. "I realize that you aren't doing this to Sam for just me and my father. Because of what he did, you will have scars on your wrists and ankles forever. You have your own debt to pay him for the time you spent imprisoned on the damnable rock. How could I have forgotten?"

"You didn't," Lloyd said, smoothing his hand down the perfect shape of her back. "You just didn't want to remember it. Nor do I."

He stepped away from her and reached for a cape made of soft wallaby hide. Slipping it around Nadine's shoulders, he secured it at her throat with leather strings. "You wear this today. From the sounds of things outside, we have more to worry about than Sam Parsons. I think we're in for one hell of a storm."

Nadine clasped the cape snugly around her, trembling when Lloyd gave her a soft, lingering kiss.

Harry Quinn sat in his hut, his dark eyes lighted by the fire as he gazed down into it. In his mind, he was reliving the past several months, hating Sam Parsons more and more by the minute. His heart beat wildly within the expanse of his chest. With shaking hands he slowly unwound the bandage on his head. His gaze shifted to the pistols beside him, and his lips quivered into a nervous smile.

Sam Parsons stood at the parlor window and pulled the sheer curtain aside. He looked up at the threatening sky, wondering if he had made a wise decision to join with Grover Grenville. The plan was to use a second stagecoach as a decoy, with himself a passenger. Captain Grenville had assured him that he and his mounted policemen would be ready to ambush the bushrangers as soon as Lloyd and his gang attacked the stage.

More than likely, Sam would be the loser, but it seemed that he was already. With Lloyd Harpster still alive and a threat, there was little hope. Lloyd

Harpster had a way of getting what he wanted. Even Nadine.

Swinging away from the window, he began to pace feverishly back and forth across the room. How had Lloyd Harpster eluded the bounty hunter? He had paid that man a lot of money to see that Lloyd was killed. And where was Harry?

"And Nadine," he grumbled. Catching sight of his own handsome reflection in the mirror, he went to stand before it.

Sam ran his hands across his expensive brocaded waistcoat, brushing the ruffled collar of his shirt. His dark breeches were perfectly groomed, and his dark hair beautifully coiffed. Swirling a finger along each tip of his narrow mustache, he smiled, satisfied with his appearance.

"Yes, and then there is Nadine," he repeated to himself, feeling a deep pain in his heart over losing her. "How could she choose a shiftless, no-good outlaw over me?"

A lump rose in his throat as he recalled how he had forced himself on her.

Swallowing hard, he straightened his back. He did not even want to think of how much Nadine hated him. He could envision her riding alongside Lloyd Harpster, stealing his stagecoaches and expensive stallions, all the while thinking of vengeance against him.

"I have no choice but to proceed with the plan," he said, shivering at the thought. He knew there was only a slim chance of surviving the ordeal, but he had something to prove to Nadine. She had branded him not only a thief but a coward.

He would show her that she was wrong, at least about that.

His finely manicured hands trembled as he placed a gun belt around his waist. As he fastened it, he looked in the mirror. He tilted his head and squinted, blinking at the vision of himself, armed, in the glass. He looked alien to himself. A sickness grabbed at the pit of his stomach.

Grover Grenville grimaced as a bolt of lightning cut across the sky above him. He sat hidden behind thick brush, awaiting the first signs of Lloyd and the bushrangers. His gaze moved over his men, who sat stiffly in their saddles, looking nervously into the sky overhead.

His eyes glinting, Grenville once again searched the dense forest that surrounded him. "No storm is going to stand in the way of ambushing Lloyd Harpster," he mumbled to himself. "I've finally got him where I want him. Soon he'll be mine, and I'll waste no time stringing him up."

His loins ached as he recalled how soft Nadine's flesh had been. He would not let anything stand in the way of stealing her back. She would be his until he tired of her.

Sam Parsons sat in the stagecoach, nervously fidgeting with the fringe on the shade of the window beside him. The road he traveled had been carved out of a high bluff, and he looked down from the window at an ocean that was churned by heavy winds.

In the sky, incessant flashes of lightning streaked across the darkening heavens. Billowing thunder-clouds rolled overhead, mirroring the rolling tide of the sea.

Sam scooted lower in the seat. He had never felt so alone. Though a hired gunman drove the coach, he did not feel confident that the gunman was as good with his rifle as he claimed. The best gunmen were scarce, for most seemed to have joined Lloyd Harpster's bushranger gang.

"Damn it, he'd better be good. I paid him a year's wages to get him to join me on this expedition. But if I don't achieve my goal, I'll lose more than money."

He edged closer to the window, watching a ship battling against the waves, its sails white against the backdrop of the stormy sky. "I'd have been better off if I'd given Harry Quinn back his money and re-turned to America," he grumbled.

The sky was darkening as though night were ap-proaching. The black stallion whinnied nervously and shook his mane, snorting as a loud burst of thunder from close by caused the earth to tremble beneath his hooves. He pawed at the ground and reared up on his hind legs. His eyes lighted with fire as he caught a glimpse of Grover Grenville through the dark foliage of the forest.

Shaking his long mane, he snorted again. Trotting away from his mares, he moved through the trees, his attention focused on his enemy.

Chapter Twenty

Nadine's cape billowed out behind her as she rode proudly beside Lloyd, trying to ignore the threatening weather. He seemed undisturbed by the approaching storm as he rode alongside her, handsome as ever.

Nadine drew her reins tight as Lloyd wheeled his horse around to a sudden stop. The road they sought was finally in view up ahead. Grabbing a pistol from its holster, Lloyd turned and gave her a wink.

"It can't be long now," he drawled, looking at the heavens. "You shouldn't have come. The storm could be fierce."

"I'd be nowhere else," Nadine murmured, unable to control the cold chill that shook her. Every nerve in her body was taut. She looked down the long, winding road in front of them. "Perhaps Sam won't even run the stagecoach in this weather."

"Or perhaps he won't because he's a coward," Lloyd growled. "He's surely smart enough to know he hasn't got a chance in hell against me and my men."

"Your description fits Sam perfectly." Nadine sighed. "He is nothing but a coward. He probably won't run the stagecoach today. Perhaps Father has won, after all."

"We'll soon see," Lloyd said flatly. He looked over his shoulder at his men, noticing the pistols in each of their hands.

He squinted and peered down the road, his insides warm with excitement. His only regret was that his vengeance against Grover Grenville had been sidetracked.

First Sam, then Grenville. One truly was as good as the other, as far as vengeance was concerned. Both were poor excuses for men.

The rumbling sound in the distance made Lloyd sit up straight in his saddle. He placed his finger on the trigger of his pistol and motioned with his firearm to his men.

As the stagecoach came into view around a bend in the road, Lloyd felt a pinprick of warning go through him. He recognized the driver of the stagecoach. He was a gunman. How many more paid gunmen followed? It seemed that Sam had prepared himself for an ambush after all.

Turning to Nadine, he frowned. "Things have just changed," he said sternly. "It seems we had Sam figured wrong after all. You must stay behind, Nadine. This ambush isn't going to be as simple as the first one. I won't endanger you by letting you be a part of it."

"What do you mean?" Nadine asked, her eyes wide. "What's changed?"

"Sam has hired a gunman to drive the coach, and there could be more following along behind," Lloyd said. "It could turn into a gunfight."

"Lord, no," Nadine groaned. If anything were to happen to Lloyd, she would be to blame, for she was at the heart of his trouble with Sam.

"I won't argue this time," she murmured, seeing how anxious Lloyd was to get this chore behind him. "I don't want to get in the way." She leaned over and touched the smoothness of his face, bronzed by the sun. "Please don't let anything happen to you, darling. You're my life."

Lloyd took her hand and gently kissed its palm before returning it. "You stay hidden in the forest," he said, nodding toward a grove of eucalyptus trees. "This will be over soon. Then I must see to Grenville." He gave her a lingering stare and spun his horse around. Shouting to his men, he galloped toward the stagecoach.

Nadine looked up into the dark heavens with a soft prayer. Urging her horse to a trot, she rode to the cover of the eucalyptus trees, trembling with fear for the man she loved. She felt as though she should be riding along beside him, but she knew that her presence would only endanger him.

Sitting straight in the saddle, she clung tightly to her reins and watched Lloyd in action, admiring him anew for his courage.

Grenville's face flushed with eagerness when he saw Nadine on horseback beside Lloyd. Never had he seen a woman of such courage and adventurousness. It made him want her all the more.

No longer did he wish to see her dead. To have such a lady at his side would enhance the vision the people of Melbourne had of him. Everyone would admire her as he now did. When he moved up in rank and became lieutenant governor of the state of Victoria, she would make the perfect hostess.

His thick eyebrows touched in concentration as he debated his feelings for her. If his men ambushed Lloyd and the bushrangers, Nadine might be killed. He couldn't have that. She was much too important to his future.

As Lloyd rode toward the stagecoach with his gang, a slow smile rose to Captain Grenville's lips. His gray eyes gleamed as he saw Nadine, left behind, leading her horse to protective cover behind the trees. She was his for the taking.

Turning his eyes to his men, he told them of the change in plans. They were to stay hidden while he personally got Nadine. They would attack Lloyd Harpster and the bushranger gang when he gave the order.

Lloyd and his gang rode toward the stagecoach, shooting into the air. "Aim over the bastard's head unless shot at!" Lloyd shouted, laughing to himself. The gunman driving the stagecoach had been caught off guard, quickly discovering that he was too badly outnumbered to take even one shot at him.

"Throw down your rifle and stop the stage-coach!" Lloyd shouted, riding alongside the white horses, his eyes alight with fire as he glared up at the gunman.

A short, paunchy man with long, dark side-whiskers, the gunman gave Lloyd a sour stare before tossing his rifle aside and drawing the stage to a shuddering halt.

"Step down!" Lloyd shouted. "Slow and easy. Don't try anything, or you'll not live to tell about it."

The bushrangers surrounded the coach as the gunman climbed down to the ground. Lloyd eyed the stagecoach warily, having caught the glint of a pistol through the window. He dismounted and edged along the outside wall of the vehicle, his pistol poised in front of him. Scarcely breathing, he jumped to the other side of the door, grabbed the latch and jerked the door open. A pistol fell from the coach at his feet.

"Don't shoot," Sam begged, his voice weak. "I'll come out peacefully."

Sam's face was pale and drawn as he climbed from the stagecoach with his hands in the air. He looked past Lloyd to Nadine, who had moved partially out from behind the trees and was watching. It seemed that he would remain a coward in her eyes. His chances of killing Lloyd Harpster and escaping alive were nonexistent.

His eyes wavered as Nadine challenged him with a stare. Where was Grenville, he wondered as Lloyd gave him a shove. Had he backed out, the bastard?

"You are an evil man, Parsons," Lloyd growled. "But I think you've just reached the end of your rope. By nightfall you'll have signed a full confession of your embezzlement or wish that you were dead.''

A great streak of lightning tore from the sky, followed by a resounding crack of thunder, as loud as a burst of cannon fire. Frightened by the sound, the horses hitched to the stagecoach bolted and galloped off down the road as though driven by the devil himself.

Lloyd's gaze moved to the steep bluff that bordered the road. The damn horses were headed straight toward it!

Quickly mounting his strawberry roan, he galloped after the runaway coach.

Captain Grenville smiled smugly as he saw Lloyd ride away. Nadine was standing beside her horse, away from everyone else, defenseless. Taking his knife from the leather scabbard at his waist, he inched his horse along behind the trees. When he was close enough, he dismounted and crept toward her on foot. His breathing was raspy with excitement as he reached the unsuspecting woman and held the cold tip of the knife blade to the flesh at the nape of her neck.

''Don't scream out,'' Grover Grenville said in a low voice. ''The knife might slip. And don't cause a commotion, not if you value your life.''

Nadine's pulse was racing, and she was dizzy with fear. Captain Grenville had come upon her so suddenly that she hadn't had a chance to cry out. The cold touch of the blade against her neck paralyzed her, but she knew she must obey him.

Staring wildly straight ahead, Nadine realized that the bushrangers were too busy watching Lloyd's pursuit of the coach to notice what was happening to her. Suddenly she felt one of Grover Grenville's pudgy hands on her wrist.

"Just come along peacefully," he whispered. "As long as you cooperate, I won't hurt you. You are much too valuable to me. I'm going to treat you like a queen."

Sam grew anxious as he looked toward the forest and no longer saw Nadine on her horse. Had she dismounted in the brief moment when he had turned to watch Lloyd chase the stagecoach? Where could she be?

Then his breath was stolen when he saw Grover Grenville leading her away, partially hidden behind the trees. Grover Grenville had played him for a fool. He hadn't come to ambush the stagecoach at all. He was after Nadine!

"That bastard," Sam growled, clenching his fists at his sides.

Sam began to run toward the disappearing couple. Nadine looked vulnerable and frightened. He couldn't let Grover Grenville harm her. He would rescue her. She would never again believe he was a coward. Perhaps he had one last chance to win her as his own.

His heart thundering in his chest, Sam rushed into the forest, stealthily following Nadine and Grenville as they shuffled clumsily toward Grenville's horse. The knife was still firmly pressed against the back of her neck, and one of her captor's huge arms circled her waist. When he reached them he lunged, grabbing Grenville's arm. "Nadine, *run*!" Sam shouted before his fear overwhelmed him. A gurgle rose from deep inside him as he felt the death plunge of the knife entering his chest.

"You stupid man," Grover Grenville snarled as he watched Sam crumple to the ground, clutching his chest.

The rain began to fall in torrents. Nadine stood rooted to the ground with shock. Everything had happened so quickly that she had no time to comprehend it. She looked in disbelief at Sam, who now lay lifeless on the ground in a pool of his own blood. He had tried to save her life. Had he cared that much? Or had he been trying to save her from Grover Grenville for himself? She would never know.

Grenville, trembling with anger, turned his attention back to Nadine. With the knife held in front of him, he moved slowly toward her, as if he didn't want to frighten her.

Like a cornered rabbit, Nadine was too scared to flee. As the madman approached her, she could do nothing more than back slowly away from him. Wiping the rain from her face, she caught a blur of movement out of the corner of one eye. She watched in amazement as the brumby of Lloyd's midnight dreams appeared out of nowhere.

The stallion flicked its stately tail, staring at Captain Grenville through eyes alight with fire.

Grenville turned in alarm as the beast began to charge. He tried to run but lost his footing and fell to the ground, the knife bouncing from his fingers. Scarcely breathing, he watched the horse edge closer and closer.

Glancing at his pistols, out of reach on his saddle, Grenville shouted to his men. "Someone shoot the devil," he whimpered. "Men! Kill that horse. What are you waiting for?"

Nadine searched through the trees for Captain Grenville's mounted policemen, but none came. She realized that they all hated him as much as Lloyd Harpster and his bushrangers did. They were not going to interfere with the horse's plan, which was surely death.

Lloyd's bushrangers, now aware of what was happening, were moving in closer, wary of the powerful wild beast.

Grover Grenville tried to inch away from the horse along the wet ground. His men were ignoring his orders. They would pay! All of them would die on Misery Rock because of their insolent behavior this day!

"Get away," he screamed, his knees too weak for him to pick himself up from the ground. He cowered as the horse followed along with him.

"By God, you are the devil," Grenville gasped under his breath, his fear having almost stolen his ability to speak.

The stallion lowered his head close to Grenville's face and blew out a loud snort. He pawed the ground nervously, first one hoof, then the other. The stallion continued his teasing and tormenting, shaking his long mane and strutting around Grover Grenville as though he were a rival.

Captain Grenville's face was pearled with a layer of sweat, despite the cool rain. His heart beat wildly in his chest as he watched the stallion circle around him, once, twice. He nervously watched the hooves getting much too close to his face. He whimpered as the stallion leaned down and began nuzzling his whiskers.

"Damn," Grover Grenville sobbed, seeing no chance of surviving what the horse had planned for him. Damn his men! Damn Lloyd Harpster, and damn this animal.

He felt the color drain from his face and his stomach lurch as the stallion turned its sleek black body and reared up on its hind legs. Whinnying loudly, the horse fell on his enemy, his legs a blur of shiny black.

Captain Grenville did not even get a chance to cry out, for the impact of the horse's hooves on his face and skull were too instant, too direct.

The stallion turned and trotted to the mares waiting for him at the fringe of the forest. He nuzzled several and then galloped into the wind and rain, the mares following close behind.

Nadine staggered backward, unable to believe what she had just witnessed. A sickness invaded her senses as she looked from Sam to Captain Grenville.

Looking up, she saw Lloyd returning with the stagecoach, his roan tied behind it. She broke into a run, sobbing.

Lloyd climbed from the stagecoach and drew her into his arms, stunned. What had happened in the short time it had taken to stop the runaway stage-coach?

"What's going on?" he gasped, looking at his bushrangers, who stood on one side of the two prone bodies on the ground at the inner fringes of the forest, and at the mounted police who stood on the other.

"Nadine?" Lloyd asked thickly, framing her face between his hands and directing her tear-filled eyes up to meet his.

Nadine sniffled. "Captain Grenville abducted me, Sam came to my rescue and was knifed to death by Grenville, and then the stallion you idolize came and trampled Grenville to death," she said in a rush of words.

Lloyd's eyes widened. He dropped his hands to his sides, stunned by the news. "The stallion?" he said in a voice that was hardly more than a whisper, rubbing his brow. "The stallion killed him?"

"Yes," Nadine said, shivering. "It was so calculated."

"Wait here," Lloyd said quietly. Walking to the death scene, he stared down at Grover Grenville, feeling a strange emptiness. The man was really dead. The horse had done him a favor in one sense, but had deprived him of his long-sought-after revenge.

"Unbelievable," Lloyd marveled. Then he swung around and called to Nadine. "He's dead. The bastard is dead!"

"And none too soon, eh?" Jon Upchurch said, walking up next to him. He placed a hand on Lloyd's arm as Lloyd turned with a start to face him. "And no one will question the death. Grenville's soldiers are glad to be rid of him and will be willing to tell the truth about you and the trumped-up charges. The charges will be dropped completely. The pardon will be easily gotten.''

"Jon, what the hell are you doing here?'' Lloyd said, clasping a hand on Jon's shoulder. "I thought you were going to let me handle this all by myself?''

"Well, now, I guess I did say that.'' Jon chuckled. "But I changed my mind. I was afraid you would be walking into a trap. You almost did, you know.''

"Yes,'' Lloyd said, glancing quickly at the mounted policemen, then at Sam. "I guess I did.''

"But now there's nothing else to worry about,'' Jon said thickly. "I'll be stepping up in rank as early as this afternoon. I will try to see to it that you have the pardon you have deserved for so long this evening.''

Nadine looked from Jon to Lloyd, reaching for Lloyd's arm. "Is this truly happening?'' she whispered, looking up into his eyes. "You will not have to hide any longer? You're not an outlaw?''

"No. I will no longer be an outlaw,'' Lloyd said, the realization just beginning to sink in. He gave Nadine a wondering stare. "We're free.'' His eyes brightened. He swept Nadine up into his arms and began swinging her around. "We're free, love! The future is ours!''

Nadine laughed gaily. Then her laughter faded and Lloyd eased her back to the ground when someone else rode toward them.

"Quinn?" Lloyd said, scratching his wet brow when he recognized Harry Quinn, his gun belt fastened at his waist. "What the hell?"

"Father?" Nadine gasped. She, too, saw the holstered pistols and noticed that the bandage had been removed from his head. "What are you doing here?"

Harry's gaze moved to the bodies of Sam Parsons and Grover Grenville. "So it's all over," he said, resting a hand on a thigh. "*Both* bastards are dead. I had planned, had hoped, to do the honors, Harpster." He gave Nadine a slight smile. "You, too, Daughter."

Lloyd placed an arm around Nadine's waist. "It is over, you know," he said huskily. He looked at Harry. "You can return to your ranch. With your partner gone, the business is yours again in the eyes of the law."

He once again looked at Nadine, reaching for her hands. "We can also go ahead with our future. Tomorrow we become man and wife." He looked at Harry, again smiling his winning, lazy smile. "Of course, only with your blessing, sir."

Harry wiped his wet hands on his even wetter breeches, then grabbed Lloyd's hand and eagerly clasped it. "Make her happy," he growled. "She's all I have left, you know."

"I'll be happy to share her with you, Quinn," Lloyd said thickly, giving Nadine a glance. "But not fifty-fifty, mind you." He turned and eyed Harry, his mouth quivering into another smile. "I won her fair and square. I'd say you'd best throw your cards away if you lose with stakes as high as this very often."

Harry chuckled. He looked from Nadine to Lloyd. "Seems I didn't lose at all," he said thickly. "I've won me a hell of a son-in-law."

Nadine's eyes pooled with tears as her father spun his horse around and went to the stagecoach. Harnessing his horse to the others, he climbed onto the stagecoach, shouted, snapped the whip and rode away in the direction of his ranch.

Nadine wiped her eyes as Lloyd reached to twine his fingers through the wet tendrils of her hair, drawing her mouth to his as he leaned toward her. "Love, let's leave this place," he whispered. "I've other things on my mind."

Then he turned and faced Jon. "Jon, if you don't mind, take charge here," he said softly. "None of this is my affair any longer."

Arm in arm, Nadine and Lloyd walked away. Nadine found herself troubled by something. She gave Sam's body a quick glance over her shoulder, then looked quickly away. She would not let herself think of Sam's fate, for deep inside her she had not wished him dead. She had hoped that somehow he would make everything right for her father, then return to America. There would be no looking back. Only precious, sweet tomorrows lay ahead for her, for her and the man she loved!

Chapter Twenty-One

The sun had willed the rain away, and it was now a wondrous day of blue skies, a day made for lovers who had just been given the right to live and to love freely.

Spilling down a limestone cliff covered with sphagnum moss, a waterfall landed in the pool of effervescent foam where Nadine and Lloyd were bathing alone, receiving the cooling spray, laughing. Nadine stretched her arms over her head, enjoying the rivulets of water running down her body like cool satin. Lloyd lifted her hair at the nape of her neck and kissed her neck, his hands slipping around and nestling both of her breasts.

He then coiled his fingers through Nadine's hair and drew her lips to his. Their bodies were wet and cool from the splash of the water tumbling down over them. Lloyd kissed Nadine gently, his free hand touching her all over, lingering at her most delicate pleasure points. His tongue softly parted her lips, and their tongues darted together in loveplay. Nadine shivered with ecstasy as she felt Lloyd's manhood swelling against her abdomen.

"Are you so sure your men are all back at the hideout?" Nadine whispered, easing her mouth from his.

"They never disobey. Trust me."

"If you say so."

His lips again claimed hers, this time with a scorching kiss. Her hands sought and found his hardness. Brazenly, with only the sky and forest as audience for their blissful moments together, she began moving her fingers around him. He moaned sensuously into her mouth, feeling the heat inflaming his insides, spreading. Nadine's breath caught in her throat when his hand went to the valley between her thighs and began softly caressing her.

Lloyd drew away from her. He lifted her hair from her shoulders and looked down at her, smiling the lazy, seductive smile that had stolen Nadine's heart the first time she had seen it.

"You are so beautiful," he said, his gaze moving over her face, then her body, then her face again. "I love everything about you. Everything."

Nadine's lips curved downward into a pout. "Even my nose?" she murmured. "You truly approve?"

He gently kissed the tip of her nose. "It's the cutest nose I've ever seen," he whispered, drawing back, again watching her, for she still seemed to be pouting about something.

"My eyes?" she murmured. "You don't think they are too widely set?"

Lloyd chuckled. He gently closed each of her eyes with a tender kiss. "No," he whispered. He studied her again with raised eyebrows. She still seemed less than satisfied with his reassurances.

"But I am so short!" Nadine suddenly blurted, yanking away from him. She swept a hand down her body, then looked up at his towering six-foot height. "Lloyd, wouldn't you prefer that I would be taller? Wouldn't I be easier to kiss? Lord, you must feel as though your back is breaking every time you bend down to kiss me."

Lloyd laughed softly, then swept her fully up into his arms and began carrying her away from the waterfall to the spongy moss that lay like a bed of green velvet on the banks of the creek. He laid her down on the moss and positioned himself over her.

"Don't you know that you are perfect in every way?" he said huskily, letting his eyes wander over her liquid curves. "Were you any different, I would not have been drawn to you so quickly."

He held her face between his hands and looked down at her eyes, now alight with passion. "Darling, I did fall in love that very first moment I laid eyes on you," he said thickly. "Never had I seen such a beautiful, vivacious creature."

He kissed the tip of her nose. "Will you stop worrying about flaws that are not there?" he said, stroking her cheek with his fingertips.

Nadine had never felt as desired as now. "My love," she said, her eyes hazing over with tears of joy. "You have to know that your eyes held me hostage that first time you looked up at me from where you lay sprawled on the sidewalk. If my father hadn't—"

He sealed her lips with a finger. "But he did," he said, smiling down at her. "I won everything that day. My life."

A peaceful languor swept over Nadine, beginning at her toes and moving upward. Her lips trembled as Lloyd kissed her, his hands gently kneading her breasts. She opened herself to him when she felt the probing of his hardness between her thighs, welcoming him inside her. His heat transferring to her, spreading, each of his thrusts set her more on fire inside. She dug her fingers into the muscled flesh of his buttocks, pulling him closer.

"Love me," she whispered. "My darling, oh, how I love you!"

"We're free to love," he said, raining kisses across her feverish face.

The word "free" caused the magic of the moment to be somewhat dimmed for Nadine. She placed a hand on Lloyd's cheek and eased his lips away from hers. "But you—*we*—are not truly free until you are handed the pardon," she said worriedly.

"It is the same as done," Lloyd said, smiling down at her. "Jon is to bring it tonight. A special celebration is planned. You'll see!"

"Celebration?"

"Don't ask questions. You'll see soon enough."

"But—"

Lloyd kissed her words away. "Hush," he whispered. "I think we've other things on our minds right now, don't you?"

Nadine nodded, then melted into him as he again buried himself deep inside her, stroking, sweetly stroking. She let herself absorb the full thrust of his virility. His kiss grew more passionate, his hands more demanding as they traveled over her, coaxing passion from her.

She laced her arms about his neck. She swept her tongue between his lips, savoring the wonderful, familiar taste of him. Then she felt the welcome splash of warmth as everything within her blossomed with the ultimate surge of rapture that came with loving him.

She withdrew her lips and nipped at his shoulder with her teeth as she felt his body harden and then shudder, filling her with his liquid heat....

Lloyd's breath quickened as his lips pressed into the hollow of her throat. "You steal my heart away," he whispered hoarsely. His muscled arms enfolded her, molding her to him. "Let's not wait long before we wed."

He leaned up over her and ran a hand over the smooth tautness of her stomach. "I wonder just how you're going to look when with child," he said, winking down at her. "But, of course, you will be even more beautiful. They say women are radiant when a baby grows within them. Perhaps you are even already with child. You've never been as radiant. It's as though you are an extension of the sun, glowing and vibrant."

Nadine's eyes widened. She scarcely breathed as she ran her own hand over her stomach. "A child?" she murmured. "Could it be?"

She placed a hand on Lloyd's cheek. "Oh, would it truly make you all that happy?"

"Yes, love, that would make me most happy and proud," Lloyd said, easing slowly away from her.

Placing an arm around her waist, he helped her up from the ground. "You aren't with child, or you would know."

He placed his hands on her cheeks and guided her eyes upward. "You *would*, wouldn't you?"

A blush made Nadine's face grow hot. "I would certainly hope so," she said, laughing softly.

She swayed beneath his gentle kiss and embrace. Then, as he moved away from her, something drew her gaze down into the creek bed. Lying in the gravel was something glistening, something *golden*.

She put her hand to her mouth, stunned, for she knew the amount of gold that was still being discovered all over the continent of Australia.

Falling to her knees, she peered more intently into the water, her heart thundering as several gold nuggets teased her from where they lay on the gravel bed of the creek. "Lloyd," she whispered, then shouted. "Lloyd!"

Lloyd was already there. His fingers dipped into the water and swept up several nuggets. He held them in the palm of his hand, mesmerized by their shine.

"By God, do you see these?" he gasped, giving Nadine a glance over his shoulder.

"Is it truly gold?" Nadine asked, her pulse racing. "Are there more?"

Lloyd's gaze swept the creek bed. Nadine's fingers dug, anxiously filtering the gravel between them. She frowned over at Lloyd. "I don't think there's any more," she said solemnly, gasping as Lloyd drew her up into his arms, placing the nuggets close to her eyes.

"Don't you see the size of these things, love?" he shouted. "Who needs any more? There is enough here to buy our own ranch."

"I'm afraid to let myself believe that all of this is truly happening," Nadine said soberly, imploring Lloyd with her eyes. "What if I should pinch myself? Do you think I might wake up back in America, having dreamed all of this from the very beginning, when you first came into my life?"

She held on to him desperately. "Tell me it's real," she softly begged. "Tell me."

Her eyes widened and she winced with pain as Lloyd suddenly pinched her buttock. She drew away from him, puzzled, rubbing the spot. "Why did you do that?" she asked softly.

"I had to prove to you that everything was real." He chuckled, his eyes gleaming amusedly. "I pinched you. You didn't wake up in America, now did you? Now are you convinced?"

Nadine's lips quivered into a smile. Then she laughed aloud and threw her arms around Lloyd's neck.

A great outdoor fire had been lighted close to the bushrangers' huts. The moon turned the treetops silver with its light, and the smell of the bush lay heavy in the air. Nadine watched, wide-eyed, as Lloyd and his men ran around waving fine nets of bark fiber and kangaroo skin in the air, catching the giant moths that fluttered in droves around the flames of the fire.

There were great whoops and shouts all around her, but Nadine did not want to join in the kill. Her heart went out to the velvet-winged creatures. She shuddered at the sight of Tipahee roasting the moths that had been caught earlier in the hot ashes of the fire.

Lloyd brought his fresh catch to Tipahee. Nadine wrinkled her nose in distaste when she heard the flutterings in the fiber net. "Lloyd, if this is what you planned for the celebration tonight, I'm not sure if I want to take part in it," she said dryly. "I can't imagine eating these lovely creatures."

"Anything that is not vegetable lived at one time or another," he said, winking down at her. He handed the moths over to Tipahee. "Do you ever stop and think about it when you're enjoying a meal of pheasant or rabbit? I doubt it. And both are lovely creatures."

"But still...moths?" Nadine said, shuddering. Then her eyes were drawn to an approaching rider. Her heart skipped a beat when she saw that it was Jon Upchurch, smiling from ear to ear as he dismounted and walked toward them carrying a leather satchel.

Nadine glanced quickly up at Lloyd and clasped his arm eagerly. "He's got it," she said excitedly. She turned to Jon, her eyes sparkling. "Jon, you do have it, don't you?"

Jon handed the satchel to Lloyd without speaking. His fingers trembling, Lloyd opened the satchel and pulled out a handwritten document, neatly signed at the bottom. Handing the satchel back to Jon, he leaned closer to the fire and eagerly read the statement exonerating him of any wrongdoing. The words became blurred as tears hazed his eyes. He handed the document to Nadine and let her read it as he turned to Jon and placed a hand on his shoulder.

"Thank you," he said hoarsely. "Damn it, thank you, Jon. I feared that you would not find it as simply done as you anticipated. But, by God, you managed it."

"Captain Grenville was the only obstacle in your way," Jon said, placing his hand on Lloyd's. "He hated you with a vengeance, you know. From the time you crossed him in England he was determined never to let you be free again. The lieutenant governor only went along with him because Captain Grenville paid him well to cooperate with him."

"And how does the lieutenant governor feel now? Doesn't he know how corrupt he appears by setting me free so easily once the man who kept him paid so well was dead?" Lloyd growled, swinging around to face the fire. "Just how free am I, Jon?"

"As free as any man can be," Jon said, taking the pardon from Nadine and returning it to the safety of the case. "As expected, the mounted policemen under Grenville's command admitted the truth. All charges against you have been dropped completely. As of this moment, you are free."

"Strange, I find it so hard to believe," Lloyd said, nervously raking his fingers through his golden hair.

Nadine put the pardon aside. Taking Lloyd's face in her hands, she forced him to look down at her.

"Why are you finding it so difficult?" she murmured.

"I imagine it's the same as you were feeling this afternoon," he said with a half smile. "I guess I need a pinch."

"I can arrange that," Nadine replied, laughing.

Lloyd chuckled and swept her into his arms for a heady kiss. Finally relinquishing her lips, he gestured with one hand toward Jon's horse. "Well? Did you bring something besides the pardon?" he asked with a wink. "This is a celebration. Remember?"

"Ah, yes," Jon said, handing the satchel back to Lloyd. "You take this. I'll get my saddlebags."

Lloyd took the satchel and tucked it safely beneath his arm, suddenly exhilarated and filled with pride. He gave Nadine a deep look and walked her to his hut.

"Like I promised, this is going to be a celebration," he said thickly. "And when Lloyd Harpster makes a promise, it is as good as done!"

Nadine smiled up at him and went inside the hut, where soft mats had been arranged around the fire pit, which was filled with glowing embers. She sat down and faced the fire, welcoming the warmth bathing her face. She rolled up the sleeves of her blouse and pulled off her boots, placing the soles of her feet close to the flames. Lloyd sat down beside her. Laying the satchel down behind her, he placed an arm possessively around her waist.

Jon came into the hut and sat down across the fire from them. He opened the bag at his side. "First we have a vintage bottle of wine," he said, handing it to

Lloyd. He withdrew a separate leather bag and eased
four wrapped long-stemmed wineglasses from it.
"Then we have the glasses."

Nadine moved to her knees to accept one glass and
watched, smiling, as Lloyd accepted another. A sweet
euphoria claimed her insides as the wine was poured
and a toast was made.

"Here's to your freedom," Jon said, looking from
Lloyd to Nadine and back again. "And to the future
and whatever it holds for the both of you."

It was a strange sound, the clinking of expensive
crystal in the primitive hut. Nadine sipped on the
wine, radiant with happiness.

Tipahee joined the revelers, carrying a wooden tray
of roasted moths. "Good," Tipahee said, his dark
eyes dancing as he offered Nadine the delicacies,
which gave off an aroma similar to roasted hickory
nuts. "I am good cook. Nadine, you eat. This is part
of *moomba*."

She smiled awkwardly up at him as he bent his
slight form over her, waiting. "All right," she murmured. "I'll try just one."

Taking a roasted moth from the tray, she slowly
lifted it to her lips and placed it in her mouth. Her
eyes widened with surprise. She was delighted with
the sweet, nutlike flavor, and could not help but reach
for another.

"So my lady has found her appetite?" Lloyd
teased.

Nadine smiled and nodded up at him. Her eyes
widened when she saw Lloyd remove the gold nuggets from the tiny leather drawstring bag that hung

around his neck like a necklace. She watched Jon's eyes widen and Tipahee take a deep breath of wonder.

"Nadine and I found these this afternoon," he said, placing the nuggets in the palm of Jon's hand. "If one were to pan for gold in the exact spot, there is more than likely a fortune to be had there." He smiled lazily over at Jon. "Well, how about it, mate?"

Lloyd reached for Nadine and drew her close to his side. "I plan to buy a ranch by the sea," he said, staring into the fire as though envisioning it. "A great spread where we can raise cattle and horses and perhaps even sheep.

"I owe a great deal to that wild stallion. One day I'll claim him as mine," he said thickly.

He looked down at Nadine adoringly. "I want a place where Nadine and I can raise many children," he said huskily.

Lloyd refilled the glasses all around. Setting the wine bottle aside, he raised his glass into the air. "Let us drink to friendship, freedom and love," he said softly.

Chapter Twenty-Two

TWO YEARS LATER...

Nadine walked between her husband and her father from the dining room of their home, smiling as she clung to both their arms.

"And did you enjoy the roast?" Nadine asked, beaming with happiness. "My cooking will never compare to Mother's, but it will do in a pinch, won't it, Father?"

Harry's dark eyes gleamed as he looked down at Nadine. "I think it'll do, don't you, Son?" He chuckled, looking over her head at Lloyd with a wink. "But I'm not so sure about that apple pie. Perhaps a little more sugar could have been added to satisfy my sweet tooth."

Nadine gave her father a quick look and laughed softly, knowing that he spoke in jest. "Well, I'm sure Tipahee will welcome the apple pie that we are going to bring him today," she said, giving Lloyd an adoring look.

Though the discovery of more gold a year ago had made them rich, Lloyd did not dress like a wealthy man. His favorite plaid shirt and fitted breeches were quite simple when compared to Harry's fancy suit and ruffled shirt.

Nadine had not changed much, either. She still enjoyed fancy dresses. Today she had chosen the same dress she had worn the night when Lloyd had first come to dinner in San Francisco. The red silk complemented the whiteness of her skin above the low-cut bodice, and the full skirt rustled as she walked.

Though she had servants, she enjoyed puttering around in the kitchen and serving up her own surprises for her husband and for her father when he came to call.

"Don't forget, we're also taking Tipahee bread," Lloyd said, interrupting Nadine's thoughts. "Tipahee's taste for food is changing, thanks to you."

"Perhaps he would like a gingerbread—" Nadine began.

"How is Tipahee faring these days?" Harry asked, swinging himself away from Nadine so that the young couple could pass in front of him and on into the parlor, where golden wooden floors shone from a fresh waxing and brightly flowered patterned plush furniture made one feel as though one were stepping into the outdoors. Huge bay windows facing the ocean were splashed with sunlight, and a fire glowed on the grate.

"Tipahee just might make it to a hundred," Lloyd said with a chuckle, going to the liquor cabinet and extracting a bottle of wine. Popping the cork, he poured wine into three glasses.

Nadine took two glasses and carried one over to her father, settling herself down beside him on the sofa. "We tried to persuade Tipahee to live here with us," she said, sipping her wine. "But he wouldn't have it. Even my cooking couldn't convince him."

She gave Lloyd a questioning look. "Do you think he might want one of my gingerbread m—?" she began again, but was interrupted by the soft cries of a child in the distance.

"Well, I think I know someone who will definitely want one of my freshly baked gingerbread men," she said, placing her glass on the table.

She rose from the sofa, looking from Lloyd to her father. "Let's go see our sweet Mariel together," she said.

"Are you sure you don't mind staying a few days to look after your granddaughter, Father?" she questioned her father as they walked down the corridor.

Harry swept an arm around Nadine's waist. "I am delighted at the chance to have her all to myself. You two stay away as long as you wish," he said softly.

He hugged gently at Nadine's waist, just beginning to thicken again with child. "Since this is your last opportunity to travel before the arrival of my second grandchild, you'd best stay as long as you can. After a second child is born, I doubt if either of you will get these foolish notions of going after that brumby again."

Nadine glided up the spiral staircase, leading the two men. "The wild stallion is only a part of the venture, Father," she murmured. "Tipahee is the main reason we are going."

Turning as she reached the top of the stairs, she gave Lloyd a knowing glance. "As far as I'm concerned, I'd rather leave the stallion alone."

"We'll see," Lloyd grumbled, recalling the flying mane and the eyes of fire that teased him in his dreams. "You know how long I've wanted that horse."

Nadine gave Lloyd a sweet smile as she reached out to gently touch his cheek. "Darling, you can't have everything," she purred.

As they continued down the upstairs hall to their daughter's bedroom, Nadine proudly surveyed her domain. Crossing an atrium open to the main floor, they made their way to the bedrooms. She smiled as she passed the bedroom she shared with Lloyd, an extravaganza of silk and satin with a canopied bed and a view of the open sea through its large windows.

It was everything Nadine had ever wanted in life and more. She had a home with love and warmth within its walls. And she had finally found the stability and roots she had always craved.

The soft whimpers of a child wafted from down the hall. Nadine hurried her steps.

Entering the nursery, she went to the crib and bent low, brushing the tips of her fingers across the pink face of her year-old daughter. Mariel's blue eyes looked up intently at her mother, and her tiny lips curved into a sweet smile.

"Oh, but aren't you just too beautiful?" Nadine cooed, straightening the child's lacy dress on her delicate body. Mariel's tiny fists swung in the air, and her bootied feet kicked. "Wouldn't your grandmother be proud of you?"

"Her grandfather is proud," Harry said, strutting across the room. Without bothering to ask permission, he stooped down and swept the child up into his bulky arms. Rocking her back and forth, he leaned down close to the baby's face and began to hum a lullaby.

Nadine stepped back into Lloyd's possessive embrace, full of happiness at the sight of her father enjoying his grandchild. One hand went to her stomach as she felt the first kick of her second child. She hoped this child would be a boy, for she knew how badly Lloyd wanted a son. So did she. A son the image of his handsome father.

A satchel filled with food and other surprises for Tipahee was tied securely to Nadine's horse. She flipped her travel skirt around as she walked arm in arm with Lloyd, surveying their property before leaving on a venture that would take several days. Attired in his fringed wallaby-hide outfit, Lloyd had to make one final check on his spread before leaving it all in the hands of men who had not long ago been total strangers. All except those of his gang who had given up their old ways to join Lloyd in a more civilized way of life.

"Everything looks just fine," Nadine murmured, looking around at the herd of cattle that stretched to the horizon, where the trees had been stripped for grazing land. The outbuildings served as bunkhouse, barn and stables. Some of them were for functions that Nadine did not even understand the meaning of.

She looked toward the house standing majestically on a bluff overlooking the sea. It was a two-story brick house with a wide porch on the north side and a view of the vast ocean to the south.

A profusion of roses surrounded the house, and a lone eucalyptus tree of staggering size stood in the spacious yard. The tree stood close to three hundred feet high, with an unbroken sweep of slender silver-gray trunk that rose more than half its height before the first branch broke its perfect symmetry. Its leaves were narrow and hung straight down and it blazed with crimson and yellow blossoms.

"Gary knows what to do in my absence," Lloyd said, resting a hand on a holstered hip as his gaze swept around him.

The ranch was more than he had ever dreamed of having in life, and he guarded it as though it were the pure gold that had paid for it. He knew the ways of greedy men. He had learned them at the hands of the masters. No one would ever take away the paradise he had found with Nadine at his side.

Lloyd waved to Gary as he approached, a frisky brown dog following at his heels. "How's it going, mate?" Lloyd asked, placing an affectionate arm around Gary's muscled shoulders.

Gary wiped a bead of perspiration from his brow. "A lot better since we got these herding dogs," he said with a smile. "They can scare a stray animal from brush so thick that a horse would never get through it."

"That's good to hear," Lloyd said, laughing huskily. "Not only do I have Gary watching out for my interests, but his dogs, as well."

Gary looked over at Nadine's travel skirt and prim white blouse. Her boots and gloves were made of the same soft wallaby hide as Lloyd's fringed outfit. "Give Tipahee my regards," he said, smiling. "I kind of miss him, you know."

Nadine laughed softly. "Yes, I think I do," she said, accepting Lloyd's arm around her waist as he stood up, away from the dog. "Ready to go, love?"

He did not have to answer her. She saw in his eyes the look of someone who had been kept from adventure for far too long.

Chapter Twenty-Three

They followed a clear stream surrounded by pale gum trees that gleamed in the dark green forest. Following Lloyd's strawberry roan, Nadine rode stiffly in her saddle. She was going to savor this moment of adventure with her husband, for soon she would be too pregnant to travel on horseback. She wanted nothing to endanger the tiny life growing inside her. She had waited too long for a husband and children. She and Lloyd had both been only children and had experienced a childhood of loneliness because of it. Their children would be part of a large and happy family.

"It shouldn't be long now," Lloyd said, looking through the foliage at the slanting rays of the sun. "It will be dark before you know it."

He looked over at Nadine, with an expression of concern. "Are you all right, love?" he asked, leaning closer to her. "You've hardly said a word the past hour. Are you having second thoughts about traveling? I was foolish to encourage it. I could have come alone."

Nadine gave him a wide-eyed look. "I wanted to come," she said softly. "You didn't have to talk me into it. Darling, I know that in the next several months I won't be able to come to see Tipahee with you."

Her eyes lowered, and her cheeks grew hot with a blush. "Besides, I wanted to make love just once more in the hut where we shared so many special moments. This may be the last time, you know."

"You are a woman after my own heart," Lloyd said, laughing huskily.

"Am I wanton, darling, because I enjoy making love as much as you?" Nadine asked, giving Lloyd a slow gaze, her lips quivering into a seductive smile. "Sometimes I do feel so wicked!"

"Wicked? Well, now, let me think about that for a while," Lloyd said, kneading his chin, pretending to contemplate her question. "Wanton?"

He reached out a hand and cupped her cheek within its palm. "Yes, love, I think you are both." He chuckled. "But I wouldn't want you any other way."

Nadine relished the touch of his hand, then slapped it away as what he had said sank in. "I'm not sure if I should take that as a compliment or as an insult," she said, laughing softly.

She galloped away from Lloyd, her coppery hair flying behind her.

Lloyd brought his horse up next to hers again, and Nadine let her eyes roam, enjoying the primitive setting that lay around her in all its loveliness. This was a memory she would cherish over the long months ahead.

They had been following a trail through steep ridges covered with alpine ash, peppermint trees and thick tangles of blackberry bushes, but they were now traveling along a winding river. Towering, mottled-barked eucalyptus grew along the length of the river. A gray koala clung to a eucalyptus, eating leaves, and a furry platypus, startled by the horses, splashed into the water at their approach.

"I'm going to miss coming here," Nadine said sadly.

"It won't be forever, love," Lloyd promised.

"I know," Nadine said softly, laughing at her own peevishness.

A movement in the vegetation just beyond Lloyd captured their attention. Tipahee moved quietly along the riverbank, blending naturally with the setting around him.

"Tipahee!" Nadine called to him with a wave.

The small figure carried several small traps made of wire and saplings and shaped like wasps' nests.

Tipahee, clutching his traps, ambled up to the horses. "You come! That is good!" he said, showing his sparkling white teeth as he smiled at Nadine and Lloyd. "You have come for dinner. Plenty of crayfish."

Nadine eyed her satchel filled with goodies for Tipahee. "Yes, we've come to dinner," she said, winking over at Lloyd. "I guess we'll have to be satisfied with crayfish, won't we, Lloyd?"

Lloyd chuckled softly at Tipahee's disappointment, knowing that he had expected some of Nadine's bread and pie. "I guess so," he said. He reached out a hand to Tipahee. "Hop on. Ride with us the rest of the way, Tipahee."

Tipahee took a step backward, shaking his head vigorously. "No, no horse," he grumbled. "Tipahee *walk*."

Without further conversation, Tipahee turned and started through the forest. Nadine and Lloyd followed him to his hut and dismounted.

Nadine took her satchel from her horse and carried it inside. Beside the simmering fire she sat and unpacked her gifts. Tipahee's smile grew as she presented the wealth of food she had prepared for him.

"Moomba moomba," Tipahee exclaimed, looking over the bread, pie, gingerbread men and cheese that Nadine had brought.

"You have crayfish for dinner. Tipahee eat this," he said, gesturing with his hands toward the feast laid out before him.

Lloyd sat down next to Nadine by the fire, and she sidled up next to him, content.

Nadine lay beside Lloyd in the privacy of their own bark hut. Outside, the moon turned the landscape a silvery gray, but in the small dwelling, the fire's embers cast everything in a faint orange light. Nadine sucked in her breath as Lloyd bent down and kissed her, moving his hand over the curve of her breast.

Looking into one another's eyes, they shed their clothes slowly. There was something about the primitive setting that seemed to intensify the passion of the moment. It was as though they were awakening all over again to the wonder and magic of each other's bodies as their hands and lips touched and explored anew.

Nadine's excitement grew as Lloyd drew her soft body against the hardness of his. His tongue slid between her lips, and his hands reached between her thighs and touched the throbbing core of her womanhood.

Her arms wound around his neck and her fingers moved gently down his back. She tried not to wince as she discovered anew the scars that crisscrossed his back. They would always be a reminder of his troubled past. A past she was doing everything in her power to make him forget. At night, when he had nightmares, she would nestle him close and croon to him as though he were a baby. Never again would he feel anything less than totally loved.

Her hands wandered lower, along his spine and across his hips. Splaying her hands across his buttocks, she guided him inside her, trembling with need as he filled the warm cavern of her femininity.

"Love me as never before, darling," Nadine whispered, breathless with desire.

She lifted her hips in unison with his masterful strokes within her. Her raging hunger spread, sparked by his mouth as it bore down upon her lips in a heated kiss and the possessive touch of his fingers kneading her swollen breasts.

His lean, sinewy body pressed against hers as his hands seared her flesh, unleashing a trembling weakness. The pulsing crest of their passion rose as she moved against him with a moan.

"Nadine," Lloyd whispered, lowering his mouth to tease her taut breasts. He could feel the pressure building and spreading a tingling heat, searing his heart and soul.

His fingers went to her buttocks and lifted her closer so that he could touch the deepest part of her silky warmness with his hardness. He sucked in his breath and closed his eyes when he felt the pleasure peaking.

Nadine let her own euphoria take hold. She opened herself wider to him, savoring the touch of his powerful body moving against hers, answering his excitement with her own.

Her hands clung to his sinewy shoulders, and her hips moved mindlessly as delicious shivers of pleasure spread throughout her consciousness, blinding her to anything but the moment.

His energy spent, Lloyd lay next to his wife, one arm resting comfortably across her chest. Noticing the soft swell of her abdomen, he leaned forward and kissed it softly.

"Hello, David," he whispered. "I hope you didn't find your parents too ambitious this evening."

He patted Nadine's stomach fondly. "You can go back to sleep now, Son. Sweet dreams."

Nadine laughed throatily, feeling a slight stirring deep within her. She reached for Lloyd's hand and placed it on the spot.

"I believe he heard you," she murmured. "Darling, your son is responding to his father's voice."

Lloyd's face glowed as he felt the fluttering beneath her skin. "Lord, I do believe he did," he said, chuckling. "That proves he's a boy. If I had called him Margaret, I would have humiliated him for sure."

"Yes, I'm sure, too," Nadine whispered, settling down into Lloyd's arms and closing her eyes. "I'm sure it will be a son."

The cockatoos awakened Lloyd and Nadine at five. Anxious to be on their way, they shared a bite with Tipahee and set off in pursuit of the wild stallion.

As the morning sun began to warm the day, the young couple entered a lush meadow. The steamy summer weather had produced a galaxy of dazzling wildflowers, and an eagle circled overhead, searching out his quarry, which would soon take shelter from the rising sun. Ahead was an emerald swamp thick with grass that grew deep into the gently flowing water.

"We should be thinking about what we're going to have for dinner," Lloyd said, giving Nadine a sly glance. "Follow me. I think I know just the thing."

The horses rode hard until they reached the windblown hills near the sea. Nadine dismounted, following Lloyd's lead, and headed after him down the steep slope. They traveled through dense tufts of grass that ended abruptly at the top of the sea cliffs.

"What are you looking for?" she asked, clinging to Lloyd as she moved alongside him, dangerously close to the rocky cliff.

"Shh," Lloyd said, putting a finger to his lips. "I think we've found one."

Nadine stopped beside him as he bent down to examine a small burrow on the edge of the cliff.

She gasped as Lloyd reached into the hole up to his shoulder and brought out a dark, fluffy ball.

"Good grief, what is that?" she asked in surprise.

"It's a muttonbird," Lloyd said, proudly holding up his catch. "These fatty fledglings make the best of eating."

Just then, something caught her eye, and Nadine turned to look. Her eyes widened in disbelief. High above them, on a windy bluff, stood the majestic black stallion.

"It's him..." she whispered harshly, pointing. "Oh, Lloyd, it's him!"

Lloyd was so stunned by the horse's sudden appearance that he lost his hold on the muttonbird. As though in a trance, he looked up at the stallion. Set free, the baby bird scampered back into his nest. The black horse stared back at him, challenging Lloyd with a snort and a shake of his proud head.

"Damn. He's as handsome now as that first time I saw him," Lloyd said, clenching his hands into tight fists at his sides.

Nadine watched the dark stallion with wonder, understanding Lloyd's obsession to claim him as his own. Suddenly a mare came into view at the edge of the bluff, heading toward the stallion. As she came close to him he reached out to nuzzle her. Nadine's insides melted at the sight. The two horses were so peaceful, so lovely.

Lloyd's fingers unclenched as he watched the two horses. The mare was as white as the stallion was black, and just as beautiful.

The mare turned her head and whinnied, and a young foal ambled into view and began to suckle its mother. Except for a pure white star upon its chest, the foal was midnight black.

"Damn, do you see that?" Lloyd finally managed in a whisper. "Nadine, do you see?"

Tears formed in Nadine's eyes. "Except for our daughter, I don't think I've ever seen anything as lovely," she murmured, easing herself into Lloyd's waiting embrace. "Do you still wish to capture the brumby?"

"Never!" Lloyd growled, taking one last, lingering look at the black stallion. "Let's go home, love."

"Yes, let's," Nadine whispered, lifting her lips to his. Lloyd kissed her as though it were the very first time.

FIVE MONTHS LATER...

Exhausted, Nadine lay in her bed, hours after having given birth to her second child. Lloyd tiptoed into the dimly lighted room and stood over the cradle beside the bed, gazing proudly down at the pink-faced infant wrapped in a blanket.

"David," he whispered, "my son."

Nadine stirred beside him. "Isn't he beautiful," she murmured, radiant with happiness.

"Yes, beautiful," Lloyd answered, rearranging the blanket more snugly around his child. "But of course he would be. Look who his mother is."

"Not to mention his father," Nadine said, welcoming him down onto the bed as he sat beside her.

Nadine lifted a weak hand to his face and touched him gently on the cheek, full of love for him. Lloyd bent down and kissed her softly on the lips.

"I'm so proud of you," he said, enfolding her hand in his. "First a daughter and now a son. What more could a man ask of a woman?"

"Thank *you* for all you have given *me*," Nadine replied.

She looked into Lloyd's sea-blue eyes and thought of all the sweet and wondrous moments they had shared and the promise of the future to come.

She was so blessed. She had children and a wonderful man who was hers forever. And she had finally found a house that she could call a home.

* * * * *

You'll flip . . . your pages won't!
Read paperbacks *hands-free* with

Book Mate • I

The perfect "mate" for all your romance paperbacks

**Traveling • Vacationing • At Work • In Bed • Studying
• Cooking • Eating**

Perfect size for all standard paperbacks, this wonderful invention makes reading a pure pleasure! Ingenious design holds paperback books OPEN and FLAT so even wind can't ruffle pages — leaves your hands free to do other things. Reinforced, wipe-clean vinyl-covered holder flexes to let you turn pages without undoing the strap . . . supports paperbacks so well, they have the strength of hardcovers!

Pages turn WITHOUT opening the strap

SEE-THROUGH STRAP

Reinforced back stays flat

Built in bookmark

BOOK MARK

BACK COVER HOLDING STRIP

10 x 7¼ opened
Snaps closed for easy carrying, too

Available now. Send your name, address, and zip code, along with a check or money order for just $5.95 + .75¢ for postage & handling (for a total of $6.70) payable to Reader Service to:

Reader Service
Bookmate Offer
901 Fuhrmann Blvd.
P.O. Box 1396
Buffalo, N.Y. 14269-1396

Offer not available in Canada
*New York and Iowa residents add appropriate sales tax.

BM-G